THE WICKED DOOR

To. Susan & Louise
Love from Auntie Mary

The Wicked Door

MARY MANION

RABY

Copyright © Mary Manion, 2003

First published in 2003
by Raby Books
The Coach House
Eggleston Hall
Eggleston
Barnard Castle
County Durham
DL12 0AG

British Library Cataloguing-in-Publication data
A catalogue record for this book is available from the British Library

ISBN 1-84410-015-4

Printed and bound by The Cromwell Press, Trowbridge, Wilts

Author's Note

The Wicked Door is a twentieth-century story set in the late 1930s and early 1940s. The Catholic Church fulfilled a need, taking in and caring for large numbers of children and orphans, homeless and children who needed a temporary home because of circumstances.

Most of them adapted to life in the orphanage but for some it was a heart-breaking experience; corporal punishment in schools and institutions was the norm. Those days are long gone. The church cares for needy children in the present day. Catholic Care in well appointed care homes, foster care or adoption providing a family environment. This is all a big improvement on the institutional upbringing of long ago.

Mary Manion, 2003

*I dedicate this book to my husband, Denis,
whose love, constant care and encouragement
enabled me to complete this book*

*I would like to thank St Gregory's
Youth and Adult Centre, Thomas Danby College,
special thanks to Therasa 'Tutor', Barbara, and
Maggie 'Staff' for their help and encouragement.
Also to all my family and friends for their interest
which inspired me to carry on to the end.*

Chapter One

The Cairnes were an ordinary working-class family: Mr and Mrs Cairnes with their three children, Peggy aged ten, Irene aged six and little Marie who was three. They lived on a new council estate called Meadowfields in the city of Lingford. Their home was a very modern one by 1938 standards. It consisted of a square kitchen which had a gas stove as well as a big black oven, heated by the coal fire in the front room. Near the back door was a pantry where all the food was kept. Next to that was a coal cellar. Coal was delivered every two weeks by a man with a horse and cart.

A wooden table was pushed up against the side wall with various chairs and buffets, all made by Mr Cairnes, grouped around it. At the far end of the room was the big window, looking out onto the garden and the fields opposite where all the children and their friends played for many a happy hour.

Under the window was a large square sink with a wooden draining board. Also standing there was a peggy tub and a mangle with its large wooden rollers. This was where all the family washing was carried out. There was also a cupboard fastened to the wall, which contained all the pots, pans and crockery a family would need. Next came the front room which had special windows that folded back when opened. This was to give Mrs Cairnes, who was mostly confined to bed or chair with tuberculosis as much fresh air and sunlight as possible. It wasn't a very big room and the bed took up much of it. It had a black polished coal fireplace and when the fire was lit this heated the water boiler and the kitchen oven. There was a small wooden table where her medical requirements were kept and a chest of drawers for her clothes. The next room was known as the back living room. It had a large comfortable brown leather sofa and two matching chairs, built-in cupboards and drawers, but pride of place went to the polished sideboard with cupboards and drawers, plenty of space to keep all their clothes and toys. Upstairs were three bedrooms and a bathroom. The bathroom had a sink, lavvy and a very deep bath; very modern indeed for 1938. Outside were the front and back gardens, always full of flowers, and there was grass to play games on.

Altogether they were a very happy household until the changes came into their lives.

The front room had its large windows open wide to let in the fresh spring air. It was a Saturday afternoon and Peggy was sitting under her mother's window in the garden reading a book. Her two younger sisters, Irene and Marie, were playing nearby. Irene was a chubby child with long straight hair which was tied into plaits by Peggy every morning to try and keep her looking tidy. But her efforts didn't last very long. Irene was always untidy, no matter how hard Peggy tried with her. Marie, on the other hand, was a small, dainty, child. She had very curly hair, tight little knots of blond curls that seemed to jump out of her head no matter how much Peggy brushed it; it always looked the same. They were playing with their dolls in a homemade tent. Their father had gone into town to buy some wood. He was going to make a dolls house for Marie as a birthday surprise.

Peggy was reading a story about a girls' boarding school. She was so engrossed in the book that she only half heard the unusual noise coming from her mother's room. Suddenly she jumped up, dropped her book and ran inside. There she found her mother making choking noises and unable to speak. For the first moment Peggy stood still with shock, then she ran towards her crying, "Oh Mum, oh Mum." Her mother waved her away. Peggy turned and ran, thoughts racing through her mind, wondering where she could go for help. As she reached the garden gate she saw her father was coming down the road and talking with one of their neighbours, Mr Oates. Not knowing or caring what she was doing, she screamed "Dad, Dad come quickly! Something has happened to Mum." There was a loud crash as her father dropped the wood he had been carrying and ran past her. Mr Oates, their neighbour, bent down to pick the wood up. He was a tall thin man with bushy hair that always seemed to need a good combing. He dashed past her carrying the wood and ran into their house.

A few seconds later he ran out again and said to Peggy, "Quick, take the children and go to my house. Tell Mrs Oates to keep you all there. I'm just going to ring for the doctor but don't worry," as he ran off down the road to the nearest telephone box. "Your Mum will be all right."

Peggy's first reaction was to run into their house but the look on Mr Oates' face had frightened her. She ran up the garden, quickly grabbing hold of the two protesting children, who did not want to leave their homemade tent or their dolls, but Peggy dragged them up the road to

Mrs Oates' house. The door was open. Mrs Oates was in the kitchen, baking. She was a chubby, red-faced, happy person, always doing something useful. She was as short as her husband was tall. A few seconds later, Peggy flew in pushing the two bewildered youngsters before her, and dropped into the nearest chair, and, laying her head on her arms she sobbed her heart out. At last, she managed to control her crying long enough to give Mrs Oates the message from her husband, and with Irene and Marie busy eating the newly baked buns, she told her what had happened to her mother and how Mr Oates was helping her father by going to ring for the doctor. Mr Oates arrived home in what seemed to Peggy to be the longest afternoon she had known, though it had only been about an hour. The Oates were a kind and homely couple. They had two sons; the eldest, Tom, was married and lived in another town. The younger one, Jim, was in the navy. Mrs Oates didn't say very much but she was very worried with all the talk of war.

Peggy jumped up from the chair that Mrs Oates had insisted she rested in, and, was ready to run home in an instant to see what had happened to her mother. But Mr Oates said, "Just stay with us a while longer and have some tea. The doctor has been to see your mother and she is sleeping now, so let her rest awhile and I will take you all home later."

"Thank you," said Peggy, "but I am quite able to take us all home myself as it is only down the street."

Mr Oates let her have her way and even persuaded her to eat a sticky bun. After about an hour he said "It should be all right for you all to go home now but I'd like you to keep Irene and Marie as quiet as possible." Peggy nodded her head and thanked him for helping them.

He walked down the street with them as far as their garden gate. "Thank you both again. I'm sure my Mum and Dad will be most grateful for all your help." He looked at her solemn little face and marvelled at her composure and the way she handled the two little ones.

On returning home he said to his wife, "She is only a child but she is too old for her tender age of ten."

Holding her sister's hands, Peggy entered the house through the back door. The first thing she noticed was the two white tin buckets of water boiling away on the cooker top. She was very surprised because these buckets were only used on washdays to boil white sheets, school socks and any other clothes that didn't come clean after a good rubbing in the peggy-tub. Their father had heard them come in. He came out of mother's room quietly closing the door behind him. The three children were still in the kitchen. Irene said that she wanted her doll from the tent as she was worried that it might catch a cold if it was left out in the garden any longer. Father spoke softly to her and Marie: "Go and bring your toys in as it will soon be your bedtime." They went jumping and skipping up the garden path oblivious of any changes in their lives.

Peggy looked at her father. He came towards her, and taking her gently into his arms he spoke softly to her. "I want you to be a very brave girl. Mum is very sick and for the time being she must not be disturbed. So you and I will make some tea then undress and wash Irene and Marie, and when they go to bed, maybe if you are not too tired you could read them a story. Just for tonight. And I will sit with your Mum in case she wakes up and needs me."

Peggy, fighting back her tears could only nod her head. Her father gave her a big hug. "That's my girl. Oh, here they come now, let them see you smiling. We don't want them awake all night. Your Mum needs all the rest she can get and the doctor said she may be a little better tomorrow."

Peggy turned from him with a smile and quickly went to the kitchen sink. There, she picked up the sponge and washed her own tearstained face, just as Irene and Marie came running in through the back door demanding their tea.

It was while Peggy was reading Irene a bedtime story (Marie was already fast asleep) that she heard strange voices coming from downstairs. As quickly as she could without letting Irene notice, she gently tucked the tired little girl up, and kissed her goodnight. She drew the bedroom curtains and crept out onto the landing.

Peeping through the banister rails she saw two men coming out of her mother's room. The first one she recognized at once as Dr Walls whom she had seen before when he had been to visit her mother. But the other man was a stranger, and much taller and younger than Dr Walls. Both men were standing just below where Peggy was crouching at the top of the stairs. She saw the younger man shake his head and hold out his hands as if he didn't know what to do next. At that moment her father emerged from her mother's room and went across to join the two men. Peggy now had pins and needles in her legs but she couldn't move. Then she saw Dr Wall's face; he looked really sad and then he turned and put a hand on her father's shoulder. Peggy tried hard to listen to the murmuring between the three men but the only word she was able to make out was hospital.

Hospital! She knelt there stunned. As far as she knew, hospitals were places where people went to die. She had never been in one herself but once or twice she had heard of a person who had died in hospital. Sometimes at school assembly the children had been asked to say prayers for someone in hospital but it had never been anyone Peggy had known.

Her first impulse was to run downstairs and tell Dr Walls that she would stay home from school until her mother was better. But at that moment she heard other voices, all speaking in whispers. Mrs Oates was there, and Mr Oates. She was so full of tears that she didn't hear her father quietly coming up the stairs. She turned and saw him standing behind her, his face pale and drawn. He guessed at once that she had heard something. Holding out his arms he gently drew her small trembling body to him. For a few moments they stood there saying nothing, then he gently led her into her own bedroom. Sitting her down on her bed he spoke in quite a controlled voice. "I want you to stay in here for a while. Mrs Oates will come and stay with you." Then, kneeling down in front of her, he said, "Dr Walls would like your Mum to go into hospital for a few days. It is only for some tests. They want to see if they can find what is making her so ill and these things can't be done at home. So we must all be brave and keep smiling. Maybe when she comes home she will be well again." He gave her a big hug and smiled. "I will need your help, my little one, more than ever now."

Peggy dried her eyes on her father's big hanky and tried to smile at him. "Don't worry, Dad," she said standing up straight. "I'll be here to look after you, Irene and Marie. I will tell them in the morning that Mum has gone on a holiday to make her better."

There was a light tapping on Peggy's bedroom door. Mrs Oates was standing there. She smiled at Peggy then turned to her father saying "Dr Walls would like to see you now. I'll stay with Peggy – maybe she can show me how to do some of those fancy stitches she makes on the fireside covers. I've always wanted to be able to embroider but was never shown how."

Father winked at Peggy as he turned to leave her room, trying hard not to show the turmoil he was feeling at that moment. One hour later, although Peggy didn't see her go, Mrs Cairnes was taken by ambulance to the isolation hospital just outside the town. Her husband, who by now was a very worried man, accompanied her. The lung specialist that Dr Walls had called in to see Mrs Cairnes had told him that she had a collapsed lung and would have to remain in hospital for some time. Meanwhile, after what had seemed to Peggy a very long day, she eventually fell asleep. Mrs Oates, gently covering the sleeping child's arms with the blankets, said to herself. "Poor little thing, she is so young to have to bear such a heavy burden." Then she quietly left the room and checked that the other children were sleeping before she joined her husband downstairs to await the return of the children's father.

Chapter Two

When Peggy awoke the next morning she couldn't think for a moment why it seemed so different. Then she remembered the events of the night before. Quickly dressing herself she ran downstairs. Holding her breath she tiptoed towards her mother's room. There she saw the empty bed, with all its sheets and blankets gone. She stood for a moment, staring at its bleakness then she ran into the living room where she found her father fast asleep in his chair. She tapped him lightly on his arm and stood there wondering what to do next. Her father awoke with a jump and, seeing her standing in front of him looking so bewildered, he stood up and, took her by the hand went to the kitchen with her saying, "We must get the breakfast ready before those two come down or else there will be the dickens to pay."

Peggy asked in a very quiet voice, "Where has our Mum gone?"

"Well," replied her father, kneeling down in front of her, "remember last night I told you that Mum had to go for some tests?"

Peggy nodded her head.

"Doctor Walls thought that the sooner she went the sooner she would be home again, so we must make the best we can of the time she is away to get the house back in order. I will paint her room for her though maybe she won't have to spend as much time in it on her own when she comes home, because we all hope that she will be much better and able to spend her time with us again."

Peggy turned away from her father and started to prepare breakfast for them all. She would have to be brave and not let her father see her cry, as she knew that it would upset him all the more. Then she remembered that it was Sunday, the day they all went to the children's Mass at their church. Each class of children sat on their own benches according to their age group and most of the teachers from their school were present. Peggy knew that you had to have a good excuse for not being at Mass when they went to school on Monday morning. Turning to her father she said, "We had better hurry up and get the other two ready if we are not to be late for Mass."

Her father wondered what thoughts were going on in her young mind but thought it best to act as normally as possible, started to rush around pretending to be busy when all the time his thoughts were with his sick wife who he had left last night in a strange hospital. Her parting words had been "Whatever happens, keep the children together."

When she came out of church, Peggy saw her father talking to her school teacher, Mrs Davey. As she approached them her teacher said, "Hello Peggy, your Dad has just been telling me that your Mum is not very well at the moment, but don't worry, we will say a prayer for her in school tomorrow and I'm sure that she will be better. Now, go and find your two sisters before they wander away."

When she had gone, Mrs Davey turned to the sad-looking man and said "If there is anything we at the school can do to help please don't hesitate to ask. As Irene is already with us in the infants class we could take little Marie as well."

He thanked her and went in search of his children.

The children's school was a large square two-storey building. Inside it was light and airy. The downstairs classrooms were for the infant and junior children aged from five to eleven (Marie would be the exception). The classrooms were bright and cheerful. There was also a nice hall for assembly, dancing and PE (if it was wet outside). Upstairs was the senior school, for both boys and girls, aged from eleven to fourteen. As well as the classrooms, there was a cookery room with all the requirements for a nice meal or buns and cakes. There was a woodwork room where the boys made all sorts of things, and a science room with glass tubes and a Bunsen burner. They too had a large hall where many activities place.

The headmistress was a tall lady who always wore her hair in a bun. She was strict but very pleasant. Her name was Mrs Marsden and she had an office at the end of the corridor. Peggy's teacher, Miss Davey, was much smaller and younger. She had very black hair and wore it tied back with a hair slide. She was kind and gentle and had a round smiling face most of the time.

Early that Sunday afternoon, Peggy wrote a letter to her mother telling her everything was all right and they hoped to see her home soon. In the meantime she would look after them all. She had to hurry with her letter because her father was going to visit her mother that afternoon. He had to go by train and then face a long walk as the isolation hospital was well out of town.

Mr and Mrs Oates had offered to look after the children for the afternoon and give them their tea. Peggy wasn't keen and wanted to stay at home but the look on her father's face as he left them was enough to make her do as he asked. Really, there was no one else the children could stay with. There was an auntie May and family but they lived in Ireland, and although she was aware of her sister's illness she was unable to help look after them. One reason was that she had no room, having a large family of her own, and there was all this talk about war. There were other aunts and uncles but they too were unable to take the children in. Father's brother was a soldier in the regular army the last time he visited his brother's family, the Cairnes. He had given his sister-in-law a prayer book with mother of pearl on the front and back. Scratched into the mother of pearl was the inscription 'To Kate from Charlie'. The children loved Uncle Charlie.

Peggy was swinging back and forth on the Oates' front gate after tea waiting for her father to come home. She was thinking of what her teacher had said that morning after church: "We will say a prayer for your Mum tomorrow at our assembly." Peggy had wanted to say "No thank you miss, my Mum is not going to die like all the other people we have prayed for." But she had kept quiet. "Anyway," she said to herself, "I'll tell her in the morning before school begins. Gosh! It does seem a long time since Friday. I must get my homework done this evening if I don't want to lose any good marks." Just as she was going to ask Mrs Oates if she could run home for her books she saw her father walking up the road. Everything else went out of her mind as she jumped from the gate and ran towards him. Grabbing both his hands in hers she cried, "How is Mum? Did you see her? Did she like my letter and when is she coming back home?"

For a moment he looked at her and said to himself, "How do you tell a child that she may never see her Mum again?"

For that afternoon the doctor who was looking after his wife had told him just how ill she was. Both her lungs were affected with tuberculosis and it was only a matter of time, maybe six months, but at the most a year. And of course she couldn't be in contact with the children at all; they too would have to go to a special clinic for tests to make sure that they had not contracted the disease. He had been told by a fellow visitor on the return journey that children could only visit parents after a years separation. But they could only view the patient whose bed would be placed on a veranda so that the children could see them from a safe distance. All they could do was wave to one another.

"Well," he said, trying not to step on Peggy's toes. "First things first.

Mum is a little better but the doctors want her to stay in the country air for a while to get her strength back. She loved your letter and the pictures that you all drew for her and she is going to write to you. So you had better watch out for the postman." He couldn't tell her that he wasn't allowed to bring paper or anything else for that matter out of the hospital because paper more than anything carried germs, and even when her mother did write a letter it would have to be fumigated before it left the hospital. "Come on now and let me thank Mr and Mrs Oates for looking after you. We must see what the other two are doing. You will have to go to bed early tonight. School in the morning. Have you forgotten that it is only a week to your school exams?" Hand in hand father and daughter led the other two children down the road to start the next and very different part of their lives.

Chapter Three

Like all children, even in a crisis, Peggy slept well that night and was up very early the next morning. She didn't have much time to brood as it was Monday. She helped her father to dress Irene and Marie and get them ready for school. Father made the breakfast and told her that he was to have a couple of days at home to get things sorted out. He was going to ask Mrs Dean (who was to sit with their mother and do a little housework), if, as well as doing a bit of cooking for them, she would come in the early mornings and stay with them until he came home in the evening. She was a very kind lady who lived on her own. He didn't know what his situation at work would be like. Everyone was supposed to work longer hours and sometimes weekends. He was an engineer and war weapons were already being made at their workplace. He was going to see his employer that morning to explain his situation. How could he leave three young children to take care of themselves?

The next morning, when Peggy arrived at school, some of her friends came to say how sorry they were to hear that her mother was in hospital. Peggy was so busy telling them all about the events of the weekend that she forgot to ask her teacher not to say prayers for her mother, so when they were all in the school assembly it came as a shock to her hearing the head teacher, Mrs Marsden, asking the whole school to remember her mother in their prayers as she was in the hospital and very ill.

Peggy could feel all eyes on her. She thought to herself, "I must tell my friends once we are in our own classroom that my Mum is not ill like the people we pray for who are going to die."

When morning prayers were over, Peggy found that she had quite a crowd gathered around her. Not knowing quite what to say, she said, "My Mum is in hospital, but she is only staying for a rest to get her strength back then she will be coming home again." Some of the girls drifted away when they thought no more news was to be had but Peggy's friends stayed with her and the talk changed to the topic of the forthcoming exams.

The next week seemed to fly by for Peggy. After school she would dash to find Irene and Marie and run with them to the local shop, for her father still made out little lists for her each morning. He thought if he kept things as normal as possible the children wouldn't find the changes to their lives too much to cope with. When she finally arrived home she let the two little ones play in the garden, then sat down and did her homework. After tea she helped Mrs Dean to wash Irene and Marie and put on their nightclothes, then she read them a story.

The big day came at last. All those taking the entrance exam for a place at the grammar school had to go to school as usual, then they were taken by a teacher to the grammar school to sit the exam. Peggy's mother had sent her a letter to wish her luck. The postman had brought it that morning. She had written that she was feeling much better and would be thinking of her today. She had also written that Peggy was not to worry, and that she and her father knew that she would do her best. With this letter in her pocket, Peggy set forth with every intention of passing the exam just to show her mother and father that she could do it and make them proud of her.

Peggy expected her mother would be home when the results came through sometime in July, and then everything would be back to normal again. But little did Peggy know that even if she passed the exam, she wouldn't be able to go to the grammar school.

After all the excitement of the exams, life for Peggy's friends seemed to settle down to normal routine again. But for Peggy it was a very uneasy time. Soon, it would be Whitsuntide, a time when all the children wore their new clothes to church on Whit Sunday morning. As long as she could remember she and Irene had walked proudly down the road in their new dresses and coats. Their mother had always made their dresses and she supposed she had chosen the coats and shoes to match. It was a problem she had not had to think about before but now their mother was in hospital and unable to do those things: what was she to do? All her friends would be dressed up and she dreaded the thought of going to church in last year's clothes. She didn't want her friends to think that they were too poor to buy any new ones. But next Saturday morning her father said, "We had better go into town this afternoon and choose your new clothes. Mum has told me what you all need and you, Peggy, have to choose the colours."

What an afternoon that turned out to be! It seemed to Peggy that father wasn't worried how much her dress cost. She was to pick the one she liked best but first they did the shopping for Irene and Marie.

When they had finished with the two younger ones, both she and her father were exhausted so they went to the big store's tearoom to have some refreshments. They had lovely iced buns and Peggy felt very grown up when her father ordered tea for two, and milk for the children. Then it was her turn. She tried on dress after dress until the lady brought out the most beautiful dress she had ever seen. It was blue with a little coat to match.

"That's the one," father said.

But when she saw how much it would cost she asked "Will I be able to have the coat as well?"

"Of course you will." The lady came back with the coat and a straw hat in pale blue and a handbag to match them all. When she had tried them all on her father said with a lump in his throat, "There now, don't you look a little beauty. They are just what your Mum would have chosen for you I'm sure." Giving her a big hug he then looked at the clock on the wall and said, "Let's all go home now and put your nice things away. Irene and Marie are getting fed up with all the shopping and want to go home and play with their toys."

Peggy decided that she wouldn't tell her friends about her new clothes. She would wait and let them see her on Whit Sunday morning. She wished that her mother would be home in time but her father had told her it would be a little more time yet before she came home as the country air was doing her good and the doctors had said that they were very pleased with her progress.

Peggy missed her mother very much. She missed the little talks they had in the evenings. She wondered why it was taking her so long to get better. Irene and Marie being so much younger seemed to have accepted the fact that she was no longer there. They cried for her when they fell and hurt themselves but so long as someone was there to soothe them and kiss them better, they were all right.

Of course Marie had had very little to do with their mother. When she was born, their mother had been very ill and Marie had remained in the hospital nursery for quite a long time; and as far as Irene could remember her mother had spent most of her time in her room in bed. So it was easier for them when she had to go away. Being young they soon adapted to the new routine of people coming and going and doing things in their home. But not so with Peggy. She would often stand in the doorway of her mother's room where she had lain so long and she sometimes wondered to herself if she would be home in time to see her to go to the grammar school if she passed her scholarship. And if she did, who would look after her two young sisters and take them to school? The grammar school was in a different part of town and all the girls who went there did so by tramcar. Peggy had seen them coming home in their uniforms long after she and her friends were home from their school.

It was now June and the evenings were getting longer and lighter. One evening when Peggy and her father were sitting on their front doorstep watching Irene and Marie playing with a ball, she mentioned her worries to him, but all he would say was, "You are a little worrier, we will cross each bridge when we come to it. You know we have to await for your results then we can start thinking of such things." Little did she know that that problem had been on his mind ever since his wife had been taken to the hospital.

Mrs Dean did the housework but Peggy still went shopping, looked after the two young ones and took them out to play with her as much as she could. But some of her friends were not very happy to have the young ones following them everywhere. Another thing that worried her was the fact that her father was coming home much later from work than usual. This left them on their own for a while and Irene and Marie were a handful. Peggy had only to turn her back for a moment and they would be away. They never went far and she soon found them but one evening she heard two neighbours talking. "Those children should be somewhere where they could be looked after proper." Peggy had only a vague idea of what they meant but all the same it made her feel uneasy. This feeling stayed with her all night.

At last it seemed that the great day had arrived. Just before home time the Head teacher, Mrs Marsden sent for each boy or girl who had sat the entrance exam. They trouped out in alphabetical order. Then came Peggy's turn. She was one of the early ones as her name was Cairnes. Once inside Mrs Marsden's room she was handed an envelope addressed to her parents. She didn't say whether she had passed or not but she just smiled and said, "You may get your coat now and go home; give this letter to your father and I will see you in the school assembly in the morning."

Peggy's mind was in a turmoil. She just said, "Thank you miss" and as if in a dream walked out of the room. She looked at the envelope in her hand. It had her name at the top but was addressed to her parents. She dared not open it and would have to wait in agony until her father came home.

Peggy rushed to the cloakroom, grabbed her cardigan from her peg and hurried to meet Irene and Marie. She was holding the envelope tightly in her hands when all of a sudden she almost fell over one of the girls from her class who had been called in before her. She was leaning over a wall, crying and sobbing. In her hand was the envelope she had been given for her parents. It was opened and a single sheet of paper was screwed up on the floor. For a moment Peggy didn't realize what had happened.

"What's the matter?" she asked.

The girl didn't answer her. Then it dawned on Peggy and she said in a whisper, "Oh, you have opened your envelope. Why didn't you wait until you got home?" She bent down and picked up the paper from the floor and tried to hand it to the crying girl.

Just then one of the teachers came up to them. She must have realized what had happened. "I'll take that, Peggy," she said, holding out her hand for the crumpled paper. Peggy handed it to her without a word and the teacher putting an arm around the crying girl led her into the staff room.

Peggy didn't know what to think. They had been told that the idea of taking the sealed envelopes home was for parents and their children to find out the results of their exams together, and therefore to make it easier for those who had not passed to come to terms with the result before the whole school was told of the results.

After that incident she hoped Irene and Marie would be ready for home and that she wouldn't meet anyone else who had opened their envelope on the way.

At last they were home. "Thank goodness," thought Peggy. She didn't have to go to the shops that day. Once inside the room she placed the envelope on the top mantel above the fireplace. Mrs Dean was still there but she didn't mention the envelope to her. It was for her father and herself to open. Oh, how she wished her mother could be there too. For the next few hours, Peggy set about her usual jobs around the house, setting the table and helping with the washing up. The children now had their tea before their father came home for he was coming home too late for the two younger children to see him before they went to bed. Peggy's eyes turned again to the fireplace shelf. How much longer would he be? It seemed to her that he was later tonight than ever before. She mentioned the fact to Mrs Dean,

"Oh, it's this war business," she said. The children's father had bought his wife a wireless last year. He had said that she could listen to all the news that went on in the world. Peggy thought they were very lucky to own a wireless as none of her friends had one and Mrs Dean used to listen to it during the day so she always knew what was going on in the world.

Among her school lessons Peggy was taught history and geography. Some of it was about wars but she couldn't imagine anything like that happening in their town so she dismissed the idea from her mind. Peggy had found to her relief that it was not always wise to listen to what Mrs Dean had to say. She was just about to look at the clock for the umpteenth time when she heard her father's voice in the back garden talking to one of their neighbours about his wife's illness. She dashed out of the door to greet him with the news that a letter was waiting for him. "A letter?" said her father. Then he looked at her expectant face. "Oh, I will read it after my tea," he said, knowing full well that she had been waiting for him to come home. Peggy stood still. She knew her manners but then she saw the smile on her father's face. "Shall I bring it out to the kitchen for you?" She was almost running in her excitement. "OK then," he replied. Then sitting down at the kitchen table he opened the envelope. Peggy could hardly bear to look at him. There was a moment's silence then her father said, "Oh won't your Mum be proud of you." She let out a big whoopee and threw herself into his open arms. "Have I really passed, Dad," she cried. "Of course you have. Your Mum and I had no doubts about you at all. We knew you could do it. Well done, you clever girl." Then he gave her a big hug. Irene and Marie came downstairs to see what all the fuss was about and joined in all the laughing and hugging although they had no idea at all why father was making such a fuss of their Peggy.

Chapter Four

Next morning when arriving at school, Peggy met some of her friends in the playground. Six other girls who were her best friends told her they too had passed and would be going to the same school as her. Everyone seemed to be talking at once and when the bell rang for assembly a great feeling of excitement was in the air. When everyone was seated in the school hall and morning prayers had been said, the head teacher Mrs Marsden stood up in front of the whole school and read out the names of the boys and girls who had passed the scholarship and to which schools they would be going. Then, all whose names were read out had to stand up and face the rest of the children. Everyone started clapping and cheering, it was quite a day for everyone.

On the following Sunday afternoon, the children's father once again went to visit their mother. Peggy had written her a letter and made a copy of the one she had received from school as her father had told her he would frame the original one. He knew to take the real one to the hospital wouldn't be fair as Peggy would lose it. It would have to be burnt once it was in contact with his wife. This time a lady from the church came to look after the children. She was very nice and kind but found Irene and Marie a real handful. They had never seen her before and wouldn't come to her when she called them, so, Peggy had to sit and read stories to them for most of the afternoon and she was very relieved when she heard her father arrive home. That evening he sat and told her all about his visit to the hospital. How her mother had beamed with pride when he showed her the letter and how she was to expect a handmade card in the post very soon, especially from her mother.

After all the excitement following the exam results, the next few weeks were pretty boring. Lessons in school seemed much easier as the pressure was off. Some of her friends had already spoken about going into town to buy their new uniforms. Peggy wondered whether to ask her father about hers. He had been so busy working, visiting their mother and looking after them all that she thought he might have forgotten all about it. What she didn't know was that her father had received a letter from the school, asking him to let them know how long the children would be without their mother, and if Peggy was to go to the grammar school who would look after Irene and Marie? There was a air of uncertainty in the country. Large engineering firms like the one where he worked were working twelve-hour shifts and he had been approached a time or two by his employers as to when he would be able to work the extra hours. Peggy knew nothing about these worries, so when one evening, two ladies she had never seen before called to see her father, she didn't question him when he told her to take the two little ones and play in the garden with them for a while. Nothing was said to her after they had gone and she soon forgot all about them. But the following weekend they were back again, this time they each carried a folder with papers in them under their arms and they stayed much longer with their father. Peggy began to wonder who they were and decided to ask her father when they had gone.

The two women were from the education department. News had reached them that Peggy had passed her exam, that her mother was in hospital, and that she was responsible for taking her two younger sisters to school. So they had come at first to see what, if any, arrangements had been made for all three children on their return to school in September. Peggy didn't know her father was at his wits' end with worry. He had promised his wife that no matter what happened the children would stay together. Now they had only one more week at school before the summer holidays began and Mrs Dean had told him she couldn't look after them all day as it was too much for her. He couldn't stay home from work as the talk of war was becoming very real and his firm was working full-stretch. So he asked himself over and over again what he should do for the best. On their two visits he had discussed these problems with the two child officers. They in turn had told him of the two options open to him. The first was to split the children up by trying to find separate homes for them. Peggy to live near to the grammar school she wanted to go to, and Irene and Marie to live as near to a primary school as was possible. It may not be not the one they were attending now. All this was if somewhere could be found for them. The alternative would be to place all three children together in a children's home where at least they would all be together. The two ladies had brought all the information about the home with them. It was an orphanage for girls aged two to fifteen and was situated just outside Lingford.

"We can only give you a week to make up your mind," they told him, "as the children could not be left on their own throughout the day during the long school holidays."

"I will think about things," Mr Cairnes told them, "and discuss the matter with my wife." Sunday was the day he always went to visit her.

Unaware of all these discussions, Peggy and her friends had been preparing for their last week at their old school. They had decided to buy their teacher a thank you present for helping them to prepare for their exams and to let her know how much they would miss her. One of the girls was chosen to collect the pennies as they were brought to school. Each girl was to do some extra jobs at home to earn the money.

When her father came home Peggy told him, "We are buying our teacher a present and we all have to earn some money." Her father laughed, but Peggy looked worried. She already did most of the jobs she could manage around the house and never asked her father for a penny.

"Right-oh," he said "I will give you sixpence for cleaning my work boots."

Peggy was overjoyed. She threw her arms round his neck saying, "Thank you Dad I didn't want to be the only one who didn't take any money." She was now smiling again and it cheered him up no end to see her so happy. If only sixpence would resolve all their other troubles, but he knew nothing would.

Another girl had an aunt who worked and lived above a sweet shop so it was decided to buy their teacher a fancy box of chocolates and to present it to her on their last day at school. Someone else suggested making her a card and for all of them to sign it. "You're the best at drawing and painting," Peggy's friend said. "So you make it and bring it to school on Friday."

Peggy spent a lot of time making that card. In the centre she drew a heart with an arrow through the middle, having seen one like it in the shops in town. She then stuck some fine lace around the edges. Two days before school finished she took it with her to the playground and all the girls wrote little messages for their teacher and each signed their names on the card.

"Ooh, it's lovely," said all her friends. They put it on the teacher's desk the morning of the last day at school. When the day finally arrived everyone seemed to be in tears. Peggy thought that even her teacher would cry when she saw the card and the lovely ribbon-wrapped box of chocolates on her desk, but first they all had to go into the school hall for the last assembly together. The headmistress Mrs Marsden and all the other teachers had said their goodbyes and wished them all well in their future lives. They then all went into their own classrooms for the final day.

The day was spent mostly clearing desks and cupboards of old books and papers, at last it was home time. Each person went to the teacher's desk to say their own goodbyes. When it was Peggy's turn the teacher placed a hand on her shoulder and said, "Goodbye Peggy. I do hope things will be sorted out soon for your family so that you will go to the grammar school."

Peggy said, "Thank you miss," but she was very puzzled. What did she mean? she thought to herself. Of course I'm going to the grammar school. She went to meet Irene and Marie, automatically fastening Marie's cardigan, almost forgetting that this would be the last time she would be bringing them home from school. Somehow the excitement she had been feeling all the week seemed to have left her. Little niggling doubts came creeping into her mind. Why had she not received her new uniform yet? Who were the two ladies who had been to see her father and why had he not said who they were? Well, she said to herself, I will ask him tonight what the teacher had meant and also who the two ladies are and why they kept coming to see him? I'm sure he will say that everything is all right.

Peggy soon had other things to think about. Mrs Dean had been unable to come that day and Irene and Marie were asking for their tea. On arriving home from school they found the doors to the house locked. Peggy trailed the two young ones under protest to see Mrs Dean and ask if she had the door key. She knocked on the door and Mrs Dean herself came to answer it "Oh, I'm sorry love," she said. "But I'm finding it all a bit too much for me trying to run two homes. I didn't realize how late it was. I suppose it will be all right to give you the key but don't go near the fire or touch the oven until your father comes home. Tell him I will be down to see him this evening after I've got myself sorted out." Peggy took the key and said, "Thank you for all you have done for us but we will manage. I'll give your message to my Dad as soon as he comes home." The three children walked back up the road to their own home. This was the first time they had been all on their own; even Irene and Marie only mentioned their tea once. They seemed to sense all was not right. Peggy unlocked the door and they all went inside. She gave the two younger children some bread with jam on it and a cup of milk each to keep them quiet and they all sat around the table in the kitchen to await the homecoming of their father. When at last he arrived home, the sight that met his eyes of the three little faces gazing expectantly at him, even stopped him for a moment of even speaking. His gaze swiftly took in the remains of the jam and bread on the table and the fact that they had been on their own for at least two hours filled him with dismay. "Mrs Dean couldn't come today Dad she is coming to see you tonight to explain things to you, so I will help you to make the tea and we will all have it together." She turned to Irene and Marie saying "Go and play in the garden and don't go out of the gate or else you will get no tea." They ran off thinking every thing was OK now their father was home.

Closing the back door a little Peggy turned to face her father, who was sitting on one of the chairs left vacant by his younger children. She wanted to ask him what her teacher had meant in her goodbye remarks but decided it would have to wait as her father didn't look very well. His face was white and he still had his coat on.

"What's the matter, Dad. Do you feel sick?"

He seemed to shake himself a little and stood up. "No love, I'm all right," he said, taking off his coat and boots. "I was just a bit shook up when I saw you all on your own. We will have our tea first then when Mrs Dean has been to see me we will sort everything out. We will all feel better after something to eat. Look in the pantry and see if there is any jelly left. Irene and Marie love jelly and custard so we will make some for them."

Chapter Five

On Sunday Mr Cairnes went to visit his wife at the hospital. On his arrival he asked to see the doctor in charge of his wife's case. The doctor took him into his room and told him he was very sorry to hear of the difficulty he was having regarding the children; then told him there was no hope of his wife coming home in the near future, and advised him to make some arrangements for them to be looked after as soon as possible. These words had left Mr Cairnes with no alternative. If he was to abide by his wife's wishes to keep the children together they would have to go into the orphanage. But how was he going to tell Peggy? The worst thing of all was that according to the two education officers, to whom he would have to give his final answer to on Saturday was the fact that Peggy would not be able to go to the grammar school. It was one of the strict rules of the orphanage that no girl could be different in any way to the other girls living there. All the girls from the orphanage went to the same school and no exceptions could be made for grammar school education.

Mrs Dean called to see him that evening. She told him how sorry she was that she wouldn't be able to continue looking after the house and children, but as with all the talk of war she was going to live with her sister in the countryside until the country was more settled. He thanked her for all the work she had already done for them and told her his decision regarding the children. Mrs Dean was quite upset but thought he was doing the right thing for them. "At least," she said, "you will know they are all being looked after and would all be together."

"Please don't say anything to the children," Mr Cairnes said. He hadn't told them anything yet. He was going to have next week off work and get everything settled. It would break their hearts and his, but they would have to go: he had tried everyone and everything but nothing else could be done.

When Mrs Dean had gone home he stood looking out of the window at the three children playing with a skipping rope and thought to himself that if only their mother had been well enough to be at home he was sure they would have managed somehow. But at least he hoped they would only be away for a short stay. Lifting the curtain he tapped on the window and waved to the children to come indoors. Peggy was the first through the door. She hadn't seen Mrs Dean go as she had used the front door, and they had been playing in the back garden. "Is everything fixed up now Dad?" she said, looking at him closely,

"Well, I will tell you all about it when we have got these two rascals to bed," said her father, playing for time. The younger ones wouldn't understand and if they saw Peggy crying they would cry too, and he didn't think he could cope with three very upset children. He had decided to try and explain their position as best as he could to his eldest daughter hoping as young as she was she would understand that he didn't want to send them away, especially to an orphanage. He wished that he could have given up work altogether until his wife was home again and looked after the children himself, but what would they do for money? How could he afford the train fare to the hospital every week? And how did you keep three healthy appetites at bay with no money? Men were enlisting for the forces but he had an idea that he would be needed at his own job as a skilled engineer specializing in machine tools. If there was going to be a war he would have to work long hours, night or day, he would not be able to work and look after his children as well. So tonight was the night when he would have to tell Peggy the worst.

Peggy was in an optimistic mood. She was amazed to realize that it was still Friday, the day when she had said goodbye to everyone at school who wasn't going with her to the grammar school in September. She glanced at her father as he helped her to wash Irene and Marie for bedtime. He seemed to be cheerful enough as he tickled Marie's toes and when they were ready he gave them a ride on his back up the stairs to bed. Peggy busied herself washing out socks and ribbons to use the next day while her father was upstairs. When she heard him coming down again she sat on the chair next to his to wait for him to tell her their plans for the long summer school holidays. He came and sat next to her, wondering how he was going to tell her they would have to go away from home and that she would not be going to the grammar school, the event he knew she had worked so hard for and was looking forward to so much. He took a deep breath and said, "Well, Peggy, what I have to say to you is not very good news I'm afraid. You know the problem I'm having to find someone to look after you all while I am at work? Well, those two ladies who came to see me were from the school inspectors department and they insist that you have someone with you all when I am not here. Your Mum is not well enough yet to come home, so next week all three of you will be going to stay in a children's home until she is better. I don't think it will be for long, maybe just for the school holidays."

Peggy looked at him in disbelief. "A children's home. Is it just for during the day while you are at work?"

"No," said her father. "You will have to live there. I'm counting on you to look after Irene and Marie for me."

There was a shocked silence.

"I'm not going," Peggy shouted. "Who will look after the house and you? What will my friends say, going into a children's home?" Then she started to cry. "Don't send us away, Dad. We will be good and stay in the house all day until you come home at night."

"It is not up to me Peggy," said her father. "I wish it was. It's the law. Children under a certain age cannot be left on their own without supervision in case they have an accident, and I must go to work, so help me, Peggy, by doing as I ask. I'm sure it won't be for long."

Peggy dried her eyes. Still sobbing, she asked, "When do we have to go?"

"Well, next Wednesday. So I want you to help me pack all your nice clothes but don't tell the other two where they are going: we will say it is a holiday for you all."

Once again Peggy was crying. "You really mean it Dad – we are going away from home."

He nodded, fighting back his own tears; he couldn't find the right words. "Your Mum wants you all to stay together and this is the only way I can grant her wishes, so you will be pleasing her by staying with Irene and Marie and before you know it we will all be home together again."

That Friday night, which should have been one of the happiest in her life, turned into one of sadness. When Peggy finally went to bed she tossed and turned all night. Her father had done his best to cheer her up and she had tried to smile for him, but deep down both of them knew how sad the other was feeling. Peggy had remembered an incident over a year ago. A young girl, living on their estate, had lost both her parents in a train accident; she had gone to live in an orphanage and no one had ever mentioned her again. Would that happen to them? She was so upset that she had forgotten all about the grammar school and how she was to get there.

The next few days were frantic and unreal. On Saturday the two children's officers called to their house with the relevant papers. The children's father signed three separate papers, one for each child, stating that he was willing for his children to be taken into the care of the local orphanage, then he was given the times of visiting, once a month only on the first Sunday of each month from 2pm to 3pm. He dared not tell Peggy this. On Sunday at the children's mass and afterwards, outside the church, Peggy avoided as many of her friends as possible in case they mentioned the grammar school. That afternoon as usual they went to stay with Mr and Mrs Oates while their father went to the hospital. Peggy had not written a letter to her mother but had drawn her a picture of their house with four figures standing at the gate waiting for her to come home.

Mrs Oates had been very upset when she heard where they were going. "If only I was younger and able to get about more," she said, "I would take you all in myself." But she knew that she couldn't be responsible for three lively children every day, she was too old to cope now: but she promised "I will come to your home on Monday afternoon to help you and your Dad to do the packing." It wouldn't take long as each child was only allowed one case and to take nothing too fancy at that. Irene filled the shopping bag with her dolls saying, that they could go on holiday too. But just before they left their home for the last time her father had hidden them under the table. He thought to himself she might settle down better without reminders of home.

All of a sudden it was Wednesday morning. The three children came down together for their breakfast. On their chairs lay their best clothes, coats and hats. Peggy was very quiet: "I don't want anything thing to eat." But her father persuaded her to eat some bread and drink a cup of milk. The three small cases stood near the front door because the girls' father had ordered a taxicab to take them to their new home. It was to come at 10 o'clock sharp He has thought it better to leave early as he knew how upset Peggy would be. Irene was very excited; she had never been in a motor car before.

The garden gate was swinging backwards and forwards as the three young girls chatted. Irene and Marie were excited. This was the day of the big adventure. First they were going to their new home and were travelling there in a taxi with their father. No one that Peggy knew had ever been in a taxi. It was a lovely sunny day in July 1938 and Peggy as well as pushing the gate back and forth was holding their coats under her arm. Father had said that they would need them later on when it became cooler but Peggy didn't think that they would be away from home for that long. The rest of their clothes had been packed into cases. Peggy didn't think that they needed to take their toys, except for Irene and Marie's dolls as they were going to a home for girls. Surely there would be plenty of toys to play with and they would all be able to play together until their mother came home? Putting her hands up to her eyes to shade them from the sun, Peggy gazed down the hill. Just turning the corner at the bottom was a big black car with a sign on its roof. She rushed into the house and shouted to her father, "It's here, Dad. It's coming up the hill."

Her father was in the kitchen. He had to compose himself and put on a smiling face when his heart was breaking, knowing his children had to go away from their home comforts. He came through the door saying, "At last. I thought it was never coming. You hold on to Irene and Marie's hands and I will carry the cases."

The big black car came to a halt outside their front gate. Peggy wished her friends were there to see them getting into and driving away in the big taxi, but their father had picked 10 o'clock in the morning knowing no one would be around. Their neighbours, Mr and Mrs Oates, had come to help them into the car while their father stowed all the cases away in the boot. At last it was time to go. Peggy turned to the two people she had come to depend on since their mother had gone into hospital and said, "Thank you for helping me to look after Irene and Marie, and we will see you in a few weeks when we are all home again."

When they moved away from the kerbside it felt like floating after the shaking tramcars that they used when going into town. She looked through the window at the familiar scene. They passed her old school then the church and the buttercup fields where they used to have bread and jam picnics. Peggy heaved a sad sigh. The scene was changing now. She had never seen this part of the city before. She wanted to ask her father where they were but the motor car had a glass window between the front and back seats. He kept turning round and smiling at them and eventually they stopped.

Chapter Six

All Peggy could see from the rear window was a large black door that seemed nearly as high as their rooftop at home. The driver and their father were putting the little cases down in front of it. There was a small window with bars across at the middle of the door and a long chain with a bell on the top. Peggy's father pulled the chain. She instantly took hold of Irene's and Marie's hands as the car drove away. Father pulled the door chain again and waited.

The little window opened and a face peered at them. "Yes? What is your name?"

Peggy's father coughed and gathered his children around him. "Mr Cairnes and daughters," he replied.

The great door opened and standing there was a tall thin nun dressed in black. "Good afternoon. Please step inside and wait in the side room. Sister Superior will be down to meet you shortly." The children's father pushed the two younger ones in front of him and picked up two of the cases. Peggy lifted her own and walked in silence through the door. It closed behind them with a great clang and the thin nun locked and bolted it before she disappeared up a long polished staircase that led to another large door. The side room was painted green and had very high windows. It reminded Peggy of the school clinic. There was a round polished table and two chairs. Peggy looked at her father but neither of them spoke, for at that moment, the door opened and in swept the most fearsome looking nun Peggy had ever seen in her life.

"Good morning," she said, sitting down on one of the chairs and pointing to their father to take the other one. "My name is Sister Superior and that is how you will address me in future. The other nuns in charge of you you will be called Sister, do you understand me?"

Peggy nodded her head but Irene said, "Sister who?" Peggy jerked her hand. "I'll explain to them later," she said, glaring at the nun and disliking her at once.

"Good," said the nun. "Now say goodbye to your father and we will get you all upstairs." She rang a little bell attached to her black apron pocket. Almost at once another nun came bursting through the door. It was as though she had been pushed in. Taking hold of Marie and

Irene's hands, Peggy held them tight. "Take them to the sewing room," she said to the other nun. "I'll be up in a few minutes."

At last Peggy found her voice. "But what about our cases?" she said. Sister Superior seemed to glare at her. "You won't be needing them at the moment. Now go along with Sister and just do as you are told." Peggy turned as though to go to her father but was swiftly pushed through the door which was quickly closed behind them. For one moment Peggy thought she was going to faint. Her head felt all swimmy and she felt her legs go weak at the knees. She had never fainted in her life but she had seen girls at church who had been carried out sometimes when it was hot and stuffy.

The nun gave her a slight push forward and pointed to the staircase. Somehow she made it to the top. Turning to the nun who was now holding onto Irene and Marie she asked, "When can I see my Dad again? I want to ask him something."

The nun looked at her and said, "Oh do get a move on. I've other children to see to as well as you three. Open that door please then follow me." Peggy opened the door to reveal a completely different kind of world to the one they had just left behind. Gone were the thick carpets and the polished furniture that had greeted them on their arrival. In their place was a long cold-looking corridor with large red and black tiles on the floor, half tiled walls and brown painted wood-work. Here the window were very high up the walls, fastened down with locks and not a curtain in sight. Walking down this long corridor was a young girl aged about twelve. She was wearing what seemed to Peggy to be a brown spotted dress covered by a wrap-around pinafore like the ones she had seen Mrs Oates wearing when she was baking on a Sunday. Her hair was brown and cut very short, all the same length around her head just above her ears. On seeing her the nun called to her "Dora, what are you doing indoors and why are you not at play?" The girl stood still, holding her hands in front of her pinny.

"I have been sent inside because I have been sick and I've just been to the washhouse, Sister."

The nun pushed Peggy, Irene and Marie in front of her saying, "Take these three up to the workroom and wait for Sister Superior. She will be along shortly so keep them quiet."

Dora came forward and tried to take Marie's hand but Peggy had grabbed hold of her two little sister's who looked as though they would start crying at any moment. Squeezing their hands tight she followed the older girl down the long corridor. Her eyes were fastened on the girl's hair and dress. What a mess she looked, thought Peggy. Dora was giving a running commentary as they walked along. "That's the lavs and basins." They walked a few more steps. "This is the playroom and that's the refectory." Peggy was only half listening. She had never heard of a refectory before. She was wondering if she would see her father again before he went home. Just then they came to a flight of steps made of grey stone with smaller dark grey squares in the middle of each step. At the top was a door partly opened, leading out into a kind of playground. Peggy just caught a glimpse a sea of a brown-spotted dresses and the sound of children playing some kind of game. It was dinnertime and the children were waiting to be called in for their meal. Then Dora pushed them forward up two more flights of steps. Facing them at the top was another long corridor. The floor was made of wood and was so highly polished that the three children had difficulty staying on their feet. Dora didn't slip, Peggy noticed, because she was wearing plimsolls - the kind she had worn in school for gym lessons or netball.

Once they had left the stairs, Dora started her commentary once more. "That's the infant's lavvies and basins." Then, opening a very large wooden door, she walked in, saying, "This is the workroom and next door is the infants' and younger juniors dormitory."

When they were all inside she told Peggy to stand next to the large table, Irene next to her, then Marie. As she tried to get them into line Marie decided that she had had enough and started to cry for her daddy. Of course Irene joined in. They were making so much noise that no one heard the door open.

Then a voice shouted, "Stop that noise at once." All four children jumped and looked around. It was Sister Superior, looking fiercer than when they had seen her before. She strode towards them, glaring at each one in turn. Dora stood petrified, hardly daring to breathe.

"You." She pointed a finger at poor Dora. "Go and help in the playground and ask Sister Grey to come up here at once."

"Yes, Sister." Dora moved in a flash and was gone before the other children realized that they were alone with the formidable Sister Superior. But Peggy somehow got her courage back and turned to face the angry woman. "When can we see our Dad again? And please don't shout at Irene and Marie. You have made them so frightened."

Sister took a deep breath, raised her eyebrows (which Peggy was to learn later to her cost was a sign of trouble) and, pointing a finger in Peggy's face said, "Don't you dare speak to me in that tone of a voice again. And you will soon learn that you don't even speak to me unless you are spoken to first: do you understand me, girl?"

Peggy glared back but was spared an answer by a knock on the door and the entrance of Sister Grey. She was the Sister who had brought them from the room in which they last saw their father. Peggy noticed the grey apron tied around her waist over her black dress. Sister Superior turned round to her saying, "Ha, Sister Grey, you can help me sort this little lot out, but first will you bring me the book." The book was large brown leather one with gold lettering on the front; it was lying on a desk at the far end of the room. As Peggy watched, Sister Grey hurried across the room. She noticed a white line painted on the floor in front of this desk. The line ran from one side of the room to the other. Sister Grey returned with the book and placed it on the table in front of Sister Superior who had now seated herself in a large chair.

Opening the book and looking at the three frightened children she said, "In this orphanage there are one hundred and five girls already and each girl has a number. This number is sewn or scratched on every single item given to that girl. You will each be given a number and you will answer to this number when spoken to by any of the Sisters. Now let me see."

She opened the large book, turned a few pages, then turning to Sister Grey who was now sitting on a buffet with Marie on her knee (Peggy was still standing up holding tight to Irene's arms as the younger girl struggled to get away) she said, "The Bean girls left us last week so we can give these three their numbers. You," she pointed to Peggy, "will be known as number forty two and your two younger sisters will be forty three and forty four."

She started to write in the book, then, looking at Marie who was trying to climb down from Sister Grey's knee to get to Peggy, said, "Of course that one is too young to stay here. She will have to go to the infants' home until she is old enough to go to school." Peggy could hardly believe what she was hearing. Hadn't her father said that the only reason they were coming here in the first place was the fact that they would all stay together? She let go of Irene's arms, took a step forward and, looking straight at the Sister, said, "Please Sister, our Dad said we were all to stay together. I will look after Marie."

"Quiet!" shouted the nun. "How dare you speak to me. You will do as you are told or else." She didn't say what the else would be but she was soon to find out.

A bell was ringing somewhere, one like they used to have rung in the playground of her old school. Sister Grey stood up. "Shall I take them down for dinner? I am on dinner duty myself today." The Superior nodded her head. She was still writing in the book. Sister Grey tried to take Irene's hand but she was too quick for her and ran to the other side of Peggy.

Sister Superior looked up from her writing and said, "Leave her for the moment, Sister Grey, just get them downstairs and I will deal with them after dinner. When they have eaten send them back up to me with one of the senior girls."

Back down the grey stone steps they trouped. Sister Grey walking as best she could with the reluctant Marie. Peggy was behind her holding on to Irene's hand. They came to the first corridor they had come to on their arrival at the orphanage that morning. Peggy wondered where all the other hundred and odd girls were. The only sounds that could be heard were coming from below them. Halfway down the corridor Sister Grey stopped, then, opening a door, ushered the three frightened children inside.

The sight that met Peggy's eyes was one she was never to forget for the rest of her life. The room was very large and high. But all that Peggy could see were row upon row of girls in brown spotted dresses covered over with wrap-around pinafores and all with the same short haircut as Dora. Sister Grey pushed them forwards to a long table at the front of the room. Not one girl moved or made a sound. There were girls of all sizes and all ages. Then Peggy noticed another nun standing in the middle of the room. She was dressed the same as Sister Grey except for her apron, which was brown (they were to learn later that you called each Sister by the colour of her apron) so this one would be Sister Brown. Sister Grey left the three of them standing where they were, then she went and stood at the head of the long table, clapped her hands once and said, "Grace before meals." Each girl joined her hands together and said grace. One more clap from Sister Grey and each girl carefully lifted her chair before sitting down. Not one chair was scraped on the red and black tiled floor. Then, row by row, and just as quietly each girl took a tin plate off the pile at the end of the serving table and held it out to Sister Grey and two older girls who were helping to serve what looked like, to Peggy, a kind of brown watery stew. And still not a word had been spoken except for grace.

Peggy was watching Sister Grey, waiting for a sign from her as to what they were to do next. She was totally unprepared for what did happen. She saw Sister Grey nod her head and as if by magic a very large girl lifted Marie up and carried her away to a low table where lots of other small girls were being helped with their dinner plates. These were being passed down the line until each little one had a dinner in front of her. The big girl sat Marie on a chair in the middle and gave her a plate of stew. While Peggy was trying to see what Marie was doing, someone touched her on her arm and pointed to a place at the end of a table in the bottom half of the room. She was pulling Irene with her when a hand came as if from nowhere and took Irene to another table. She could hear Irene protesting, "I'm not sitting there. I want to go with our Peggy."

Peggy sat down in fright more than anything else. She had not seen anything like this before. It reminded her of a book she had read at home called *Oliver Twist*. She remembered how sorry she had felt for the boys when they couldn't have any more food. Without being told, all the girls at her table stood up together. Peggy followed them to the top table and received her first meal in the orphanage refectory.

From where she was sitting, Peggy couldn't see Marie or Irene without turning round. But she soon found out that this was not allowed after receiving a poke in the back when she had tried to look for them. She could hear Irene's voice shouting, "I won't eat it. I don't like it so there." Nobody took any notice of her. Sister Grey clapped her hands once and everyone leapt to their feet. Peggy was wondering what would happen to them next when she felt a tap on her shoulder. Should she turn round or not? Was someone trying to get her into trouble again? Then she felt her arm being pulled and a voice saying softly in her ear, "I have to take you and your sisters upstairs. Sister wants to see you all now."

As she turned to leave Sister Grey shouted, "Stop! how dare you leave the room without saying thank you to the Lord for giving you good food to eat?" Peggy looked down at her plate which had hardly been touched and thought to herself, "If this is good food what will the bad food be like?" She would find out soon enough that when you were hungry anything tasted good.

After grace had been said the three of them were taken once more to the workroom to face Sister Superior. She was sitting just where they had left her, still writing in the book. Also in the room were two older girls standing near some cupboards that ran the whole length of one side of the room. The girl who had brought them up was nowhere to be seen. Sister stood up and called the three children over to her. Peggy had to pull Irene over to the table. Irene was protesting. "I don't like you," she said, looking straight at the Sister's face.

Peggy saw the nun's face start to go red with anger and her knees went weak with fear. "She doesn't mean it, Sister," she cried, trying to shield Irene from the look on the nuns face. But Irene had a mind of her own. "I do mean it, and I want to go home now!"

Peggy was desperate. She was sure Irene would be in awful trouble if she didn't keep quiet. But what could she do? Sister solved the problem by saying to the two older girls who had been standing watching them, "Take these two," pointing to Irene and Marie, "next door and find which beds are empty, then stay with them and keep them quiet until I call you." Peggy's instinct was to protect her two little sisters but the look on the nun's face froze her to the ground. She could hear them crying but was unable for the first time that she could remember to do anything to help them.

"Well," said Sister. "We have quite a rebellious little family here have we not? We shall have to see what we can do about it, won't we? So, number forty two, you now must know that you will not see your sisters for the rest of the day. It will give them a chance to settle down and learn to do as they are told. It is obvious that you have all been running wild while living at home with no one to teach you what good manners are."

"That's not true," cried Peggy before she realized that she had spoken without asking.

"You see what I mean." A thin smile was on the nun's face. "You will soon learn to obey without question and the sooner you do all this the better it will be for you all." She pulled on a long red rope hanging at the side of the window just behind her back. Almost at once the door opened to admit another girl. She too was older than Peggy. Walking towards Sister she never spoke a word, just stood there and waited for her instructions. The nun pointed towards Peggy. "This is Cairnes," she said. "She will now be known as number forty two." Peggy was dumbfounded. She had never been called by her second name before. Only boys were called by their second names and then only by their friends at school.

Sister turned to the silent girl standing beside Peggy and said to her, "Go and find Sister Brown. Ask her to open the store cupboard and to find the articles and clothing belonging to number forty two, then bring them to me."

"Yes Sister." The girl swiftly left the room as quietly as she had entered it. Taking a large bunch of keys from her apron the nun walked over to the long cupboards, signalling to Peggy to follow her. Opening the first one she said, "I will sort you out for tonight. You may as well keep on the clothes you are wearing for today. No use in causing more laundry than is necessary." With these words, she reached into the cupboard and brought out, what looked to Peggy like a faded blue shirt with a flap at the back. "You can sew I hope?" Peggy nodded her head. "When I have finished fitting you with clothes you will sit and sew your number on to each garment, picking out the old number first. When you have done your own you can then sew both your sisters' numbers on to their nightclothes for the time being. Do you understand me, girl?"

"Yes Sister. But we have brought plenty of clothes of our own including our nightdresses."

"Well, you won't be needing them here, my girl. Every girl wears the same here – good clothes that our benefactors have paid for. We aim to teach you above all else to be modest and obedient. Do you hear me? Neither I, nor any of the other sisters in charge here, never ever want to hear you speak of things that belong to you, except what you are given from today onwards in this home." The nun handed her the faded blue garment and told her to go and sit at one of the tables and unpick the number already sewn in large red stitches on the bottom flap. Fortunately for Peggy, the time she had spent sewing with her mother came to her aid. The nun gave her a needle and just enough thread to sew in the number forty two.

While she was doing this, the girl who had been sent to find the articles returned with a bag of some kind of white linen.

"Come here Cairnes," said the nun. Peggy went and stood in front of her wondering what on earth she had to do next. Opening the bag, the nun took out a small towel, brush and comb and a toothbrush. Handing these to Peggy she said, "These are your belongings. Mark each one of them with your own number. They will be inspected every night so woe betide you if any of them are lost. Now go with Warton here; she will show you where you are to sleep and where to put your belongings."

Peggy's head was in a whirl. Was this really happening to her? Maybe it was all a dream and she would wake up and find herself back home in her own bed, wearing her own pretty nightdress. But she must have done as she was told because once again she found herself out on the corridor walking towards more steps. This time she had to climb three more flights of the same stone steps leading into a room which was the most incredible sight. This room was filled with beds, more beds that she had ever seen in her life. Rows and rows of them, all exactly the same. The colour green swam before her eyes. Green bedspreads, green walls and even green doors. Only the floor was different. It was as highly polished as the workroom one downstairs. In the middle of the room was a narrow aisle and near one wall was a row of beds which had a rail going all the way round them with curtains that could be drawn. Peggy was to learn later that these beds were for the senior girls.

At each end of the room there was a box-type partition. The top was open and the top half was made of frosted glass and the bottom half was polished wood. Opening another door, "This is the wash and lav room," said the older girl. "But no one is allowed to come up here during the day unless one of the orders send you."

Peggy let her eyes roam around the room. Here, the floor was made of the same red and black tiles as the ones she had seen downstairs on the first corridor. At one side of the room were six or seven toilets cubicles, all with their doors open wide, and around the other three walls were tiny wash basins. Above these were little wooden rollers, each with a small towel hanging from it. Above each one there was a number scratched into the wood from one to a hundred. Standing like a row of soldiers were the toothbrushes, each one pushed into a hole all facing the same way. "Here is your number," said the girl whom Peggy knew only as Warton. "I'll lend you my hairgrip to scratch your number on your brush and comb and other things. If you don't they will be gone by this evening as some of the other girls are always taking things that don't belong to them. They use them for 'favours'."

By this time Peggy was becoming very worried. 'Orders.' 'Favours.' What did she mean by all these things? Turning to the girl she asked, "What is your first name? I can't call you Warton all the time."

"My first name is Alice and my number is fourteen. As I am older than you I can only call you by your number when I am in charge of any group you may be in."

"What do orders and favours mean?" said Peggy. "I don't understand half the things you are telling me."

"Oh, you will learn soon enough. Now we had better get back down to the workroom before Sister sends someone looking for us. Then we will both be in trouble. Come on," she said, pulling Peggy's arm. "Oh, and your bed is the third one down on the second row from the window." Peggy's mind was in a whirl. How was she to remember all these things and look after Irene and Marie as well? On returning to the workroom Peggy started to worry about what had happened to her two little sisters. She hadn't seen them since the nun had sent them out of the room but she dared not ask in case she was shouted at again. On the table was a pile of spotted brown dresses that Peggy had seen all the other girls wearing. Sister Superior was sorting through them. "Come here," she said to Peggy, holding up one of the dresses in front of her. "This one looks about your size. I have left you some cotton on the table so sew your number on this one and you can wear it as from tomorrow."

As she was saying this she was looking down at Peggy's dress and shoes. Her dress was pale pink with a white collar and puff sleeves and was trimmed with white piping. Her shoes were the black patent leather ones that her father had bought only a few weeks ago. Her socks were pink and white to match her dress. "Those clothes you are wearing now will be put away to be used on special occasions." She then handed Peggy a pair of old worn pumps telling her to take off her own shoes and put them at the side of the table to be taken away later.

By this time Peggy was almost in tears. She had never had to wear anyone's shoes before, especially old ones like these. Then came the worst moment of all. The nun handed her a pair of dark blue knickers and a very off-white vest and something she had never seen or heard of before. It was a 'chemise'. The idea was that you placed this thing over your head and took all your clothes off underneath it, thus keeping your modesty. She was to find out later that the beds she had seen with the curtains that could be pulled around were for the senior girls. Those over thirteen could undress in private. In a daze, she heard the nun saying to Alice, "That will be all for the moment. When she has done her sewing take her down to the playground until the bell rings."

Peggy turned back to the sewing table. She had never felt so miserable in her life. After pricking her finger several times she finally finished her sewing. The thing that was worrying her the most was what had happened to her two little sisters. As soon as the nun had left the room she asked Alice where they could be. "Oh, I expect that they will be in the playground by now. Babies' and infants' clothes are taken care of by the senior girls."

Chapter Seven

The playground. Thank goodness, thought Peggy. That was where Sister Superior had told Alice to take her next. At least she could see that they were both all right and not crying. At last she had finished sewing number forty two on all those horrible clothes. At least she wouldn't have to wear them until tomorrow. Maybe she might be able to run away tonight when it became dark. She would try and find her way home. She was sure her father didn't know about all the horrible things that had happened to them since he had left them that very morning. When he did know she was sure that he would have them home again.

With these thoughts in her mind, Peggy followed the older girl once again down the stone steps, coming to a door that she had seen earlier. As they went through, the older girl turned to her and said "Don't call me Alice in the playground; whatever you do, don't forget."

Peggy just nodded her head. She had other things on her mind. She followed Alice through the door into the sea of brown spotted dresses. She soon picked out Irene who was wearing a bright blue dress. She was standing near a wall all by herself. Peggy started to make her way over to her when all of a sudden her dress was almost pulled from her back. "Where do you think you are going?" said a very gruff voice. Peggy swung around and found herself facing a very mean-looking fat girl, who was obviously a senior. Peggy glared at her. "I'm just going to see my little sister, and please let go of my dress. You will tear it." The fat girl glared back at her, still holding on to her dress. "So, we have a rebel here have we? What is your number, junior?"

By this time Irene had seen Peggy and she too was being held by a senior girl. "I'm not doing anything wrong. I only wanted to see if my sister was all right," defied Peggy. "Well you can't. If you cross the line I will have to send you inside to Sister Superior." Peggy stopped struggling. Send her to the nun! She had just had as much as she could take of her and had no intention of meeting her again so soon.

"What do you mean, don't cross the line, What line?" she asked the fat girl who had let go of her dress and was standing in front of her. She seemed very surprised that Peggy had not been told about the lines.

"Now you listen to me," she said in a very bossy voice. "In this playground there are two thick painted lines dividing it into three sections. The one over there, where your sister is, is for infants only, except for the senior girls like me who have to look after them. This middle piece is for the likes of you, the junior girls, and the end bit near the railing is for seniors only. Now if you cross either of those lines in the future you will be in serious trouble because I have told you the rules, and what's more I shall tell all the other senior girls I have done so." With this saying she pushed Peggy in the back. "Now move away from the line."

Peggy was frightened. This girl looked as if she wouldn't think twice about sending someone inside to face the wrath of the nun. She walked away towards the wall. Standing there all by herself she felt like crying but all the other girls were watching her to see what she would do next. So, she crossed her arms and leant against the wall. Soon, the other girls went on with what they had being doing before the fat girl had shouted at her. She could still see Irene who was now busy learning to skip with some senior girls. Irene would be all right, thought Peggy. She liked playing with other children. But where was Marie? Peggy had not seen her since this morning. She wasn't in the infant part of the ground. Maybe she is asleep thought Peggy. After all, they had all been up very early that morning and Marie sometimes went to sleep at the most unusual times. Once, she had fallen asleep at a Christmas party just before Father Christmas had come through the door and when they had woken her up to see him she wouldn't speak to him.

While these thoughts were going through her mind she felt a light tap on her arm. Looking round she expected to find someone telling her not to do something else. Instead, she saw a girl about her own age standing looking at her. "My name is Josie," she said. "Do you want to play with us? We are not doing much but we would like you to join us." Peggy just stared at the girl.

"Do you mean that you want me to be a friend? Oh I am so glad. I was beginning to think that no one was allowed to speak to me. Are you sure it will be all right if I join you?"

"Come on," said Josie, "and meet the others." Taking Peggy by the hand she walked over to where three more girls were sitting on the playground floor playing with some wool.

"This is Peggy," she said, sitting down and pointing to Peggy to do the same. "And we are going to be her friends aren't we?" The other girls nodded their heads and told her their names. They were all dressed in the same brown spotted dresses like the one she had been sewing her number on that morning. Sheila had fair hair. Winnie and May were twins and both had jet black hair. And Josie's hair was the same colour as Peggy's own, a golden brown. The only difference was that Peggy's hair was still long and a bit wavy. But for how long, she wondered.

One of the twins was holding onto Peggy's dress. "I once had a pretty dress like yours. It was when I had to go to the hospital after cutting my thumb." Peggy was bursting with questions that she wanted to ask them. Why did they all wear the same kind of dress? Why did everyone have their hair cut so short? When would she see Irene again and what had happened to Marie? What had the older girl meant when she said 'favours' and 'orders'? One of her questions was answered without her asking. Josie said, "Marie will be going to the infants' house in the morning." Seeing the look on Peggy's face she said, "Oh, don't worry about her because it's lovely in the infants' home. Some of the older girls who had lived there a long time and had left school lived in the infants' house and helped to look after the babies. Josie herself had had a baby sister living there when she had only been two years old. But Peggy said that Marie had been used to going to school with her and Irene and she was sure that she would cry for her.

Winnie changed the subject. "I expect that you will have your hair cut this evening if Sister Brown is on orders."

Peggy looked at her in dismay. "What do you mean by orders? And what was meant by favours?"

"Oh, they haven't told you much." So if anyone asked her if she knew all the rules she was to say no. In the meantime they would tell her.

Josie joined in. "Orders mean that when one of the nuns or an older girl is in charge of a group and gives you an order to do something, if you don't do it at once you will be punished in certain ways. One of the ways is that you have to scrub the stone steps with soda and water while all the other girls were out in the playground."

"Yes," said Sheila. "And there are lots of other punishments that we will tell you about later."

"Favours," said Josie, "Mean that some of the older girls steal your belongings and to get them back before inspection time you have to do them a favour. It could be anything, from polishing their shoes to darning their socks." All these things Peggy would find out soon enough, Josie said.

Just then a bell began to ring. As if by magic all the girls were in their separate lines. Winnie pulled Peggy after her. "Don't say a word. Just stay behind me and do as I do," whispered Winnie. Peggy found herself doing as she was told and as she watched the lines of brown spotted dresses weave their way indoors she thought that they looked like a line of caterpillars that she had seen on the fields at home. Only last week Irene had brought one home in a matchbox and kept it in the garden to wait for it to turn into a butterfly. Peggy had just remembered it. She must ask her father to let it loose or, better still, when she ran away that night she would do it herself.

Following the long line of girls she found herself once again going down the stone steps, this time to a large room. It was the barest she had ever seen. Winnie's voice was saying softly, "This is the playroom. We are all gathered here every time the bell rings. We each answer to our number before going to do our jobs. You will be given yours soon." The room was large and looked as much like a playroom as a graveyard. Looking round Peggy could see nothing but a wooden bench, highly polished, that went all the way round the room. High windows, once again without curtains, glared down at her. The floor was the same red and black tiles as the refectory and the corridor she had seen earlier. Down at the far end of the room was a very large bookcase which seemed to be filled with lots of books. This gave Peggy hope because she was an avid reader but she was soon to find out that it was only for show and not for using. Next to the bookcase stood a large tall wooden cabinet. What was in it she couldn't guess. Whatever it was it had a large lock on the door.

Someone was calling numbers out. Peggy realized that the line she was in was getting smaller. As each girl's number was called she went and sat on the bench. All this was done in silence. "Forty two. Forty two. Are you deaf, forty two?"

Someone gave Peggy a push in the back. It was Josie. "That's your number. Say 'yes Sister' and go and sit next to Winnie." All this was said in a whisper.

Peggy mumbled, "Yes Sister," and walked across the floor to where her new friends were sitting. She sat down, more bewildered than ever. Winnie whispered, "We will now be going to work – just do as you are told and you will be all right." Just then Peggy saw Marie. She was being brought into the playroom by a senior girl and her dress had been changed. Instead of the bonny blue one Peggy had dressed her in that morning she now had on a dark blue spotted one not unlike the brown ones everyone else was wearing. Her ribbons were gone and her hair had been combed back to try and make it look straight, and was fastened back with a black hairgrip. Peggy's impulse was to rush across the room and hold her little sister to her, but she sensed the look from Sister Grey's face rather than saw it, so she stayed still. But not so Irene, She too saw Marie and, breaking away from the group she was sitting with, ran across the room to her saying in a loud voice, "Where did you get that awful dress from?" For a moment Peggy thought that the senior girl holding on to Marie was going to slap Irene on her face but Sister Grey's voice rang out, "Sixty four! How dare you let one of your infants behave in this way? Take her back at once." A senior girl whom Peggy had seen playing with Irene that afternoon dashed to her side and almost dragged the protesting Irene back to her place. "If there is any more disturbance from your group, sixty four, you will see me after washdown. Peggy waited for her number to be called, but Sister Grey clapped her hands twice and everyone who was left in the room sat down again. Then she noticed the drawers. They had been behind her and therefore out of her sight. Now she watched in fascination as groups of about ten infants and one senior girl went in turns to the drawers. The senior girl would open a drawer and take out two small pinafores and place them over each of the infants' heads, then the next group would go until all were attired in the same type of pinafores over the same kind of dresses.

As Peggy was watching the ritual the girl sitting next to her pushed herself forwards on the bench, almost knocking Peggy to the floor. She hadn't noticed that all the other girls in front of her had moved forward and none had spoken a word. Then she found that she was the only one left on the bench. What should she do now? Sister Grey called her number and told her to join the end of the line of girls now waiting in silence to enter the refectory for tea.

Chapter Eight

Teatime ritual was a repeat of dinnertime, except when everyone was sitting down two senior girls, each carrying a large wooden tray, went from table to table. Peggy watched to see what everyone else would do. She couldn't believe her eyes when each girl was given one slice of bread and margarine. Then, another girl came round with a large teapot and poured half a cup of watery tea for each person.

Dare she ask what they would have next after the bread? She decided against doing that as no one else was speaking. She assumed that meals were eaten in silence. She quickly ate her piece of bread. It was the first time that she had felt hungry since leaving home that morning – but there was to be no more to eat at that meal.

Two claps of the hand and everyone was on their feet again saying thank you for such a good meal. This time she didn't have to leave the refectory to see Sister Superior as she had done at dinnertime. So, what was she to do now? Everyone seemed to be going somewhere. Irene and Marie had disappeared again and Peggy felt very lonely. Even her new-found friends seemed to have disappeared as well. Then she heard her name being called, and her first name at that. She turned her head to see another Sister standing behind her. She had a kind face and was even smiling at her. She too had on a grey apron but she was not the same Sister she had seen before. In fact before the night was out she would see three Sister Greys. But, thought Peggy, this one looks different. She was holding out her hand to Peggy and asking her to come with her. Not shouting at her to go, but actually asking. She felt herself to be too old to be held by the hand so she just smiled back and went to follow the Sister out of the room.

Out on the corridor it was quiet and Sister Grey turned to her and said, "I suppose that you are a little bit bewildered by all this activity, and upset that you have had to leave your home and father so suddenly."

At this point Peggy could not keep back the tears that had been welling up behind her eyes all day. It was the first time that anyone had spoken to her in a kind voice since she had left her father in that little room. "Oh, I want to go home," she cried. "I don't like it here at all."

"There, there. It will be all right once you have got to know the different way of life. We have to have rules, you know, with over a hundred girls living here. If not, it would be chaotic, don't you agree?" Peggy just nodded her head. She wasn't bothered how many girls they had, all she wanted was to go home where life was normal.

Sister Grey took her arm. "Come into the playground for a while and after evening prayers I will see you again."

Still crying, she walked up the stone steps and out into the so-called playground again. This time none of her friends were there. Neither was Irene or Marie. Where was everyone?, she thought. Then, drying her eyes she tried to think of a way she would be able to run away that night. She was deep in thought when she heard that wretched bell once again and was just wondering what to do next when a line of girls came out of the door and the ones that were in the playground started to line up and go inside. This time the twins and Josie had come out. When they saw her standing all alone by the wall they came over to her.

"What's the matter? Has someone been at you?" said Josie.

She told them about Sister Grey and added, "I have a plan to run away tonight. Can you tell me which is the way out of this place, because the way that we came in is out of bounds for everyone except the Sisters and those senior girls working in that part of the building."

Peggy knew this because there was a big notice on the door saying so. It was one of the first things she had seen when they had arrived. Her friends were horrified. No one ever ran away from the orphanage. If you did, the nuns told the police who then went and found you and when they brought you back no one was allowed to speak to you for at least a week. And, if you did it again, then you were sent away to another place where they kept you locked up forever. And you never saw your family again. This made Peggy very frightened. If she ran away and they locked her up she would never see the two little ones again and she had promised her father that she would look after them.

"Anyway," said Josie, "the Sister Grey who is on duty tonight is smashing. She hardly ever shouts at anyone and she is always smiling. So come on and let us go and play at something before the bell goes again."

They started to play a game of stones. The idea was that you had five small stones, threw one in the air then tried to pick as many of the other ones up before catching the first one. Peggy had seen boys at her own school playing such a game but had never had a go herself so she was soon 'out.' Standing once more near the wall she was soon joined by Josie who was also 'out'. Josie asked her how old she was.

"I'm ten," she answered.

"Maybe you will be in our class when we go back to school in September. You are the same age as Sheila, the twins and myself."

"Do you go to the grammar school," she asked Josie hope rising in her heart at the thought of getting away from this awful place even if it was only during the day at grammar school.

Josie said, "Whoever heard of a girl from the orphanage going to the grammar school? Don't talk daft. We all go to the school just around the corner and a senior girl goes with us to make sure we get there. Who gave you the idea that we went to that kind of school?" Peggy didn't know what to say. Then, in a small voice, she told Sheila, Josie, and the twins who had now joined them, "I have passed my scholarship to go to the grammar school in September."

"Well, you won't be going now," said Josie. "But why don't you ask Sister Grey who is doing orders tonight? She is very kind and I'm sure she will tell you if you are going or not. But don't ask Sister Superior as she will only shout your head off." Just then the bell went. Everyone scattered into lines, Josie pulling Peggy after her. Peggy, like any other little girl, had always liked to ring the bell at playtime at her school or, more important, to ring it in the corridor for hometime. But she thought now if she never heard another bell again it would suit her. The lines of girls walked back into the playroom and sat on the benches according to their numbers. Peggy found that she was sitting next to the fat girl who had been so mean to her that afternoon. No one spoke. Then, a very senior girl who seemed to be much older than the other girls clapped her hands and once again they all lined up after their numbers had been called. This time it was for supper. Thank goodness, thought Peggy. I'm starving. She followed her line into the refectory and sat down by mistake. Before she knew what was happening, she found herself dragged to her feet by "Fatso" (the name that the girl was always known as).

"You're lucky it's your first day," she whispered in Peggy's ear. "I'm in charge of this group at mealtimes – so don't you forget. Next time you only sit when you are told and not before."

The very senior girl said grace and they all sat down. There was no sign of Irene or Marie, and she was wondering if they too would get any supper. She knew how hungry Irene always was at bedtime. Their father used to tease her and tell her that she would grow up to be a

44

pudding. Then out of the corner of her eye she saw two girls moving around the far tables with trays. Each girl reached up and took something out of the tray.

When one of them arrived at her table the tray was held above her head and the girl sitting next to her said, "Hurry up and get your piece before they pass us by." Peggy reached up and took a quarter of a slice of bread from the tray. She looked at it in amazement and whispered to the silent girl sitting next to her, "Is this all we have for supper?"

The silent girl nodded. She looked around at the other girls who were slowly eating their bread. Then someone clapped their hands and the girls sitting at the first table went to the cupboard, took out their own numbered tin cups and walked to the top table where the senior girl was pouring something into each cup. When it was Peggy's turn she followed the other girls and was given a quarter of a cup of watery milk to take back to her table. She noticed that no one had started to drink theirs yet and it wasn't until all the girls were served that a sign that she could not see was given to start.

Almost at once, the senior girl clapped her hands and once more they were all standing up again for grace. Grace for what? Peggy was really hungry and hadn't even managed to drink the so-called milk yet. Two more claps, and they all started to move away in lines. Some went back to the playroom, others were going through the door leading to the corridor, two girls were collecting the empty cups in a kind of basket and still not a word was spoken. Peggy stood, not knowing what to do next, when a girl she had seen in the playground came up to her and said, "Sister Grey wants to see you. Go up to the top dormitory to see her at once." Peggy looked at her in surprise,

"Do you know where it is?" the girl asked the bewildered Peggy.

"No," she said, fearing it was another kind of workroom like the one that she had experienced that afternoon. "Oh well, I will take you then" she said, starting to walk away. Peggy followed, then she remembered what Josie had said to her that afternoon. "Ask Sister Grey about the grammar school."

Once outside on the corridor she caught up with the other girl and asked her, "Do you know what happened to my young sisters? They were not in the refectory to have any supper." The girl laughed at her. "Infants don't have supper, they go to bed after tea. It's hard enough looking after them without having to supervise supper as well. Now don't talk when we are on the stairs or we will both be in for it. Come on, we had better hurry up as Sister Grey wants to see you before everyone else comes up. She will want to look in your hair and inspect your body to see if you have anything like spots etc."

At this remark Peggy was speechless. Her hair was her pride and joy – she used to brush it a hundred times a night to keep its golden gloss, and her body: what did she mean, see if you have any spots? She had never had a spot in her life and neither had Irene or Marie. The only time she could remember them having anything was when Irene got the chicken pox and that was two years ago. She would tell Sister Grey this when she saw her. At last they had reached the steps and began climbing what seemed to Peggy to be hundreds of stone steps. About half way up they came upon two girls scrubbing a flight of steps. They never even lifted their eyes as the two girls walked over the ones that they had just washed. She was just about to say something when a look from the older girl stopped her. This, she thought, must be one of the punishments for speaking on the stairs. When they reached the top she found herself back in the long room with its rows of beds that she had seen earlier that afternoon. It was then she noticed that at the side of each bed was a small locker, but she had no time to look further as the older girl was saying, "Hurry up. You must never keep any of the Sisters waiting once you have been sent for." Peggy followed her into the washing room where she had left the brush, comb, and all the other things given to her that morning by Sister Superior.

Sister Grey was sitting on a tall stool at the far end of the room. She had a large white apron over her grey one and her hands were on her knees. She smiled at Peggy saying, "Come and stand in front of me. I am going to cut your hair the same length as all the other girls. This is necessary to stop infection. With so many girls in one place long hair is too much trouble for the staff to cope with."

Peggy held both hands around her hair. "No," she cried. "I won't have my hair cut. I look after it myself and have never had any trouble with it before."

But Sister Grey, still smiling, pulled her towards her and held her in a firm grip between her knees. Then, as if from nowhere, she produced the largest pair of scissors Peggy has ever seen and before she could do anything to stop her, hair was falling to the floor and curling round in little circles. By this time she was crying so much that she nearly choked on a lock of hair that fell into her mouth.

Sister Grey said no more to her about her hair but instead she said, "Go and stand by your bed, put the chemise over your clothes and undress, then bring me your clothes back here to the washroom." When

Peggy walked into the room full of beds, she stood in the middle crying so hard and so upset that she didn't know where her bed was. She didn't hear Sister Grey come up behind her. Gently tapping her on the arm, she pointed to Peggy's bed. Walking across to it she could see the faded blue nightshirt that she had sewn the number forty two on in the workroom.

"Oh, where are my own nightdresses?" she cried.

But Sister Grey was very firm and told her, "Hurry up and undress before all the other girls arrive as I have to inspect your body."

Peggy felt like a piece of rag with her short hair and the horrible blue garment that was suppose to be a nightgown. She had had awful trouble with the chemise thing, she couldn't get her clothes off underneath it and in the end she threw it on the floor. She folded her best clothes and carried them into the washroom and Sister Grey put them in a cloth bag. Little did she know that was the last time she would ever see her lovely clothes again. She had to return to Sister Grey whether she wanted to or not. She hardly remembered what happened next she was so upset and all Sister Grey would say was, "All the girls are treated the same way when they first arrive. It is just a precaution."

When she had finished with Peggy she told her, "Go to the wash basin and wash yourself, then I will speak with you for a while if there is time before all the other girls arrive." Over some of the little sinks were small sections of broken mirrors. She was to learn later that the ones who got to the basins first got to look in the mirrors.

She hardly dared look at herself. When she did it was to see a completely different person from the girl she had been that morning. She hardly recognised herself. Her hair had never been cut like that before, and what with that, and her swollen eyes from all the crying she had done that day, she really looked a sight. She was in two minds whether to ask Sister Grey about the grammar school. What would her friends say when they saw the mess she was in? For a moment she wished that she had never heard of the grammar school.

Then Sister Grey clapped her hands and beckoned her to come over to the high stool. She asked her, "Is there anything you don't understand or want to know about?"

Peggy could have asked a hundred things but she found herself with one thought on her mind. "Will I be going to the grammar school in September?" she whispered, holding her breath while waiting for her reply.

"Oh no," said Sister Grey in a surprised voice. "You will be going to the local school with all the other girls of your age group. What gave you that idea?"

Peggy looked her straight in the eyes. "But I passed my scholarship," she cried. "And my Mum wants me to be a teacher - I only have to get my uniform, I'm sure that my father will be taking me for it soon."

Sister Grey told her that she would not be going to the grammar school and she thought that her father would have told her this before she came. He had been told that there would be no exceptions to the rules of the home. Peggy didn't believe her and told her so in no uncertain terms.

"My Dad does not tell lies!"

Sister Grey was annoyed. "Go and sit on your bed if you haven't anything else to say without being rude."

Peggy said, "I'm sorry for being rude and could you please tell me where Irene and Marie are and what Sister Superior meant when she said that Marie would have to go to an infants' home." She thought that they would all be staying together as that's what her mother and father had told her.

"Your youngest sister is very small and with so many girls milling around at once little ones could get hurt, so they stay just down the road in a smaller house with just a few of the senior girls and two Sisters looking after them. Then, when they are old enough to go to school, they come back and stay here. But you won't be seeing her as from tomorrow for it is best that she settles down with the people who will be looking after her. As for Irene, she will be sleeping in the infants' room downstairs, also looked after by senior girls and Sisters." Sister also said that tomorrow, when Peggy was told what her duties would be, maybe one of them would be to look after the infants as she seemed to know a lot about younger children. But Sister Grey couldn't promise her anything because it was Sister Superior who gave out all the orders and she must be obeyed at all times.

Then came the noise of shuffling feet - it was the other girls coming into the dormitory. Sister Grey told her that she could stand by her bed until the other girls were ready for bed, then they would say prayers.

Chapter Nine

Going to her bed with a very funny feeling that that was not the end of the bad things to come, Peggy saw out of the corner of her eye one of the small wooden partitions that she had seen earlier that day at the end of the room. Standing at the door was another Sister Grey. She was standing with her arms folded watching everyone in the room undressing under their 'chemises'. To Peggy they looked like a sea of wriggling white fish but somehow, they all managed to be finished together. The new Sister Grey clapped her hands and one by one they all trouped into the washroom without a word being spoken. As Peggy watched, she turned and went into the little room. Peggy later found out that that was where she slept, and that another Sister slept in the other one at the other end of the room. When she came out again she saw Peggy standing near her bed and shouted to her, "What do you think you are doing standing there? Why are you not in with the others getting washed?"

Peggy stared back at her and said nothing. She wasn't going to get caught this time answering back to someone she didn't know, and, by the look of her she wouldn't like either. Sister Grey came storming over to her, weaving in and out of the other beds but Peggy held her ground. The other Sister Grey had told her to stay by her bed and that was what she was doing. The Sister towered over Peggy and had a big booming voice. "Are you new?," asked the nun. "I have not seen you before. When did you arrive?"

Looking her straight in the eye Peggy answered her, "This morning, Sister."

Just then the senior girls arrived in the room. Each went into a bed space where the curtains were already being pulled around and the shuffling began again of people undressing. Sister Grey turned from Peggy to stand and watch the curtains closing. "No whispering!" she shouted at them. "And hurry up with those curtains."

All this time Peggy had been standing as still as a statue by her bed. She dared not move in case she caught the attention of the nun. When, one by one, the other girls came out of the washroom and walked towards their beds she looked around to see if any of her new friends

49

would be sleeping near her but they were nowhere to be seen. As her bed was the third one down from the window she had beds all around her. Each girl was facing the bottom of the room and with one clap of the hands from Sister Grey they all knelt down and joined their hands ready for evening prayers. Peggy followed suit and found that she was saying her prayers as she had never said them before. She closed her eyes tight and prayed that they could all go home. She told God that she didn't like it in here and would he please send their father for them as soon as possible. She was so intent on her prayers that she failed to hear the command to stand up but she was soon brought back to reality by a sharp push in the back by the girl in the next bed.

Opening her eyes, she found that the whole room was watching her. Josie told her later that no one stayed on their knees longer than was necessary as they sometime spent long periods on their knees if they did something wrong. She jumped up, half expecting to be in trouble again but Sister Grey just nodded her head and everyone got into bed without a sound.

At home Peggy's bed was in the centre of the room and sometimes she would lie on her side watching the little birds flying to and fro in the large tree in their front garden. So she automatically turned onto her right side until she felt a poke in her back. "Turn over and face the other way" said Sister Grey. It was then she realized that everyone in the room was facing the same way towards the little room that she had seen the Sister Grey going into earlier.

She turned and lay there, thinking of all the things that had happened to them since that morning and also wondering what had happened to Irene and Marie. Maybe, she thought, when everyone was asleep she could creep downstairs and find out where they were. But she must have fallen asleep because the next thing she heard was a loud ringing of the bell and a voice shouting, "Up, up." She opened her eyes and saw that all the other girls were out of their beds and kneeling down on the floor, facing the large cross on the wall that she had not seen last night. Being only half awake, she didn't know what was happening but she soon found out as the next moment a hand pulled her out of her bed and pushed her to the floor. It was one of the senior girls. They were already up and dressed and some had already left the dormitory. Their curtains had been pulled back and the beds were so neat and tidy that it seemed no one had ever slept in them. The Sister Grey who had seen them to bed last night was standing at the end of the room. She clapped her hands and morning prayers were said. Peggy rose slowly from her knees and glanced about her. Sister Grey was coming over to her and she didn't know whether to sit or stand.

In a deep voice she told Peggy to take the clothes she was wearing yesterday and place them in a linen bag that was hanging on a nail behind the room door. Then she was to hurry up and get herself dressed like all the other girls, and, when she had washed her hands and face, she was to go with two other girls down to the kitchen until Sister Superior had sorted out the work she was to do. Peggy gathered her own clothes into a bundle and started to walk towards the big sack and placed them in as neatly as she could. She could see a mass of girls all under their 'chemises' trying to dress themselves without becoming detached from the thing. She hurried back to her bed and tried to do the same as the others but found that she couldn't get the old blue nightie over her head while the chemise was draped over her body as well. She glanced about her and saw that all the other girls were ready except her. They were forming two lines at each side of the washroom door.

"Are you not dressed yet?" said a voice in her ear. Peggy stopped struggling and peeped out of the chemise. It was the fat girl who had caused her so much misery yesterday. "You know that you are in my group, number forty two and I will not have any one going slow so hurry up and get into that line."

Peggy buried her face in the rough chemise and the tears started to flow. At that moment she felt a gentle tap on her shoulder and looking up she saw the Sister Grey who had cut her hair but who had been kind to her last night. "Don't cry," she said. "If you do it this way it will be much easier" and with that she started to show her how to cope with the chemise and to make her bed so that it looked just like all the others. Then she gently pushed her into her place in the line. "This is the place you will take every morning and you will soon get used to the routine." With that she walked away and started to send a few girls at a time into the washroom. When Peggy's turn came she went in and washed her face and hands and brushed her teeth as best she could. She watched the other girls to see what to do next and, lucky for her, she found herself next to Sheila so she just copied her, and when she had finished she stood in line with the rest of the girls to wait and see what happened next.

Sister Grey started to call out numbers and different girls went to do their work before breakfast. She had been told earlier that her work would be in the kitchen and that didn't bother her too much as she thought how accustomed she was to getting the meals ready at home, but she was unprepared for what she saw when arriving at the kitchen door.

They had walked down the stone steps in silence. Peggy was pleased to see that Winnie, one of the twins, was with her. Standing in the doorway of the kitchen was another Sister. This one had on a purple apron and she was very tall and thin, not at all like someone who worked in a kitchen, thought Peggy. One of the senior girls was standing beside the nun and it was her who told the other girls to get on with their jobs. Peggy found herself standing all alone once more.

Sister Purple looked down at her, "What is your number, girl and how long have you been here?"

She held her head high. "My name is Peggy Cairnes and I have been give the number forty two."

"Well miss forty two, we had better find you something to do," she said, beckoning her over. On entering the kitchen she stood still. Facing her was the biggest mixing bowl that she had ever seen and standing in front of it were two small girls with very large wooden spoons stirring something in it round and round for all they were worth. All around the kitchen, girls were working. Some were filling the large teapots with hot water, others were cutting large slices of bread into two halves and placing them on large wooden trays. Sister Purple told Peggy to go and help with the plates and trays. At the far end of the kitchen was a large wooden box that had a sliding front. Into this box were being placed the trays that she was to help with. She was soon to learn that it was a lift that led from the kitchen to the refectory and it was worked by ropes. When it was full, a senior girl gave a tug on the rope and someone upstairs would haul it up, empty it, and send it back down again to be refilled. All this was done at a fast and furious pace and Peggy was dizzy before she was finished. She was hot and sticky but at long last the final dishes were placed in the shaft, as the lift was known as.

There was a large clock on the wall, like the one in her old school. Glancing up at it she was surprised to find that it read only ten past seven. Peggy thought that it must have stopped but it was July and the mornings were light at an early hour. In the kitchen when no one was looking, girls were talking to one another. Winnie was standing near her now; she had been very busy filling large tin dishes with what Peggy thought looked like porridge, but like none she had ever seen before. When they had first entered the kitchen, each girl had been handed a light purple pinny to put over her dress. Most of the girls were now taking them off again. Winnie gave Peggy a nudge and nodded to the large cloth bag hanging behind the door where all the girls were putting their used pinnies. She quickly took hers off and followed her friend to the bag. "What do we do now? And has that clock stopped?"

"No," replied Winnie. "And we do nothing until we are told. Just follow me and no one will notice you." With these words she walked back to the kitchen door and joined a group of girls already waiting for more orders.

When all the junior girls were ready one of the senior girls marched them upstairs along the corridor and into the playroom. Here they were sent one by one to the 'drawers' to get their wrap-around aprons and then to sit on the bench to wait for whoever was in charge that morning to call them for breakfast. Peggy didn't have an apron so she slipped past the senior girl and went to join her friends, Winnie and Josie. As she sat down, Josie asked her if she had seen her younger sister that morning and pointed to the other side of the room. It took Peggy a few seconds before she spotted Irene. On the long bench, at the top of the room, near the refectory door sat the infants in groups of ten to a senior, with a space in between each group. Irene was in the second group and Peggy hardly recognised her. Gone were her bright golden ringlets, her lovely pink dress and shiny buckled shoes. Instead she saw a little girl with her hair so short that she hardly seemed to have any at all. She was dressed in a brown spotted dress just like her own and on her feet was a pair of gym shoes that had a hole in the toe of one shoe. The only reason that she had seen her so soon was the fact that she wouldn't sit down on the bench. From where she was sitting Peggy couldn't hear what she was saying but it looked as though she would be in trouble before the morning was out.

Peggy rose to her feet, and was just about to set off to try to defend her young sister when Josie pulled her back. "Don't," she whispered. "You will only get into trouble, and as your sister is only an infant she won't come to much harm. They usually allow infants to carry on a while when they first come here. She will settle down better if she doesn't see you just for the present." Peggy sat down, and both her friends put their arms through hers and started swaying on the bench, singing softly to themselves as "Fatso" came over to join them to see if they were all ready for inspection before breakfast.

Sister Brown appeared in the doorway and clapped her hands twice

– to signify that it was time to line up for breakfast in numerical order. Peggy was thinking to herself what a long time it had been since they had first fallen out of bed and how hungry she was. She lined up with the other girls, remembering to get into her right place, and walked into the refectory. In the doorway was a senior girl, and each girl had to take a plate of porridge-like stuff from her, go to her place at the table and stand quietly to await Sister Brown to say grace. Looking down at the table, Peggy noticed that each place was set with a tin plate, a tin mug and a spoon. Sitting down with the rest of the girls she started to eat the porridge that was turning into a hard lump on her plate. It was awful! She just couldn't eat it. As she put down her spoon she felt a dig in her back and a voice saying, "What is the matter with your breakfast, number forty two?" It was Sister Brown. She had been walking round the room while they had been eating.

"I just don't like it Sister, I never did like porridge," she answered, not turning her head round, and knowing full well how much she did like porridge when it was made at home.

"Well if you don't want it I'm sure someone else will." And, saying this she moved the plate from under Peggy's nose and gave it to a girl on a different table. She heard one or two quiet groans from her own table. Josie was to tell her later that if at any time she didn't want her food, she was to pretend to eat it and pass it on to someone on her own table when no one was looking. In the background she could hear Irene protesting that she wasn't going to eat that awful stuff. Then there was a crash as a plate went spinning across the floor. It was Irene losing her temper and a rare one she had too. Father said that she had the most Irish temper in the whole family. Peggy didn't know what would happen to her but she knew that she would be in trouble. At that moment a girl arrived at their table carrying one of the trays of half-slices of bread that she had been loading on to the shaft that morning. She noticed that each girl only took one half-slice each but as she had had not eaten the porridge she thought that she was entitled to at least two pieces of bread. Sister Brown appeared from nowhere. "How dare you?" she cried. "Put one back at once and when you have been to see Sister Superior this morning, report to me at once."

By this time Peggy was beginning to feel very sick; hardly any breakfast and now she had to face Sister Superior again. She slowly ate the bread; it felt hard and dry but at least it went down with a drink of the watery tea that was to follow. After grace had been said in thanksgiving for a good meal, she was led out of the room by "Fatso" and told to wait in the corridor until she was sent for. It was while she was standing there wondering what would happen next that she saw Marie. Not the Marie who had been the lovely little girl the day before, but a poor little thing, dressed in a spotted cotton dress which was much too big for her. Her hair too had been cut so short that Peggy hardly recognised her. It was her crying that made her notice her. Marie had a habit when she cried of saying over and over again, "Ming ming." She had once lost a doll that she called Minny in the woods one day when they had gone on a picnic. Father had gone back later to try and find it but it had never been found. Marie had cried for a week after that for her Minny and every time she was upset she would say the word to herself in a whimper. She was crying now, but before Peggy could get to her she disappeared through the door that they had come in by yesterday morning. Then the door was shut with a bang.

Standing there on the corridor all alone, Peggy started to think of all the things that had happened to her since they had come through that door and wondered if there would ever be an end to the misery she was now feeling. If only she could see her father – she was sure that he didn't know they were separated like this and that they had hardly had anything to eat; and when he saw how their hair had been cut and the clothes that they had to wear she was sure that he would take them home at once. When she saw Sister Superior she would ask her when was their father coming to see them. She felt very brave standing there but, a few minutes later when a senior girl came and told her that Sister Superior would see her in the workroom, her knees turned to jelly as she followed the older girl up the stairs.

Chapter Ten

It seemed to Peggy that Sister Superior was sitting just where she had left her yesterday. She was sitting with a book in front of her, staring at it as if she had never seen it before. Peggy had learned her lesson, not to speak until spoken to, and so, she just stood inside the door and waited for the command from the nun to come over to the table.

"So here you are again, Cairnes. I have had some reports that your sisters are not behaving themselves and that you refused to eat your good breakfast."

Peggy said nothing, but just stood there waiting for her to go on.

"What have you to say for yourself? And what are you going to do about it?"

At last she found her voice, "Please Sister can you tell me when our father will be coming to see us? And I can't do anything about Irene because I am not allowed near her."

She held her breath. Sister's face was going very red and angry looking and when she answered it was in a whisper of a voice. "Number forty two, you are an insolent and very disobedient girl. You will not see your father for another two months, and as for the way your sisters behave, I can only blame you as it was you who was supposed to teach them their manners while you were at home. If I hear any more nonsense from any of you, you will be punished accordingly." With that she slammed the table with her hands which made Peggy jump with fright.

Turning towards the book Sister Superior gave Peggy her orders for the weeks to come. Her head was in a whirl trying to take in all the nun was saying. The first thing she had to do after dressing in the morning was to wait until all the other girls were finished washing, then, with another girl she was to wash all the hand-basins and toilets, make sure that all the towels and toothbrushes were straight, then wash the floor and polish the doors. All those things were to be done before breakfast. Then she was to come down to the playroom, put on her pinny and help to keep the infants quiet. But not her sister's group.

After breakfast she was to go down to the kitchen and she would be told what her orders were by the Sister in charge there. After that she could go into the playground for a while until it was her turn to go back in and help with the tables in the refectory. After dinner she would once more go to the kitchen to help with the washing up, then into the playground once more until it was time for her to go to the wash-house. There she would be told what to do by the Sister in charge. Before tea she was to polish the upper corridor floor and sweep a flight of steps. Which one would depend on the senior girl in charge of the orders for that week. After tea, she would do the sewing in the workroom. Here, all the socks were darned and the underwear mended and anyone who failed to do their sewing properly would soon know about it. The nun finished by saying that that would be all for the moment, and if there were to be any more orders, she would be told by a senior girl. Sister Superior did not believe in idle hands as she said that they made mischief.

Peggy was wondering how anyone could find time for mischief or for playing out for that matter. As she was about to answer her, Sister stood up, walked all around Peggy and said, "Right: number forty two, can you sing or dance?"

This came as a great surprise to Peggy. Whatever did singing and dancing have to do with washing floors and polishing doors? She didn't know whether to say yes or no. Was this another trap, she asked herself? If she said yes, would Sister say that she was showing off?

"Well," said Sister. "can you or can't you?"

Taking all her courage in both hands Peggy answered that she was very good at dancing and that she had been in her school concerts many times, ever since she was very small. She had even been to a dancing school before her mother became ill but she had to give it all up to look after the two younger ones.

To her great surprise, Sister Superior told her to report to the playroom that evening after she had done her orders. She went on to explain that every Christmas the orphanage put on a big concert for all the people who helped to keep the home running, friends and benefactors of the home and that every girl was expected to play her part, doing whatever she was good at. She went on to say that she hoped Peggy was telling the truth and that they would soon see that evening when a lady would be coming to play the piano and she would listen to each girl sing. Then she dismissed her with the first kind words that Peggy had heard her speak since they had arrived here. She said that she hoped that they would all settle down to their new way of life. She knew it wasn't easy for children who had been used to running wild at home. This really upset Peggy. To think that people thought

57

of them all running wild and out of control was heartbreaking, but she decided to say nothing. What she would do was to tell her father when she did see him and before he took them home; he could tell Sister what kind of children they were. With these thoughts in her mind, she turned to leave the room, trying to remember where it was that Sister had said she was to go, but the nun's voice followed her saying that when she arrived at the kitchen she was to tell Sister Purple that she had been with her. Peggy gave a sigh of relief as she closed the door behind her.

Peggy was so busy that the day passed very quickly, she even ate the stew and rice pudding she was so hungry. When evening came she found herself in the playroom with lots of other girls, some of whom were seniors.

They stood apart from all the junior girls and even "Fatso" was there. But the gentle Sister Grey was in charge so everyone seemed to be talking and laughing. Some of the girls who had been there a few years were telling Peggy and a few more newcomers some of the funny things that had happened in other years at these concerts. Suddenly the door opened, and in sailed Sister Superior, followed by a tall thin lady dressed in a light blue dress and still wearing her hat.

"Oh no," she heard someone whisper behind her. "Not her again." Sister walked into the centre of the room and by this time all the girls were sitting on the benches around the room. Clapping her hands twice she said in a friendly voice, the one that Peggy had only heard for a short while in the workroom, "Now girls this, as some of you know, is Mrs Watson. She has kindly offered once more to come and help us prepare for our lovely Christmas concert. Now for those of you who have not taken part before, Mrs Watson will hear each one of you sing a few lines of a song, you will then be grouped according to how she would like you to sing."

Then, with a wave of her arms, she pointed to the piano standing in the corner of the room. This was the first time Peggy had noticed there was a piano. She didn't remember seeing it before. Sheila was sitting next to Peggy as for once they were not forced to sit according to their numbers and she told her that it was kept in the nuns' home and only brought over here when someone like Mrs Watson came.

One by one the girls went up to the piano and sang a few lines of a song that Peggy had never heard of. Then it was her turn, and she walked as quickly as she could without getting a frown from Sister who was sitting next to Mrs Watson.

Standing in front of her she said, "I'm sorry Miss but I have never heard of this song as I have only been here a day."

"That's all right dear, just sing something that you know. It is only for me to see which key you sing in." Peggy closed her eyes and started to sing one of the beautiful songs her mother used to sing to them at home when she was well. She forgot all about where she was and it was only after she had finished the whole song that she realised that Mrs Watson had not been playing the piano and that she had sung more than two lines. She opened her eyes to realise that the whole room had gone quiet and that everyone was waiting to see what would happen next. What did happen next was to put her in the bad books of some of the senior girls.

Mrs Watson said, "You have a lovely voice, go and stand at the other side of the piano." She found that she was the only one so far to stand there. Her friends told her later that usually only the senior girls got the solo parts and that she had better watch her step as they didn't like any junior girl taking their place. But for the moment, she wished that she had never sung the song and that she was at the other side of the room with her friends.

When everyone had had a turn, she found herself with three other girls, all senior to her, facing the nun and Mrs Watson. The two women were discussing the different kinds of songs that were to be performed that year. Peggy was told to go and join the other juniors who were lining up to get ready for bed. She found her place in the line and walked in silence up the stairs and to the side of her bed.

This time she wasn't classed as new and had to take her place in the queue for the sinks and the toilets. Sister Brown was on orders that night and she was sitting on the high stool that Sister Grey had sat on to cut her hair last night. Each girl lined up in numerical order, and had in her hands all her wash things, towel, toothbrush, comb and hairbrush.

Sister Brown looked in their hair and examined their belongings. If everything was all right then you passed, but if the girl standing in front of you had lice in her hair you had to clean it for her. At the far corner, near the big sink, was a row of small stools. There the poor unfortunate girl had to kneel while her hair was cleaned. This was something that Peggy knew nothing at all about. She had known of girls at her own school being sent home from school for having dirty hair but she had thought it was because their mothers had not washed it for them. She knew nothing about lice or how to get rid of them.

Luckily for her that night the girl in front of her was clean but it was not always to be so.

When she had been blown, (which was a term used by the girls when they were to wash and have their har looked into. If you were clean then you were "blown") she went and placed her belongings back on the shelf. It was then that she saw her friend Winnie looking very worried. She was looking for something - her hairbrush was missing. One of the senior girls must have taken it. This was what Winnie had been warning her about only that afternoon that you had to do a favour to get your things back. At that moment Winnie managed to slip out of the room and a few minutes later was back with her brush and just in time to get into the line. Peggy was wondering to herself what she had had to promise to get it back. She vowed to herself that if at any time her things went missing she would never bow to do any of those mean girls a favour, no matter what it cost her. She was to be tested many times in the weeks to come but despite all the punishments for not having her belongings at blown time she never once gave in to them.

Peggy walked out of the washroom and went to kneel at her bedside, where she would have to stay until all the other girls were ready. Placing her hands together and leaning her elbows on the bed she began to go over all that had happened that evening. Her thoughts were miles away, so she didn't notice that the mean Sister Grey had come into the room. It was the rule that whoever was on orders for that week slept in the two little box-type rooms that were placed at each end of the dormitory. This week it was the Sister Brown and the mean Sister Grey's turn. When prayers had been said and everyone was in bed the lights were turned out at once and the two sisters went into their rooms. But it was only July and the nights were long and light. At home Peggy would have been sitting on their front doorstep reading a book or doing something else that she liked. But here she was lying on her right side trying not to move, just looking at the girl's back in the bed next to hers and wondering to herself if she would never get to sleep.

Chapter Eleven

The following morning she woke with a jump – someone was poking her in the back with something hard. This turned out to be the window pole, and Sister Brown was doing the poking at every bed where the girl had not jumped straight out of bed at the sound of the bell. This was a ritual every morning. Peggy soon found out how hard a pole was through the thin bedclothes. Falling to her knees for morning prayers she glanced at the large round clock high up on the wall; it was a quarter past six. She tried to think which day it was and why they had to get up so early. Then she remembered that this was the second day that she had woken up in this room so it must be Friday. But what could be so special about that? Friday had always been a nice day at home – the start of the weekend, the visit to the shops with her father and lots of other times when she had sat with her mother and read a book. Everyone was standing up so prayers must have ended and she had not even heard them.

Sister Brown was making everyone hurry. Sheila was going past her to get into the line and she whispered in her ear that Friday was church day during the holidays. Peggy was struggling under the chemise to get herself dressed in time. She emerged ruffled and untidy but all in one piece. Hurrying over to join the others in the line she wondered when they were going to church and would it be after breakfast as she was very hungry. But a shock was in store for her. When they were all washed and inspected, she was sent by Sister Brown to get on and do her work in the washroom and not to be late in coming down to the playground door. The girl who was working with her was a year older; her name was Pam and her number was twenty-three. Peggy found her a bit bossy but she was not a bad sort to get on with. While they were working in the washroom they were on their own so talking was allowed unless one of the senior girls was still in there.

But this morning everyone had gone so Pam told her, "We go to church on a Friday morning to pray for peace so that there will not be a war." The most astonishing thing was that they went before breakfast after doing their work so they had to get a move on or they would be late.

When their work was finished, they hurried down the stairs to join the others and to find their places in the line. At last all were ready and they trouped out into the playground. Standing at the far end where the senior girls had their part of the playground was Sister Grey. She was holding open a small wooden door that Peggy had not seen before. It was the same colour as the walls and didn't have a handle, only a big lock. This door had been named "The Wicked Door" by the girls, so called because there was no way out unless it was opened by a nun or very senior girl with a large key. As the lines of girls reached her she passed them one at a time through the door, each girl giving her number and Sister Grey crossing them off.

Peggy whispered "Forty two" and passed quickly through the door to the other side. In front of her was a long passage and at the end of this was a senior girl. The long line came to a stop when it reached her and when all were through the door, she led the way round the corner and into the church. It was large, dark and even in summer, very cold. The girls had on only the brown spotted dresses and the coarse underwear, thin white socks and old plimsolls. There didn't seem to be anybody else inside the church, except three old ladies and themselves.

The priest was asking them all to pray for peace but all that Peggy could pray for was that she didn't pass out before the mass was ended. How she got through that first early morning she never knew, as there was still her work to do in the kitchen before they could have anything to eat. That morning at breakfast she forced herself to eat the porridge as she was so hungry. The rest of the day passed with bouts of work and visits to the playground where she saw Irene. She was busy playing with some of the senior girls and a group of little girls around her own age. Peggy thought that she looked happy enough for the time being. At least the infants didn't have to do any work, she thought to herself.

After dinner when she was in the playground, she was joined by Sheila and Josie. Sheila told her, "Josie and me have to go to the wash-house in the afternoon."

"What kind of work is done there?" Peggy asked.

They both started to giggle and Josie said "Well, of course all the washing and ironing is done there but, we are lucky going in the afternoon as Friday is change over day and bath night as well."

Sheila joined in, "The twins are on orders right now placing clean sheets and a pillow case on every bed. Also, someone else will put the clean nightgowns in order in the entrance to the bathrooms."

If she stayed close to one of them they would see that she knew what to do. Then Sheila said, "Come on it's our turn to go in now."

She wondered how they knew when it was time to go in as no one had rung the bell. But Josie said, "Each group has a lookout and when the group in front of them comes out from wherever they've been, then its time for the next group to go in."

She followed them down the steps that led to the same place as the kitchen, but at the other end of the corridor. Here was a very heavy double door, Sheila opened it and pushed the startled Peggy inside. It was thick with steam and she couldn't see a thing. The noise was deafening. A senior girl wearing a blue apron appeared out of the mist, nodded her head at the other girls who had come down with her and then, taking hold of Peggy by the arm she guided her over to where three girls were folding sheets that were coming out of the biggest pair of rollers she had ever seen. It was impossible to speak, the noise was so great.

One of the other girls gave her the end of a sheet and she started her work in the wash house. As her eyes became used to the steam she glanced around the room. It was much larger than the kitchen and there seemed to be large white bags full of washing in every spare place. Down the centre of the room were six very large boilers with lids on. These were pouring out the steam as, from time to time, someone lifted the lid and gave the contents a stir. The ironing machines, ones like she was working on, were at each end of the room. Two girls were feeding sheets into them and four were at the other side folding them and placing them in rows of twenty. Someone else would then come and take them away. She was so busy trying to keep to the rhythm of folding that she failed to notice the Sister standing at her elbow. When she did it was to see a very thin nun wearing glasses and a dark blue apron. She was known as Sister Bluey; she looked very kind and Peggy didn't feel at all afraid of her. Sister Bluey just smiled at her and went to inspect one of the boilers that seemed to be overflowing with water. When at last they had finished folding what had seemed to her hundreds of sheets it was time for them to go back to the playground.

After the heat of the wash house the fresh air was like a tonic to the girls. They just flopped down on the ground and lay there. "Whew," said Peggy, "Do we have to do that every day?"

Her friends laughed and Sheila said that they had orders to every day but they were changed every month. Then she remembered the upper corridor floor and the flight of steps that she had to do before tea. Josie said, "Wait a few more minutes and then go and get it done as this is your first time you might get behind."

None of her friends was on that order at the moment so she would have to do as the others were doing. Sheila told her, "Don't forget to ask the senior girl who is on order duty which steps to sweep as some are worse than others."

After a while she left them and walked across the yard to the door. Standing just inside was a senior girl. "Where do you think you are going?" she shouted at Peggy.

She nearly told her to mind her own business but thought better of it. "On orders, miss."

She had decided to go along with whatever she was told to do until she saw her father again, then she was sure he would do something about it. When they got home she would tell someone about all the other girls who had no homes to go to. On reaching the upper corridor she was met by Sister Brown, who seemed to be everywhere that she went. She gave her a piece of cloth with a smear of polish rubbed on it and pushed her down on to the polished floor. She was to start at the top on her knees, rubbing the polish into the first three boards. Another girl knelt in silence beside her as did the other three. When they got so far, still more girls came and followed them with very long polishers. They swung them from side to side making the floor shine like a mirror and from time to time giving her a smack on the shoulders if she got behind the other girl. She was glad when that long job was over. But what about the steps? No one had said anything to her so she just quickly went back downstairs to join her friends.

After tea that evening, Peggy was getting ready to go to the workroom, wondering what sewing she would have to do this time when, whenshe noticed that all the infants and most of the junior girls were lining up near the playroom door. It was then that she saw a new Sister wearing a white apron, she was the bath Sister and also the nurse if anyone was ill. She found herself pushed along into the line. She was just about to tell the senior girl who was pushing her that she had to go to the workroom when the older girl asked her, "What is your number?"

"Er, forty two."

"Well get in line over there. We have no time for messing about on a Friday. Bath night is bad enough without juniors being awkward." Saying this the girl walked away to the front of the line where Sister White was sorting the infants into small groups. When she had finished, a senior girl opened the door and they all trouped upstairs. This time it was just one flight of steps up from the playground door. Peggy had not noticed this door before, it was painted the same colour as the walls and having no handle on the outside, just like "The Wicked Door", and one could pass it quite easily and not know it was there at all.

Sister White had opened the door and the activity began almost at once. Although Peggy couldn't see what was happening, she could hear Irene's voice, "Get off me with that wet towel, I won't go in that bath."

Peggy was worried, she knew what a temper Irene had and was waiting for her to get into trouble, but somehow they must have bathed her for she went quiet. Peggy didn't see her come out either as she was up two flights of steps and the infants were disappearing about five at a time. When they went into the bathroom they were fully dressed and in a matter of a few minutes out they came, hair wet through and dressed in their nightdresses.

When she had been at home it had taken her and her father ages to bath Irene and Marie what with playing with the clay pipes, blowing bubbles and father pretending to let them swim. It was a night's job! But here they were in and out before she could think how they did it. When all the infants had disappeared, it was the turn of the juniors.

She heard a girl behind her saying in a whisper, "I hope the water is a bit warmer this week."

Peggy turned her head, the girl was smiling at her. "This is your first turn in the bathroom isn't it? I hope they change the water before it is our turn."

Just then a senior girl came on the scene and told the girl to report to her after bathtime for punishment for speaking on the stairs. But Peggy's thoughts were on other matters. What had the girl meant by 'changing the water?' Surely she wasn't to be bathed in someone's dirty water, it was unthinkable. Of course at home Irene and Marie went into the bath together but then they were sisters and it was more fun for them to play together. But, Peggy had as long as she could remember had her bath to herself. She was remembering Saturday nights when their father had stoked the fire up and pulled out the damper to get the lovely hot water for them while the two younger ones were playing. He would tell her to watch that they didn't go down the plughole while he went to put more coal on the fire for her water.

She dragged her thoughts back to the present and found that she was in the next group to go in. By this time she could see inside through the slight steam. The sight that met her eyes was unbelievable.

Sister White was standing in the doorway and about three senior girls were just inside the small tiled partitions. Each one had a bath in the centre. Altogether there were six such baths and there were no doors on any of them. There were at least five girls all wriggling to get their clothes off under one of the 'bath chemises' She watched in horror as one girl came out wrapped in a towel and went to stand near the wall. Sister White asked her number and then she was handed a clean nightdress. Somehow she had to get this on without losing the towel, but the sight that was holding Peggy's gaze was one of the senior girls wringing out the wet chemise and then placed it over the head of the next girl waiting to be bathed.

Six more girls moved forward and she watched their every move as it would be her turn next. First, they took off their dresses and shoes and socks and put their socks in a large white bag hanging on the back of the door. The wet chemises were placed over their heads and they had to take off their remaining under-wear and stand there shivering until it was their turn to go in. She moved forward with the next five girls. Now it was her turn; standing near the wall she had to take off her dress, shoes and socks. When everyone was ready, one of the seniors pushed her in front of the entrance to the bath cubicle. Another girl was just standing up while the senior girl held the towel in front of her. She wriggled about until the wet chemise fell into the bath. Then out she stepped and passed Peggy dripping wet. Peggy felt rooted to the ground. The senior girl who turned out to be Alice (the one who had taken her to Sister Superior just two days ago) called her into the cubicle, at the same time wringing out the wet chemise, then placed it over her head and told her to remove the rest of her under-wear and step into the bath. The cold wet chemise took her breath away and it was a few moments before she made any move at all.

"Hurry up! You are not the only one to be bathed tonight."

Still she didn't get into the water, just stood there looking at it. There was about three inches of water and she knew that the other girl had just got out of it.

"Well, what are you waiting for?"

"I'm waiting for the water to be changed."

Alice laughed, "Don't be so fussy, I don't change the water until the sixth girl had been in and you are only the fourth, one so get in."

By this time she was shivering with the damp chemise clinging to her so she had no choice but to step into the dirty water.

"For goodness sake, sit down," said Alice, pushing the unwilling girl down into the cold water and starting to rub some brown soap onto a wet flannel. She scrubbed at her arms and legs and then started to wash her over the chemise, until she came to her neck and face. Peggy had never felt so ashamed in her life. When she looked up there was another girl waiting her turn, standing, watching her struggle.

"Stand up" said Alice and holding out the wet towel. She told her to drop the chemise. "Go and stand near the wall and dry yourself and hurry up with the towel as the next girl is waiting."

"Number forty two," called out Sister White. Peggy was handed a clean cream-looking nightdress, just like the blue one she had been wearing. She placed it over her head but her body was still wet. She felt something hit her feet and looking down she saw it was her wet underclothes. They had been thrown from inside the bath cubicle. Sister White came over to her just at the moment when she was about to put on her shoes. "Put your dirty clothes in the white bag and don't put on your shoes. Stand with the other juniors outside and wait for the orders." Picking up her wet clothes she did as she had been told, following another girl out into the draughty stairs – it felt very cold after the closeness of the bathroom.

A line of juniors was standing near the wall from the top of the next flight of stairs and halfway down the ones outside the bathroom door. Peggy went to join them at the end of the line. She was cold and hungry and almost in tears, when, at that moment, the kind Sister Grey appeared at the top of the stairs. She clapped her hands once and the line of girls started to move upwards. What about supper time? Peggy was thinking to herself. It only consisted of a quarter slice of bread but that was better than nothing when one was so hungry but, she was soon to learn that Friday night was bath night and that there was no time for such things as supper.

When they arrived at the dormitory, it was to find that all the beds had been stripped bare and at the end of each bed was a pile of clean bedding. Each girl went to stand at the side of her bed and when Sister Grey was ready she gave the order to start making up the beds. When everyone was finished and all the beds were made Sister Grey moved up as each row was finished. It all seemed so silly to Peggy but she liked Sister Grey and wanted to do something right for her. When she had turned to helped the girl behind her she had noticed that she had to sleep on a piece of rubber. This, she found later, was because she wet the bed a time or two. Those poor girls who did it regularly had the last two rows of beds and every morning the beds were inspected before they were made up. If they were wet, the girl had to wash out her sheets in the large sink in the washhouse. This was done by hand and they were very heavy to wring out. They then had to take them to a small yard just outside the kitchen where hopefully they would be dry before bedtime.

As the weeks went by she was to see sometimes as many as six girls all standing miserably holding their bundle of wet sheets, waiting their turn to wash them. She was also to learn that those poor girls were not allowed the wishy-washy milk that they had for supper and only a drop of tea at tea-time. Another thing that bothered her was the fact that once one was in bed there was no getting up to visit the lavvy. If someone was found doing this the punishment was very hard. When she had spoken about it to Sheila and Josie, they told her that Sister Superior said it was to teach them discipline.

Chapter Twelve

The following day was Saturday and Peggy was hoping that they would be able to stay in bed a little longer, but she soon found that Saturday was different in another way, one that she was to dread in the future weeks. As she lay in bed that night, she was thinking of the happy times she had had at home. Even when she had most of the work to do when her mother was ill, Saturday had always been special. Father was always at home at the weekend and she never had to get up until at least nine o'clock and then there was the fun of going to the shop to choose her sweets and maybe a comic. She also had more time to spend with her friends when her father was at home. He would also look after Irene and Marie while she went into her mother's room and sat on the end of her bed or, if she was up and sitting on a buffet, she would tell her all the things that had happened at school that week. It was a lovely time and what a long time it seemed to her since she had done these things. She rose with the others at the usual time, six thirty, and set about her orders until it was time to go in to breakfast.

Some of the girls were talking about the dreaded drink that they had before breakfast. Peggy was wondering what this could be. She didn't think that anything else could shock her after all that had already happened since she came to this place. When Sister Brown, who was on orders that morning, came into the playroom to line them up for their entry into the refectory, little did Peggy or her younger sister Irene know of the ritual of every second Saturday that was to come. Every girl was standing in her place at the table, and in front of them was a cup half-filled with what looked like cold tea. No one moved until Sister Brown clapped her hands then, still standing, cups were raised and amidst a lot of choking and spluttering sounds, all the cups were emptied at the same time. Peggy took one sip of hers and was almost sick on the spot. She had never tasted anything like it in her life. She glanced quickly to the girls, right and left of her. They had replaced their cups on the table without uttering a sound.

The voice of Sister Brown boomed in her ear. "Drink it, Cairnes, everyone is waiting for their breakfasts."

"I can't its awful. It makes me feel sick." Peggy didn't care that it

69

was Sister Brown that she was answering back to, although she knew that it would spell trouble.

"So you feel sick. Well in that case you won't want any breakfast. You will stand there until you have drunk every drop. You need senna pods to clean the insides as well as a bath to do the outsides."

She clapped her hands and the rest of the girls sat down. Breakfast went ahead but Peggy was left without anything at all. She tried sipping the stuff but it was no good, it just wouldn't go down at all without her disgracing herself in front of everyone.

Breakfast was finished, grace was said, and everyone went about their orders. Sister Brown accompanied by "Fatso" came and stood either side of Peggy. Sister Brown took the cup from her hands and quick as a flash "Fatso" dragged her head back and pulled her jaw open while Sister Brown poured the horrible mixture down her throat. It was all done so quickly that Peggy had swallowed it before she knew it.

"There," said Sister Brown, "the next time you refuse your medicine I will give you a double dose, now get out of here and attend to your orders."

The room was spinning round and round as somehow she made her way to the door. She managed to make her way to the infants' lavvies where she was violently sick. As she emerged, shaking all over, one of the girls on orders in the washroom came up to her saying, "You were lucky no one saw you do that, otherwise you would get another dose of senna. There was a small wooden bench in the corner and she sat down on it. She didn't know the girl who spoke to her but she seemed friendly enough not to tell on her.

The rest of that day was just as bad; it was work as usual, but everyone seemed to have the runs, and pains in their stomachs, with long queues at the lavvies. Peggy didn't feel too bad as she had managed to get rid of most of her senna that morning. All she could think about was the fact that it was Sunday tomorrow, and she hoped to have a visit from their father even though some of the girls had told her she wouldn't have any visitors she didn't believe them. She was sure that he would take them home when he heard all the things that had happened to them since he had last seen them.

Sheila came and sat next to her in the playground. "We go for a walk this afternoon to the park, it has swings, slides and roundabouts." This lifted Peggy's spirits. Maybe she would see her two little sisters today and be able to look after them.

"Do we actually get out of this place, on our own?"

"No, don't be so daft," said Sheila. "The seniors and one of the Sisters go with us, you will see."

They were still in the playground when the bells started to ring at noon. Everyone stood still and started to say a prayer that she didn't know. She had heard it yesterday but didn't know what it was for. When it was over she asked her friend Sheila. "Oh, it is the Angulas. It is said every day at noon and again at 6pm, and don't forget, whenever you hear it stand still no matter what you are doing, and for heaven's sake don't get caught in the lavvy."

It was dinnertime. Sister Grey rang the hand bell, and they all trouped into the refectory. 'What will it be today?' thought Peggy. She was soon to find out. Taking her plate, she followed the rest of her table to the senior girls and Sister Grey who was serving from a long table. She held out her plate, and Sister Grey, holding a big ladle, slapped a dollop of brown stuff on her plate. One of the senior girls put a tiny piece of potato next to it. "Go on forty two, what are you waiting for?" She went back to her place carrying the horrible-looking stuff and placed it on the table. When everyone had been served, and all were standing behind their chairs, grace was said and quietly everyone sat down. Not a word was spoken. Peggy picked up her fork and tried to eat the cold stew, but it tasted awful. Oh she was so hungry, not having had any breakfast. She ate the potato and a bit of the stew but it was horrible.

"Don't you want that stew?" whispered Sheila.

Peggy shook her head.

"Quick, change plates with me, I'll eat it."

Plates were changed over in a flash, and so the stew was eaten.

That afternoon, all were assembled near "The Wicked Door" ready for their trip out. Peggy looked around for her sister Irene. She was with a group of other infants and some senior girls. At least she is not crying, thought Peggy, as she lined up with her friends Sheila and Josie. "How far are we going?" she asked them. "Oh, you will soon see," they answered and "The Wicked Door" was opened. They all went out in a long line. As they walked along, she realized that they could speak to one another. She had such a lot that she wanted to say. First she asked Sheila the question most on her mind. "Do we have visitors tomorrow, will our Dad be coming to see us?" "Oh no," said Sheila. "You have to be in the orphanage for two months before you can have a visitor, that is to let you have time to settle in." Peggy started to cry. "Oh, I do want to see my Dad, I am sure that he will take us home when he sees how unhappy we are." Sheila put her arm through Peggy's. "Come on, we are your friends and will help you all we can." She dried her eyes on her sleeve and walked on with them. She was so disappointed; how she had looked forward to seeing her father. What she wanted most was to find out how her mother was as no one at the home told her anything.

After they had been walking for about half an hour, they came to the park gates. The front of the line came to a stop, until they were all in a straight line. It was true! There were swings and roundabouts as her friends had told her.

"Can we go on them?" she asked in wonder.

"Oh yes, so long as we stay in sight of Sister or one of the seniors," said Josie. Just then she saw Irene. She was waiting for her turn on the infant swing. Slowly she made her way across to where she was standing.

"Hello, Peggy," she cried. "Where have you been all this time? I wanted you to find you but that big girl won't let me find you."

Peggy put her arms around her little sister, "Don't worry love, our Dad will be coming to see us soon and maybe we will be going home soon."

Just then a senior girl came over to where they were both hugging one another and dragged Irene away to join another set of girls.

"Get off me you big bully. I want to go with our Peggy."

"Now look what you have done," cried the older girl. "We were just getting her used to her new surroundings and you have set her off again. Go away and leave her to us." Peggy returned to her friends with the sound of Irene's voice in her ears.

The afternoon soon passed, but Peggy managed to ask Sheila, "Do you know where our little Marie is? I need to know before Sunday when we will see our Dad."

"Oh, don't worry about her, she will be staying at the infants' home not far away but you won't see her until Christmas, that is when the babies come back to the home for the holidays."

"But, we wont be here at Christmas. Our Dad will have come for us before then." Josie just smiled. She had been in the orphanage all her life and had seen it all before. Peggy was silent all the way back to the orphanage. Surely Marie would be brought back to see their father? What if she wasn't? He would demand to see her, she was sure. Better wait until tomorrow. She didn't want to make any fuss and then not be able to see him. She was pinning all her hopes on Sunday. It

72

was the same routine when they got back, pinnies on and work to do before tea. Saturday. What would they have for tea today? At home, Saturday had always been a special day; it was the day that they had their treats and Peggy always bought a new comic and sweets, and had a good time with her mother and father. But here it was just the same routine, work, work, and more work.

That night in bed Peggy found that she could not sleep, as thoughts were running around in her head. What would she tell her father first, and what would he say when he saw their hair? She was soon to find out what visiting meant. She must have fallen asleep because the next thing she knew was someone poking her with the window pole and shouting. "Forty two, get out of that bed at once, you lazy girl."

She rubbed the sleep out of her eyes and jumped out of the bed; everyone else was standing by their beds waiting for prayers.

Sunday, at last! She stood by her bed and vowed not to get into any trouble that day. Her father was coming and Sheila had told her that if there was any trouble she would not see her father if he came. After prayers, she was the first one to be dressed and ready for orders. No one was going to stop her from seeing her father. Breakfast was the same routine, one slice of bread and half a cup of watery tea, with lots more prayers. This was after they had been to church at a very early hour The Mass had lasted over an hour. She was getting used to not having very much to eat, but today she couldn't care less. The morning dragged on with silence and lots more work. After dinner, they were all sent out to the playground. Peggy and her friends were in a little group playing stones.

"What time will my Dad get here and how long will we be able to stay with him? I am going to tell him all about how we are treated and ask him to take us home, I am sure we will manage somehow."

Josie took her arm. "Don't hope too much, you may not be able to see him, you see, you have only been here a few days and as a rule you have to be here for two months before you can have a visit."

Peggy didn't say a word, not see her father if he came all this way to see them, she was nearly crying. "But I must see him."

Just then a senior girl came to the playground door. She shouted, "Number twenty two and twenty three come forward" Two small girls walked slowly forward, "Your visitors are here, don't forget what you have been told, go in now."

Peggy looked at her friends faces, they looked blank. "What have they been told to do? I don't want to do anything wrong now we have come so far," A few more numbers were called then everyone went on playing.

"Where is my Dad? I know he will be coming today." Sheila and Josie, linked their arms in hers and tried to comfort her. "Don't get upset, I tried to tell you that no visits are allowed for two months, maybe next month you will see your Dad." By this time Peggy was in tears, she had tried to be so brave but, this was a great blow, she would run away as soon as she found a way out. There must be someway of getting a message to her father but how?

The rest of the day went by in a blur. She went about her work and prayers. That night she lay awake in her bed, still crying, but dare not let anyone see her. How cruel the world seemed to her, two more months before she could see her father again, what was he doing, leaving them here in such misery, little did she know how he had pleaded with the nuns to let him see his daughters but, they were having none of it. Every girl in the orphanage had to be treated the same, no exceptions. Two months before a visit, there was nothing he could do. Their mother would be so upset if he told her that he decided to tell her that they were all right, and settled in to their new surroundings.

The days wore on, Peggy was always in trouble for something or other, she had been hit with a spoon on the back of her knuckles, whipped across the back of her legs and spanked with a hair brush on her hands, all for nothing as far as she could make out. She just lived one day at a time in misery.

Chapter Thirteen

At last it was late August, and Peggy had been thinking about school, What would her new school be like? She had been told that she was not going to the grammar school that she had worked so hard to get her scholarship at her own school, but it was now all in vain. Her father had told her she would be able to go there when she came home again, but, when would that be, she wondered.

It was Sunday again, and they were all out in the playground.

"Number forty two, go up to the sewing room, Sister Superior wants to see you," It was "Fatso's" voice, it sent a chill down Peggy's back,

"What have I done now?" She asked her friends,

"Oh just go and see, you never know, it might be something nice" said Sheila. She hurried as fast as she dare across the playground and up the stairs, she was shaking all over, Sister Superior was sat on the tall stool where Peggy had first received her orders and told to do her sewing. Knocking on the door she waited, holding her breath.

"Come in forty two I need to have a few words with you."

Peggy just nodded her head.

"Today your father is coming to visit you and there are one or two things you must know."

Peggy's head was in a whirl, her father coming today, it wasn't even visiting – maybe he was coming to take them home.

"You must not discuss anything that happens in this home, anything, do you understand?"

She nodded her head, she couldn't care less.

"If I find you have spoken about anything to do with your upbringing, you will be severely punished and will not be able to have visitors for a long time, do you understand me girl."

Once again she nodded her head. Little did she know that her father had demanded to see his children.

"Go back to the playground and wait for a call."

Peggy went back downstairs in a state of excitement.

"What did she want you for, what have you done now?" Her friends crowded around her.

"Our Dad is coming this afternoon to see us, but I can't tell him the things that happen here or I won't be able to see him again for ages."

"But it is not a visiting day," said Sheila, "I wonder why he has been able to come today? I am so happy for you Peggy." She placed her arm in hers and they all did a little dance.

Peggy couldn't eat her dinner, she passed it on to Josie who was sat next to her, there were no clocks in the room so she had no idea of the time. After dinner she did her orders in a dream-like trance, and once again, found herself in the playground.

"Will we be able to change our clothes? Our Dad won't like to see us in these old dresses."

"Don't be daft, we never change our clothes unless it is someone important coming."

"But our Dad is very important," Peggy said in scorn. "He and Mum are the most important people in our lives." Peggy nervously awaited the call to say that her Dad had arrived.

At last, "Fatso" came over and pushed her in the back. "Get moving forty two I am to take you to Sister Brown."

Oh no, thought Peggy, not her she walked as fast as she dare across the playground and into the corridor where Sister Brown was waiting for her. She glared at Peggy "Well forty two your father has arrived. Now don't forget what Sister Superior has told you, I will be just outside the door any nonsense from you and it will be the last time you will see him for many months to come." Peggy ignored her. Surely her father had come to take them home. Sister Brown opened the door that led to the nuns home, inside was just as she has remembered it, warm and highly polished floors so different to the cold red and black tiles on the floors of the orphanage and the long hard benches in the so called playroom. They arrived outside the small visiting room, the same room where she and her sisters had first met with Sister Superior on their arrival at the orphanage. It seemed like a lifetime ago.

Sister Brown opened the door and almost pushed Peggy through it, her father was standing near the small table, she ran to him not caring about Sister Brown or anyone else. He sat her down on one of the chairs.

She whispered, "Have you come to take us home Dad? I am not suppose to tell you, but I am so unhappy."

Her father didn't say anything for a few moments as he tried to find the right words to say to her. He took a deep breath. "I'm so sorry Peggy, but it won't be possible for the time being, I've come to tell you today that your Mum is very ill now and the doctors are sending her to another hospital where we hope she will receive some different treatment to help her recover more quickly."

Peggy said nothing, she was so upset she was sure that they would have been going home and now her father was telling her that her mother was to ill to come home. What would happen next? She started to cry. "Oh please Dad take us home I will look after everyone until Mum is better."

He placed his arm around her shoulder. "If only I could, love, but the child care officers won't let me do that. Have the nuns told you that there is going to be a war with Germany and if I don't have to go and fight, I will be working long days and nights helping to make tanks and aeroplanes to defend England?"

Peggy stopped crying, and looked up into her father's face and noticed how thin and drawn he was looking. "What's a war, Dad, we don't have one here perhaps the nuns won't allow it."

He smiled down at her. "Maybe they won't, love, don't worry about anything just you look after those sisters of yours. I will have a word with Sister Superior and make sure you are all right."

She nodded her head, she knew the nuns would take no notice of what he would say. "I am leaving ten shillings for each of you for your keep and two and sixpence each to buy some sweets."

Sister Brown must have been listening very near the door. She appeared before them in a flash. "I will take the money to Sister Superior,"

Peggy hung on to the half crowns. "No sister, this money is for sweets for my sisters and me." The nun glared at her out of the corner of her eye.

"That's all right dear, the money will be entered into the sweet register, you will be able to buy your sweets and the money will be deducted from your amount."

Peggy didn't believe her but she handed the precious money over to her.

"Well now say good by to your father, it will be nearly teatime."

She gasped. Say goodbye? Her father had only just arrived. Taking a piece of paper from his pocket he handed it to Peggy. "This is your Mum's new address, I am sure that she would like you to write to her as soon as possible." (He knew that those who had relatives or friends could write a one page letter every second Sunday, he also knew that they were all checked before posting to make sure nothing wrong was written about the orphanage.)

"Tell her that you are all right, we don't want her to be worried at all it will only make her worse if she thought you were unhappy so will you help me, Peggy? And try and be cheerful." He knew the situation that she was in and only hoped that she was up to coping with the heavy workload that she had on her young shoulders.

"Don't worry Dad, I'll do as you ask, and I won't say anything to Irene or Marie as they seem to have settled down." Peggy vowed that she would make the best of her circumstances for her father's sake and join in with the other girls. Some of them had been living in the orphanage since they were babies. To them it was their home and they loved the place because they didn't know what it was like to live in a real home with a mother and father, as she and her sisters did. So she would have to try and be more like them, accept the rules of the home and try not to get into any trouble.

Some of the nuns were kinder than others, especially Sister Bluey. She worked in the wash-house but she also taught them Irish dancing and led them in sing-songs, which was a change from some of the other nuns who were known to the girls as "Holy Terrors".

Her father gave her a big hug and a kiss, then Sister Brown almost pulled her out of the room. Crying, Peggy slowly made her way back to the playground and found her friends waiting for her.

"Did you see him, are you going home?" asked Sheila.

Peggy wiped her eyes on the corner of her dress. "No," she whispered. "Our Mum is too ill to come home yet but it won't be long before she is better, because she is going to a new hospital for some better medicine."

Sheila placed an arm around her shoulder. "Come on then, let's play a game before our next orders."

A few minutes later the bell rang and everyone quickly lined up for tea. She wondered what they would have today; it was Sunday, so maybe they would have something nice for a change. Suddenly, a girl whose name was Julie came running towards them. She gasped, "I've just been working on orders in the kitchen and I've got some good news to tell you."

"What is it?" asked Josie. "Tell us quickly!"

Julie smiled. "I've been helping to set the tea trays with our bread and guess what we're having – jam on our bread!" She gazed around her to see what effect her news had on the girls.

"Hoorah!" shouted the girls as loudly as they dared.

Peggy smiled at the sight of her happy friends and burst into song.

"There is a happy land far, far, away where they had jam and bread three times a day."

"That was good," said Josie, "where did you learn that, Peggy?"

"Oh, at my school. Some boys who came from a poor family used to sing it in the playground. They were so poor that they wore their boots without socks. Some of the other boys said that they got their boots from 'Boots for Babes'. These came free from the council because their father was out of work. They were brothers and were always laughing and singing funny songs – they were poor but always happy."

A few minutes later the bell rang for tea. Would it be something nice? But no, her hopes were soon dashed. The only difference was a small blob of jam, hardly big enough to cover the one slice of bread that they received each teatime. "Never mind," thought Peggy, doing the best she could with it.

That night when she lay in bed, the singing of that little song in the playground turned her thoughts back to her happy home life of not so long ago. She thought especially about her mother. Lying awake she remembered a warm sunny evening in May. She had just finished her school homework and was sitting near her mother in her room. Mother was looking at a lovely mother of pearl-backed prayer book given to her by their Uncle Charlie, a favourite uncle of theirs. The windows were open wide, when all of a sudden a lot of noisy lads gathered in the field opposite their home. They were about to start a game of football. There was lots of shouting and arguing about who was going to play in which team.

"It's some lads from our school; they can be very noisy," said Peggy. "Shall I close the window, Mum?"

"Oh no, I love the sound of children playing. Do you know, Peggy, when we received the keys for this house on this new estate it was the answer to my prayers. Where we lived 'down the old end' everyone was friendly and helpful and would do anything for each other, but living conditions were shocking. The colour black and grey everywhere, grimy back-to-back, one-up one-down houses, worn flagstones and grey cobblestones outside the doors: not a very healthy place to grow up in." Her mother paused for a drink of water. "Here it is so different, lots of greenery, fields and hedges, privet and gardens. The bright red bricks of the new houses with their contrasting white window sills. It all looks like Paradise to me and what's more, it is a much healthier place for you all to grow up in." She stopped once again. "Are you all right Mum?" Peggy asked, knowing her mother wasn't very well. "Oh yes, Peggy, it's too late for some people but I am happy for you young ones; listen to the sound of those healthy boys out there. Yes, Peggy leave the window open wide."

Peggy at last drifted off to sleep, and dreamed of her mother sitting in her room, looking and listening through her wide open window. A skylark was hovering and singing high in the sky above the fields and in the dream mother smiled, nodded to Peggy and whispered the word 'Paradise'. Peggy slept on with a lovely smile on her face.

The weeks slipped by slowly. There wasn't a day that she didn't wish she was at home, but she remembered her father's words, "do your best."

It was late August and every girl had been fitted with her school clothes. Peggy had been hoping for a better type of attire, but again she was very disappointed. Blue spotted dresses, slightly thicker than the ones they were wearing now. She was soon to learn that they were worn for school summer and winter, and changed every two weeks for a brown version, regardless of the weather. But the shoes she was given were the worst: hers were an old, much-mended pair of black once-shiny patent leather ones. They were pushed onto her feet by "Fatso". They hurt her toes but she dared not say anything. At home she had always been proud of her shoes. Every night before going to bed she had polished and rubbed them until she could see her face in them, and she and Irene had always been bought new shoes and clothes for their first day at school after the long summer holiday. She still wondered where all their good clothes and shoes had gone to.

It was Sunday, visiting day; she would ask her father if he had taken their good clothes home.

After dinner, when all orders were done, Peggy made sure that she did not get into any trouble. She wanted no delay in seeing her father because she had so much to ask him. At last she heard her number and Irene's being called. She walked over to her little sister and took hold of her hand. This was the only time that she was allowed to do that. Irene was playing a game of 'ring-a-roses' and she didn't want to go with Peggy but she pulled her to her side and hurried her through the door.

When the visitors first arrived they were taken by a senior girl to the refectory to await the arrival of the children. Peggy saw her father waving to them as soon as she entered the door. Irene was skipping at her side. But Sister Brown was sitting on a high stool near the food shaft, so she only dared walk slowly towards him. He soon had Irene sitting on his knee and Peggy, with her arms around him, leaning against his other knee. She smiled at him. "Hello Dad, is Mum getting any better? Are we any nearer to coming home yet?"

He hugged her to him. "Not just yet, love, she is still very ill, but we can only hope." "Oh Dad, we have to go to our new school tomorrow. The nuns have told me that I can't go to the grammar school, so what shall I do?"

He looked down at her expectant face. "Peggy, just do as you are told and everything will be all right. You may be able to go to the grammar school when you come home." He didn't know why he was saying these things to her, but she was so desperate for some good news that he felt he had to say something to cheer her up.

Then, with a swift look in the direction of Sister Brown, he put his hand in his coat pocket and brought out a bag of sweets. Irene shrieked with delight and tried to take the bag from his hands. The noise alerted Sister Brown.

"Oh no," cried Peggy, watching the angry look on the nun's face, "I am in trouble now." The nun glided over to where they were sitting. She smiled at their father and at the same time she reached for the sweets. "I'll take care of those, Mr Cairnes; it is very near to teatime and we don't want to spoil appetites, do we?" She walked back to her seat putting the offending goodies in her large brown pocket.

"Never mind, love, I will get some more sweets to you the next time I come to see you." Irene was happy; she had been quicker than Peggy and was busy sucking away at a big boiled sweet and enjoying every minute of it.

In no time at all the bell rang for the end of visiting. Peggy clung on to her father's arm. Irene, having finished her sweet, was pulling at Peggy. "Come on, I want to go back outside to play." Peggy turned to her father. "Goodbye Dad, don't let them work you too hard. Are you going to see Marie now?"

"Yes," replied her father, trying to stop his voice from wavering, "I am going straight from here; don't you worry about her, she is doing fine and seems to be very happy." She kissed him on his cheek. With a last wave she made her way back to the playground. She handed Irene back to the senior girls. Her own friends were sitting on the ground; none of them had had a visitor and she felt really sorry for them.

Chapter Fourteen

The sound of girls' voices, twittering like a flock of birds in a tree, slowly died away. At the sound of the ringing bell Peggy turned to her friend Sheila. "What happens now?" she whispered. "Shush," said Sheila out of the corner of her mouth. "We will be in a lot of trouble if we are seen talking, just do as I do; now come on."

This was Peggy's first day at her new school, and she was wearing the uncomfortable dresses that they had all been issued with that Sunday. She had spent all playtime sewing her and Irene's numbers on them. One more clang of the bell and the girls arranged themselves into straight lines. Not a word was spoken, although there must have been at least a hundred girls in the room. Peggy was worried about Irene; she craned her neck to try and see her but it was hard to pick her out from the sea of blue spotted dresses. Then she heard her: "I don't want to stay in this line. Why can't I go to school with our Peggy?"

Peggy looked to see where the voice was coming from and saw Irene being pushed back into line by a senior girl who seemed to be in charge of the infants. "I had better go to her," she whispered to her friend. "No," hissed Sheila, "you will both be in trouble if you do that, leave her to the seniors; as this is her first school day she will be all right." Peggy wasn't so sure, she knew Irene's temper would get the better of her but it seemed that there was nothing else she could do about it.

The bell clanged once more and the lines of girls started to move forward through the playroom door, down the corridor and out into the playground. They next came to 'The Wicked Door'. Sister Grey was there with a big book. As each girl passed through she had to give her number and was counted out. They were marched, like a battalion of soldiers, round the corner to the local schools.

The infants and lower junior schools were just across a cobbled yard. Peggy just saw the back of Irene going through the school gates. Peggy was worried about her, but what worried her more was, where was Marie? To Peggy Marie was still only a baby; she had had her third birthday just before they had left their own home. She knew that she wouldn't be old enough to go to school, but what had happened to her? Where was she, was she crying for her Peggy? Maybe Sheila might be able to tell her if she was ever allowed to speak to her again.

The first sight of her new school brought Peggy to a standstill, and the girl behind her almost fell over her. It was a small black square stone building with a large iron gate as an entrance. Once inside she gazed around at the sloping playground and the grim look of the place. It consisted of a two-storey block and, just like at the orphanage, its large windows were high up in its walls. There were four outside lavvies and nothing more. Once everyone was inside, the gates were closed by the senior girl who had walked them to the school; she then left them and returned to the orphanage.

It was then that she noticed some other girls, gathered in little groups. She noticed that they were wearing their own clothes, pretty dresses and cardigans, and some even had coloured ribbons in their hair.

Later she was to learn that these girls lived in their own homes with their families and were known to the orphanage girls as the 'Other Girls'.

Sheila and Josie seemed very excited by it all but Peggy could only think of the school that she had left behind with its airy classrooms and fields to play in. Here there wasn't a blade of grass to be seen; how could they ever begin to learn anything in a place like this?

Someone was ringing a bell. Two teachers came through a door, both middle-aged with grey hair. Mrs Ryan was in charge. She was a very large lady and her hair was drawn back from her face and fastened in a bun at the back of her neck. She looked very fierce, and Peggy was frightened of her at first sight.

Miss Banner was quiet-looking. She was very tall and thin, and she had glasses that wouldn't stay on her nose; she was forever pushing them up into place. Both the women wore light-grey dresses with blue cardigans on top.

Mrs Ryan began reading out names indicating which line each girl had to take her place in. Peggy was hoping that she would not be in her group, but no such luck. One thing did go in her favour; she found herself in the same line as Sheila and Josie. Once everyone was sorted out she noticed that there were equal numbers of girls from the orphanage in both lines. Mrs Ryan led their group into the downstairs classroom. "It's very different," thought Peggy. Everything looked so old. At the front of the room, right next to the teacher's desk, was a blackened fireplace, then three rows of highly polished desks and benches filled the rest of the room. Closed cupboards were fitted around the two main walls and the rest were painted a dull yellow.

They were allocated their seats and she noticed that the orphanage girls were put at the back of the room. In the winter, when the fire was lit, the back of the room was the coldest. One of the other girls was giving out reading books. Peggy was looking forward to having something to read after her time in the home with no books at all.

"When I call out your name, please stand up." Mrs Ryan's voice boomed out at them. As Peggy's name was Cairnes she was one of the first. "Now girl, you are new to this school so tell me a bit about yourself." What should she say without getting herself into trouble? "Yes, miss. I am nearly eleven and want to do well in my new school." There was silence in the room and every girl was staring at her. "We all do well in this school: do you understand me, girl?" Peggy nodded her head: she was in trouble again. "Sit down and remember what I have told you. That goes for all of you." She carried on with her register and the rest of the class stood up in their turn.

It was playtime and her first visit to the playground. The ground sloped downwards at one end. Girls were running around like little ants. Peggy was soon to learn who could stand where and when; the best places near the wall of the lavvies was taken by the other girls who met in little groups and whispered among themselves. Peggy and her two friends were leaning near the railing that surrounded three sides of the playground. "Oh Peggy, you should not have put Mrs Ryan in a bad mood this morning. The best thing to say is to say 'yes miss' and then sit down."

"But she asked me to say something about myself; what was I to say?"

"You will soon learn not to say anything good about yourself, but never mind, let us play at something before the bell goes again, and whatever you do, don't say anything to the other girls unless they speak to you first." This was all so confusing to Peggy. Why were they called the 'other girls' and why should she not speak to them? This was something she was to learn about in her days at her new school.

Chapter Fifteen

Peggy knew that Christmas would be different that year. Things had not been the same since she and her two young sisters had had to leave the comfort of their own home, and had been brought to live in the local orphanage for girls.

Christmas time. Irene and Marie were still young enough to believe in Father Christmas. And Christmas had always been a very exciting time in their home. On Christmas Eve, father would string the paper chain decorations across the ceiling and blow up balloons. He would pretend to be out of breath and make his face go red and funny to the delight of the children. Next would come the Christmas tree. This would stand in a big tub in the corner of the room and have lovely coloured bells and streamers, with little candles on the end of every branch. Next would come the sweets that could be eaten after the excitement of Christmas was over. Peggy used to like Christmas Eve best of all, for when it was dark, father would light the candles on the tree and the flickering lights would cast a lovely glow onto the manger, where the baby Jesus lay in his crib with Mary and Joseph watching over him. The crib always stood in a place of honour on a little table near the fireplace. To Peggy, it always seemed that the baby Jesus was smiling up at his parents, and that they in turn looked with wonder on their little baby lying on a bed of straw.

After a little while, father would gather the children together and they would all gather around mother's bed and then father would re-tell the story of that first Christmas Eve. The next exciting thing to happen was the moment that Irene and Marie had been waiting for all day. Each child had been given a pillowcase with her name pinned on the front. These were hung by the fireplace to await the arrival of Father Christmas, then one by one father would give the little ones a lift on his back to bed. It was just after Marie was born that mother had not been the same healthy person, so for the past two years Peggy had gone with her father to choose the lovely dolls, colouring books, pencils, oranges and apples, plus all the other wonderful surprises that would go into Irene and Marie's Christmas sacks. Father also let her help him choose a present for mother and somehow, in secret, he managed to buy her the things that she most wanted. She could never remember saying to father or mother that she would love to have a fancy sewing box with little drawers that opened to reveal lovely bobbins of cottons and pieces of coloured silks, a tiny pair of scissors and even a tape measure. And enough silks and satin material to make dolls' dresses for her own special doll and Irene and Marie's too.

Their mother was a talented dressmaker, and she used to make all Peggy's long white dresses for the church processions, and lovely summer dresses and gymslips for school. Even while lying in bed, she had still made things by hand and had shown Peggy how to do lots of fancy sewing and make clothes for her dolls, even a handkerchief for her father's birthday with his initials sewn in the corner; but all that was behind her now and she knew that this year would be a very different Christmas for them all.

"Stop daydreaming, Peggy Cairnes, and get on with your work." Mrs Ryan's voice penetrated Peggy's thoughts. "Sorry, miss," she said, bending her head over her schoolwork. She tried hard not to think of the conversation held at playtime with Josie and Sheila about the different Christmas that she and her two young sisters would have this year as girls from the orphanage. It was the first week in December 1938, six months since they had had to leave their home.

Peggy's class consisted of thirty six girls aged ten and eleven, twenty of whom were living at the orphanage. The rest of the girls – the 'others' – lived in their own homes with their parents and families. They dressed as they pleased but the girls from the orphanage stood out in their blue spotted dresses.

"The school party will be in three weeks' time on a Friday" was announced by Mrs Ryan at the morning assembly and this was the reason for Peggy's troubled thoughts. At the morning playtime Peggy, Josie and Sheila were grouped together near the school wall. "What do we bring for the party?" Peggy asked her friends. There was a puzzled look on the faces of her friends. "We don't," sighed Sheila. "No one from the home is given anything to contribute to a party." There was a shocked look on Peggy's face. "Well, what happens to us on party day?" Josie and Sheila looked at one another; both the girls had been in the home since they were babies. "We do favours for the other girls and hope for an invite to one of their groups."

"What kind of favours?" The other two exchanged glances again. "Oh, you know," Josie answered rather quickly. "Writing compositions, copying times tables, polishing desks and benches" – she stopped speaking as Peggy was staring at them both in disbelief. She was very particular regarding the polishing of her desk and bench in her classroom on Friday afternoons and she wondered why it was always the girls from the orphanage who did all the work; she never saw any of the other girls rubbing at desks, washing paint brushes and jars or any other jobs. She did her own desk then went out to play, but most of her friends were still using their 'elbow grease' doing favours. Peggy was determined not to grovel to any of the 'others'.

Peggy was the top of her class. She had done the work they were doing last year at her own school. The other girls soon realised this and they were more than friendly towards her, but she would still have nothing to do with their favours; let them do their own work, she thought to herself. That was until one day, when Sheila said to her wistfully, "I wish that I was clever, I have never been invited to a party all the years I have been at the orphanage."

"How long has that been?" Peggy asked.

"Oh, ever since I was a baby."

Peggy was astonished. Never been to a party? She couldn't believe it. So she was determined to get her an invite this year, but it wouldn't be easy now. The Christmas exams were over and no one wanted any work doing, and there were more polishers than desks, it seemed; she would have to think hard.

Two days later, she walked up to three girls who were talking together in a corner of the school playground. This group, she had found out, always had the best party. One girl even had a mother who was a teacher in the infant school, so they must be very rich, thought Peggy. All the other girls were nicely dressed; one had long hair, tied up with lovely ribbons.

They turned when they saw her standing there. "What do you want, Cairnes?" said one.

Peggy gritted her teeth. She still hadn't got used to being called by her surname. Looking them in the eye she said, "I would like you to invite my friend Sheila to your Christmas party please. If you do, I will do all your favours for you after the holidays. One for each of you and I don't care how hard they are. I give you my promise, I will do them." The three girls stared at her in surprise; this was the first time anyone had actually asked them outright for an invitation for themselves, let alone for someone else. They usually did the asking; it was they who said who could come to the party and who couldn't.

No one spoke for a moment, then the girl with the long hair started to laugh. "Why are you asking for someone else? Who has invited you along?"

"No one," answered Peggy. "But Sheila has never been to a party before, never, since she was a baby. I'm not bothered myself, I have been to plenty of parties before I came to this school, and I will be going to plenty more when I go home. But Sheila there has no home to go to so she will never ever go to any parties unless someone like you invites her. Will you do it?" The three girls looked at one another and began to shuffle their feet. No one had ever spoken to them like this before, especially about someone from the orphanage; they had never given a thought about the girls who never got invited to a party, they were just orphans, someone to look down on. Maureen, the girl whose mother was a teacher and who herself had failed the entrance exam to go to the grammar school spoke first. "I have another chance next year to sit for my scholarship. If you will help me with my work I will invite your friend." Peggy agreed, but said, "On one condition. Sheila is not to know that I asked for her." Maureen said she would ask her herself the next day, when Peggy wasn't around. Peggy walked away around the corner to where her friends were busy playing a game of stones. "Where have you been?" asked Josie, looking up for a moment from the floor. "Oh, just around," she answered in an off-hand way and sat down to await her turn.

That same afternoon, the girl with the long hair, whose name was May, approached Peggy while she was busy washing paint brushes in the staff room sink. She stood for a moment not speaking, then she asked, "Would you like to come to our party with your friend Sheila?" Peggy said, "No thank you, as another of my friends will be left on her own this year, so I will stay with her." This was Josie. The twins had already been invited by another group, so Peggy couldn't leave Josie, who had been the first person to befriend her at the orphanage; she would never forget that.

May stood looking at Peggy. She had never known a girl from the orphanage like her before, especially one who asked favours for others and refused to come to what May considered to be the best party in the school, just because one of her friends would be left out. She hurried back to her own friends, but she had an uneasy feeling in her mind that she wouldn't enjoy the party at all.

For the rest of that afternoon, Peggy saw May glancing her way every few minutes. She hoped that they would not change their minds about inviting Sheila; if so, she would just have to find another group to ask.

When the final bell went for hometime, the other girls left the classroom first, to get their outdoor clothes.

Girls from the orphanage did not wear coats for school no matter how cold the weather was. When the cloakroom was clear, Mrs Ryan let them out with the usual words: "No speaking until you are outside, please." Once clear of the room, Peggy was walking with the twins when she felt a tap on her arm. It was May and her two friends. "Can we speak to you a moment, Peggy?" she said. It was a moment before she realised that they had used her first name. She pushed the twins on ahead, saying, "Wait for me at the corner, I won't be long." She turned to the three waiting girls ready to do battle with them, but it was Maureen who spoke first; she seemed almost shy and embarrassed "Er ... we three have decided to ask you and your friends Sheila and Josie to come to our party." She pushed a lock of hair behind her ear. "We thought of asking you first and you could tell the others yourself." There was silence from the three girls. Peggy looked them straight in the face. "Thank you very much, but it would be nicer if you asked them yourselves, just like you asked me: I'm sure they will be overjoyed to be invited to what is thought to be the best party in the class, and thank you, I would love to come."

"Of course," said May, looking a bit sheepish. "It's just that we never thought before about the ones not invited, I think we have been rather mean, but this year we will make sure no one is left out of a party, just leave it to us." There were smiles all round, and Peggy felt a warm glow inside her. At least Sheila would get her wish. "I'll have to dash or else we will be locked out," she said, turning to go. "And thank you all very much." She ran towards the corner, just nodding her head at the many questions the twins were asking. "Just wait and see, and we had better hurry up now if we don't want to be in trouble again."

Chapter Sixteen

The next few days at school passed very happily for Sheila and Josie. They were both surprised and delighted at being asked by May, Maureen and Kathleen to attend their party and even more so when they heard that Peggy was coming too. The 'other girls' had kept their promise and many other orphanage girls found themselves unexpectedly invited to other parties. Sheila and Josie spoke of nothing else in their free time. Peggy tried to make it appear that she was joining in the excitement, but she had other things on her mind at that moment. Unknown to her, their father had been in touch with Sister Superior regarding the children's Christmas presents. Sister had sent for her that very morning and told her she was to go shopping with her father the following Saturday, but to say nothing to anybody about her trip into town.

She would even be excused the 'Saturday Senna.' Peggy was glad and sad at the same time. Glad that she would see her father again, as they had only seen their father a few times since they had arrived at the orphanage, but very sad at the thought of not spending Christmas at home. Father had told them at his last visit that their mother was still not well enough to come home, but maybe when the weather was warm again she would be better. In the meantime he was relying on Peggy to look after Irene and Marie for him. On his last visit, he had looked so tired and upset that she didn't tell him half the things she had planned to. She decided to wait until they were all home together, which she didn't think it would be long now, then she would tell him how all the girls were treated, and ask him to do something about it.

Arriving back from school on the Friday afternoon two weeks before Christmas, Peggy felt a buzz of excitement in the playground. She hurried indoors to change her clothes, but in the playroom the atmosphere was electric. Standing just behind the door was the biggest and tallest Christmas tree she had ever seen. It was standing in a large barrel of soil, and as she looked up she saw that it reached the ceiling, but no one could go anywhere near it because thick ropes were fixed all around forming a barrier. Sister Brown was in charge and told everyone to get on with their orders. As Peggy made her way to the drawers to change her school clothes and put on her pinny she bumped into Sheila, who quickly explained that a tree of that size always came at Christmas and that later that evening Sister Superior and the senior girls would be filling the tree with lovely toys and trimmings, but no one must touch them. Anyone leaning over the ropes would be severely punished! Peggy's orders for that time of day were working in the refectory, lifting plates and cups out of the crockery cupboard and setting the infants' places after she had washed down all the table tops. The door between the refectory and the playroom had been left open and she was trying to see if Irene had come in yet; she would love to see her face when she saw the big tree. Marie, of course, was still at the infants' home and would be coming to the main orphanage when school was finished for the Christmas holidays. Peggy had only seen her twice since she had been sent there. She had seemed happy enough, but then, thought Peggy, she was only a baby, and babies soon forgot things, but not herself and Irene; they would remember last Christmas when they had all been at home. Only last week Irene had told her that she was asking Father Christmas for a black doll and a pram as well as the many other things. Peggy took notice of what she said because when she went shopping with her father on Saturday, she would tell him Irene's wishes and remember the black doll.

It came to her then in a flash that since they had been here she had never seen one child with a toy or doll of any description; as she herself was past the doll stage and all her time seemed to be taken up with orders, she hadn't given it a thought. At the bottom end of the playroom was a floor-to-ceiling bookcase, full of exciting and interesting books, but now she thought about it she had never seen it open or any books removed from it. "I will ask Sheila and Josie at rehearsals tonight," she told herself. Then she heard the clap of hands and everyone was lining up to go into tea, so she had better get a move on. The food lift was working early tonight. She saw the trays of bread being lifted out of it. Only the senior girls were on orders at that time and she saw some of them pushing slices of bread down the fronts of their dresses. Peggy pretended not to notice, but couldn't help wondering who would go short this teatime as only the exact amount of bread was sent from the kitchen according to the number of girls present each day. She just hoped it would not be her or Irene; as it was, each girl only received one slice of bread each and the infants just a half-slice.

When tea was over, Peggy went with Josie down to the kitchen. They were both on washing-up orders. As soon as she got the chance she asked her the question that had been puzzling her for some time: why did no one have any toys to play with? At home the three of them still had lots of books and dolls as well as games to play with from birthdays and other Christmases. Here no one seemed to have anything, only stones, and even they were guarded and kept secret in hiding places in the playground. "But we never have anything of our own," replied Josie.

"Well, I am going into town on Saturday with my father to buy presents for my sisters and me. Irene wants a black doll and all sorts of things, but keep it a secret, no one else must know or I will be in trouble and might not be able to go."

Josie didn't believe her at first; she had never known anyone who had done anything like it before. When Peggy told her about the hanging up of pillowcases on Christmas Eve, Josie's face was a blank; she was sure that she had never heard of anyone hanging up a pillowcase before. "Oh, forget all about it," said Peggy, thinking that here in the orphanage, things must be done in a different way at Christmas; and how right she was.

Saturday arrived at last. Her father was coming at one thirty to take her into town shopping, but before then, she still had all her orders to do as usual. After dinner on a Saturday, infants and those not employed on orders were sent out into the playground for an hour even in the coldest weather. The kind Sister Grey had been in charge that morning. She had told Peggy to wait in the corridor after dinner. Down one side of this corridor were many built-in cupboards which were always kept locked. Peggy had polished them many times but had not taken much notice of them. When all the children were clear of the corridor, Sister Grey came out and produced a bunch of keys from her apron pocket.

She called Peggy to her side. "I think this cupboard should fit you up with everything needed for your outing." As Sister Grey opened one of the polished doors, Peggy gazed in amazement. The long cupboard was divided into three parts. A shelf at the top held dozens of round brimmed grey velvet hats, trimmed with a purple and yellow band round the crown. Hanging just underneath were grey matching coats of different sizes. At the other end of the rail was a row of yellow and white striped dresses. At the bottom were dozens of black patent shoes. Sister Grey was holding first one set of clothes after another up to Peggy until she was satisfied that everything would fit her including the shoes. She closed the door and told Peggy to follow her up to the top dorm to get changed. When Peggy had got her breath back she asked Sister Grey, "Where are all our own clothes, the ones we brought with us from home?" She was sure that her father would be expecting to see her wearing her own clothes. But Sister Grey told her to stop fussing; all the girls from the orphanage wore these clothes on special occasions; they were very smart and all the big shops in town knew the uniform and had often brought back girls who had got lost; and now would she hurry up and get dressed if she wasn't to keep her father waiting.

At last she was ready. Following Sister Grey downstairs she was hoping to see some of her friends but saw only a couple of senior girls who didn't seem interested in her changed appearance. Then, for the first time since she had arrived at the orphanage, she found herself passing through the door that led to where the nuns lived. Once again she was in the small room and standing there was her father. Whatever his thoughts were at the sight of his eldest daughter dressed like that, he managed to keep to himself. Sister Grey was explaining to him that they must be back by five o'clock. He was nodding and smiling and said of course they would. Sister Grey opened the big locks and chains on the heavy black door and Peggy and her father found themselves alone together at last.

They had so many things to say to one another that they both started speaking at once and just ended up laughing. They were going to town on a tramcar. Memories came flooding back to Peggy of last year's shopping trip with her father when they had bought toys, fruit and sweets to take back home for Christmas, and the excitement of hiding the toys from Irene and Marie.

"A penny for your thoughts, Peg," laughed her father as the tramcar came to a halt.

"Oh, I was just wondering how I can buy you and Mum a present when I had not got one penny in my pocket. We don't get any money to spend like we did at home."

Her father smiled. "That's all right, we will choose a present for Mum and she has sent you some money to buy me a present." When they arrived at the big store he said, "Don't worry about things; let's start thinking what we will buy for Irene and Marie first."

Once they arrived at the toy department, she soon forgot to worry because everything was so exciting, and although she half-insisted that she was too old, her father still took her to the fairy grotto to see Father Christmas. Standing in front of him he asked her what she would like for Christmas. She had no hesitation in answering him. "I would like it so much if my Mum, father and me and my sisters could all be home for Christmas." He answered, "I'm sure you will be," and gave her a large wrapped present from the fairies' basket. Father was waiting for her at the exit, and she dropped her present in his large carry-bag. They paraded around the rest of the store. On the first floor they saw a counter with lovely fluffy garments. They chose some pink and blue bedsocks for her mother, and while father was having them wrapped, she chose a nice fawn scarf for her father. "Will you wrap it for me," she asked the smiling lady. She did so and even put a nice little card on the front with "Happy Christmas Dad from ..." Peggy wrote her own name as well as Irene and Marie's. When her father turned round, she put it in his pocket and told him not to open it until Christmas day.

Next it was the toy department. She told him Irene wanted a black doll with a pink hat; they both laughed. There were so many dolls to chose from. At last they found one they both liked, she was black with a lovely smile, blinking eyes, dressed all in pink knitted clothes. For Marie they bought a baby doll in a long nightdress and shawl. Father bought lots of smaller things: a knitting set, crayons, books with magic paints, little games and puzzles For Peggy, while she was wandering around, he bought the latest girls' annual, a new type of wooden pencil box with lots of secret drawers in it, a pink hairbrush and matching comb and a box of fancy hankies.

By this time it was nearly four o'clock, and they were exhausted so they went for something to eat. Peggy was hungry as she had hardly touched the stew that they always had on a Saturday. They found an empty table and she sat down surrounded by bags of goodies and parcels while her father went to get some tea and buns. He came back with a tray of tea, buttered scones and a large cream bun for her. The last time she had seen a cream bun was at Mrs Oates' house the day her mother took ill; how long ago that seemed now. Breaking into her thoughts, her father asked her, "Are you going to eat it, or just sit and look at it until the lady clears the table?" Peggy smiled and began to eat the bun but the thoughts of her mother were still uppermost in her mind. She would ask her father for the latest news after they had finished eating.

Soon it was time to go back. They sorted the presents into different bags and father wrote the children's names on each one. Father made sure that his and mother's presents were in his pockets and carrying the bags between them, they set off to catch the tramcar out of town and back to the orphanage. On the way back, her father took her hand and told her, "Your Mum really looks forward to your letters." He added that she was responding to the treatment but not well enough to come home yet. He had been told last week by the specialist not to hope for much; he could spend Christmas Day with his wife but of course none of the children could visit. He didn't tell Peggy these things as she had enough to worry about. He had a good idea how the orphanage was run and was very annoyed about it, but for the time being the girls would have to stay there as most of his time was spent at the hospital. He felt almost torn in half between his wife and children.

All too soon they were ringing the bell at the big black door. It was Sister Brown who let them in and showed them to the small room. Sister Superior appeared as if by magic, saying, "Say goodbye to your father quickly as tea is about to be served, and you must change your clothes beforehand." She saw Peggy's eyes looking at the bags of presents and said to her father, "These will all be put away until Christmas; say goodbye now and I will let you out myself."

As Peggy turned to leave the room, she had tears in her eyes. She didn't like the look on the nun's face. It gave her an uneasy feeling. Sister Superior closed the door and turned to the children's father, who was still standing with the parcels all around him.

He spoke first. "The children's names are on each present. I hope they will be all right. How are Irene and Marie? My wife has become very ill in the past few weeks, but don't tell the children."

Sister Superior nodded her head. "The children are all well and I am sorry to hear your bad news, but can I remind you to pay for the children's keep for this month?"

Because their father was working he paid five shillings a week for each child. He gave her the money saying, "I have given Peggy ten shillings to share between them all." What he didn't know was all money had to be handed in to Sister Superior, and the amount was entered in a book.

Chapter Seventeen

Every evening, when orders were finished, one hour was spent on rehearsing for the Christmas concert that was given every year on 6 January. As it was a thank you concert for the friends and benefactors who gave money to the orphanage it was a very important event, and every girl from the eldest to the youngest took part in one of the events whether it was singing solo, duets, song and dance routines, four-hand reel dances, or poetry. Even the babies played in a fairy scene. At the end everyone came on stage together according to age groups and a special song was sung to end the concert. One week later, the same concert was performed again for the parents or guardians of the children; that was, for those who had any.

Peggy had been chosen to both sing and dance and every spare moment was spent in practising her steps. She was to dance "Autumn" in the ballet of "The Four Seasons" This meant walking round and round the playroom in old ballet shoes that had hardly any padding left in them and trying to stay up on her toes while Mrs Watson played the piano. She came three times a week now that it was getting near to Christmas and even the infants stayed up half an hour longer to practise their pieces. Irene's group was dancing the "Teddy Bear's Picnic", and from what she could see of her she was doing all right and seemed to be enjoying the whole thing. One evening Peggy was sitting watching the infants when Irene came and sat next to her, and pointing to the Christmas tree said, "I have asked Father Christmas in my prayers to bring me a lovely black doll and lots of other nice things." Peggy gave her a squeeze. "Hurry up and join your group or you will get nothing if you are naughty."

It was one of those occasions that Peggy saw the large polished cabinet that stood at the top of the playroom between the drawers and the locked bookcase. This too was always kept locked but it was the first time that Peggy had seen it opened. It was a beautiful gramophone and radio. Four girls were dancing a four-hand reel to the music from a record. In the centre of the playroom, Sister White, who was a very good dancing teacher, was in full swing and in charge of all the dancing for the concert including Peggy's "Autumn" ballet. She liked Sister

White and tried hard to do everything right for her but it was difficult without proper shoes, though she thought maybe they would get some better ones for the actual concert.

As she was putting her shoes away that night, the thought came to her that she had not found out what happened on Christmas Day regarding receiving the presents that her father had bought them. She hoped that they were somewhere with their names still on the bags they were brought in.

The Sunday following the arrival of the great Christmas tree in the playroom, Sister Brown, Sister Grey and some of the senior girls had started to decorate it with beautiful bells and baubles, shimmering tinsel and coloured lanterns that appeared to have lights already inside them. Sitting on the top was a silver fairy holding a golden wand and sitting in most of the branches from top to bottom were wonderful collections of dolls, beautifully dressed in either silk or knitted outfits. There were large, small, white, black and baby dolls, teddy bears, fluffy dogs and rabbits. Gaily wrapped boxes of all sizes that looked as if they contained exciting presents and conjured up in the mind of any child the wonders of Christmas. There were also games, books and fancy packets of sweets. As Peggy let her eyes gaze up and down the tree, her heart gave a small jump, and she decided to move a step closer.

Sitting in the middle of the tree was a black doll dressed in pink, exactly like the one they had bought for Irene; she was sure it was the same one, the thin piece of ribbon hanging from its arm that had held Irene's label was still round the doll's arm but the card with her name on it had been removed. The lady in the store had tied the ribbon in a special way so that it didn't fall off, so she knew that it must be Irene's doll. Then she started to look closer at the tree and sure enough, Marie's baby doll was lying in its cradle with a frilly cover over it. One by one she recognized the presents that she and her father had brought here only last Saturday. Even her new pencil case was tied to a branch. Her mind was in a whirl, but she decided not to say anything to anybody. Then a thought crossed her mind; maybe they would be given them on Christmas Day.

It was Friday, the day of the school party. The girls from the orphanage went to school as usual, wearing the same blue spotted dresses made from flannel with long sleeves. The other girls arrived wearing a variety of pretty party dresses with ribbons or headbands to match in their hair, and most wore fancy shoes. There was a general buzz of excitement all around the playground, girls were flitting in and out of the classrooms taking in tins and dishes containing lots of sandwiches, buns, and jellies of red, yellow and green. There was always great competition between the groups of girls about who had the best parties. Lessons still had to be done first but only for about half an hour, then their teacher gave them a talk about behaviour during the party and clearing away afterwards. The afternoon usually ended with the singing of Christmas carols.

Sheila, Josie and Peggy were even invited to help set out the spread. Maureen had brought a tablecloth for their group. Everyone enjoyed themselves so much, especially Sheila: she talked about that afternoon for months afterwards. As Peggy looked around the gaily set-out room she was very pleased to notice that not one orphanage girl had been left out of the festivities. She just hoped Irene had found a party to join. Josie told her that the infants all had biscuits and milk. When the time came to clear everything away, Maureen, May and Kathleen insisted that Peggy and her friends take home with them any buns that were left over. Whether they would be allowed to keep them was another question. When the time came for them to go home at last there were many shouts of, "Have a happy Christmas and see you after the holidays!" Peggy wondered what kind of Christmas they would have on this their very first time away from home.

Now that school was finished, everyone had to concentrate on the big concert. Any time left between orders was spent learning dance steps and words to the songs. A group of men had arrived on Saturday, and erected a wooden stage at the refectory end of the playroom. Sister Grey and Sister Brown, watched over by Sister Superior, had fitted curtains that could be drawn across the front of the stage just like a real theatre. Two of the senior girls were put in charge of pulling the ropes as each turn went on and off the stage; it was all getting very exciting. The sewing room was littered with costumes and dresses of every description. Each girl was sent for and fitted with whatever dress, shoes, parasols, baskets, or kilts that she required for her act. Peggy had to spend one evening pinning numbers on the items that each individual girl required. The large cupboards at the end of the sewing room were where all the concert clothes were kept. Peggy's hopes of getting a better pair of ballet shoes were not to be fulfilled. Instead, Sister Brown gave her a piece of orange chalk to rub on her shoes to cover any scuff marks, but only to be used on the night of the concert.

Her dress looked as though it had hung in that cupboard for years. It had a plain yellow top and the skirt was made from orange, brown and yellow leaf-shaped pieces of material that hung from a narrow waistband. The headdress was made from paper leaves, sewn onto a piece of elastic. Sister Brown said that they would curl stiffly on the night. Peggy sighed: well, at least it fit her and she didn't have to spend hours sewing like some of the other girls, whose dresses were either too long, tight or short. Sheila and Josie were to dance with a group of girls dressed as gypsies, and they had a cardboard campfire for the centre of stage. The twins were to be two wooden dolls in a puppet show.

One day passed into another and with all the work that she had to do plus rehearsals, Peggy didn't notice the days slipping by until one afternoon, returning from one of her orders she looked into the playroom and there was Marie, happily playing with some other little ones, watched over by Sister Grey and two senior girls who lived at the infants' home. She hesitated for a moment, and then went inside to take Marie in her arms.

It was quite obvious from the look on Marie's face that she had already forgotten who Peggy was. Twisting herself round she clung to one of the senior girls and cried, "Go away, I don't like you." Peggy was stunned: this was her baby sister who she was supposed to look after for their mother and father. She had forgotten the short hair and the dingy spotted dress that Marie was wearing. All her curls had been cut off and her hair had been left looking spiky.

Sister Grey looked up from her sewing. "What do you want forty two, get back to your work."

Peggy pointed to Marie, "I want to see my little sister please."

Sister Grey was kind and said that it would be better if she was to leave Marie alone for the time being, as she was quite a happy little girl and that babies soon forgot about the past. By this time Marie had run off again to play with her friends. Peggy walked away with tears in her eyes. Sister Grey had told her that she could see Marie any time that the infants were at play but she had to treat her like all the other infants. She would be going back to the infants' home the day after the concert but she promised that she would be back for the parents' and friends' concert the week after. Sister Grey's smile and nod of the head meant "dismissed".

Peggy took one last look at Marie, who was dancing around in a circle, and left the playroom to go and do her orders in the refectory. Tears were running down her face she had been so looking forward to seeing and holding Marie again, and now she didn't even know her.

This made her determined to tell her father when she saw him again. It was one thing not to worry him with things that happened to her and her friends, but Marie not knowing her was something she couldn't cope with.

Josie was already in the refectory and asked, "Why are you crying Peggy?" She tried to explain about Marie but all Josie could say was not to worry, it would be easier for them both once Christmas was over. Then she pointed to the ceiling, and looking up Peggy saw that coloured streamers had been festooned from the corners, with a large bell holding them together in the centre. Josie explained that these were put up every year for dinner on Christmas day. She chattered away in an excited voice telling how Sister Superior and all the other nuns served the children their Christmas dinner, they came round the tables carrying large dishes and served each child separately. Christmas pudding and custard followed. Everyone put on a clean dress and no pinnies were worn. There would be fancy hats too but they must be left behind when the meal was over. Josie chattered on and on.

This brought Peggy's thoughts to the fact that it was Christmas Eve and no one had mentioned a word about presents. The toys their father had bought were still on the big tree in the playroom. She decided to wait and see what happened on Christmas morning. Things were bound to be different here with all those girls to cope with. In the meantime, Christmas Eve or not, she still had her orders to do and after that evening there was to be a dress rehearsal for the forthcoming concert in January. Even the infants and babies were to take part so she might see both Irene and Marie together.

The evening passed very quickly. The babies dressed as fairies danced in and out of a fairy bower. One of the senior girls was the fairy queen and seemed to be leading them to dance to the music.

Irene's group was funny to watch, "The Teddy Bear's Picnic" had never been meant to have bears falling over one another because some of the headpieces were too big and fell over their eyes, but Irene managed to stay on her feet. Peggy did her Autumn ballet and later sang with two other girls, then came the grand finale where everyone came on stage in order of age group. They sang the final song, all bowed together and last came God save the King. Everything had to be cleared away and put back in the cupboards, and it was quite late when they got to bed that night. Peggy had a quick look around the dormitory before getting into bed but could see no evidence of Christmas.

Chapter Eighteen

They were woken up earlier than usual on Christmas morning. As Peggy knelt saying her prayers she peeped as far as she could see, but there were still no signs of any presents. A few thoughts crossed her mind: maybe after breakfast, in the playroom, Sister Superior gave them out herself; she would just have to wait and see. Her main worry was Irene. Last night she had not seemed to notice that it was Christmas Eve and hopefully she wouldn't realize that it was Christmas Day until she received her presents.

Just before the holidays, their teacher had told all the class that on Christmas Day, there was to be a special service for children of all ages in the church at ten o'clock. Peggy had been looking forward to meeting some of the new friends that she had made at the school party, but the children from the orphanage were marched out to church at eight o'clock, and she was so disappointed. As far as Peggy could see it was orders as usual, just like any other day. She was on orders with Sheila in the top dormitory before and after church. It was almost time to go down for breakfast, and Peggy felt a little tingle of excitement but looking at Sheila, who showed no sign of anything being different, she had her misgivings, especially when Sheila said, "Whoo! I'm glad that I am not working in the kitchen today, it will be like a boiler room."

Apart from the decorations that she had seen yesterday, the refectory at breakfast was just the same as usual. They had the usual porridge, still no sugar or milk, with usual slice of bread, eaten in silence. Sister Brown was on orders and rapped the knuckles of some girls that she had caught turning around or speaking. After grace was said at the end of the meal all babies, infants, junior and senior girls were to assemble in the playroom after breakfast orders were finished, change into their good dresses and put their pinnies away in the drawers. This is it, thought Peggy, at last something is going to happen. She and Sheila were on infant dormitory orders. The beds still had to be made, floors polished, but today she went to work feeling much happier. Although it was Christmas Day, there was still no talking on the corridors or stairs. Senior girls were still on the lookout just the same hoping to catch someone out and to bribe them into doing favours for them.

Despite the fact that she was bursting to ask Sheila what would happen in the playroom after orders, she passed the senior girls in silence.

When at last she and Sheila met while making the beds, Peggy asked her, "When do we receive our Christmas presents – will it be in the playroom or after dinner?"

Sheila's face was a blank. "What Christmas presents?" she asked. "I have never received presents."

Now it was Peggy's turn. "But what about all the presents our Dad bought us, the ones on the Christmas tree? Surely Sister Superior will give Irene and Marie their dolls?"

"No," Sheila replied. "Those will stay on the tree until after the big concert then they will be put away until next year." What surprised Peggy was that Sheila didn't seem at all upset at not receiving any presents. She went on to say, "After the big concert has finished, each girl is called off the stage by order of age and then they all receive a present, but that isn't until 6 January when all the important people come and one of them will be asked to present the gift to each girl."

Peggy didn't know what to say, she was so upset. She asked Sheila, "Will Irene and Marie receive the presents that Dad has bought them?"

Sheila paused for a minute. "I don't think so, juniors and seniors usually get a new jumper or school cardigan, a new pinny and maybe a book."

On the night of the concert the long tables from the refectory were placed down the side of the playroom and covered in crêpe paper. On them in order of presentation would be their gifts; each one had an old Christmas card with a girl's name on it stuck on the front. When your name was called you stepped down from the stage, smiled, said a "thank you sir" or "madam" and then returned to the refectory. There, Sister Brown or Sister Grey would remove the card and place it in a big box to be used again next year. Peggy listened to her friend in disbelief, but Sheila went on to say that maybe one of the babies and infants would receive a doll or woolly toy in a decorated basket, as they were called out first and led by a senior girl back to the refectory. Very few people saw what they received; the dolls, teddy bears and other things were taken from them and never seen again until next year.

At this point Peggy began to cry. But Sheila carried on: "As for our things, we come from the playroom, lay our gifts on the tables left in the refectory, and once all the guests have left the tables and chairs have been carried back to the refectory, we go to change our concert clothes, everything is put back in order for next week's concert then it's off to bed. Next morning the only things remaining are the jumpers, cardigans and pinnies and we have to sew our numbers on them that afternoon. But come on, we will be late for the playroom meeting. We sing carols and one or two of the senior girls sing on their own, but whatever you do don't laugh or giggle otherwise you will be sent out to kneel in the corridor." Peggy couldn't even speak after hearing all the unexpected new information, let alone think of laughing or giggling. She followed Sheila in silence down to the playrrom where they managed to squeeze between Josie and May on the far bench. Was this really Christmas Day? She gazed across the room and saw Irene, who was clapping her hands with everyone else and seemed to be enjoying herself. Marie was sitting on the knee of a senior girl who was holding Marie's hands and clapping them to the music of the singing, but Peggy herself was very sad. How long ago it seemed to be since last Christmas when they were all at home having such a wonderful time. What would their father say when she told him on his next visit? He was coming to the concert for relatives and friends in three weeks' time but it seemed to be such a long time away.

The singing went on until Sister Grey rang the bell. As they lined up each girl was called to make sure her dress was clean and tidy before leaving for the refectory. The great moment had arrived; every other girl seemed to be very excited and happy, but none of it rubbed off on Peggy.

As they marched into the refectory there was a buzz of excitement. Everything seemed so different that even Peggy lifted her head and took notice. The long refectory tables were covered with different coloured paper, and a fancy hat had been placed between each girl's knife and fork. Sister Brown seemed to be in charge and grace was said. "Girls, please sit down and place your hats on your head." Her next words were a big surprise to Peggy. "You may talk quietly among yourselves while dinner is being served, but no turning round or shouting across the room."

It had always been a punishable act to speak at mealtimes. Depending on who was on orders punishments varied from six slaps on the back of the hand with a large spoon, to kneeling for a stated length of time on the cold corridor floors, to washing down a flight of stone steps when everyone else was in recreation. Therefore it was a few minutes before murmurs were heard.

Suddenly every head in the room turned as the refectory door opened.

Sister Superior herself entered wearing a large white apron. Behind her came four other nuns, two of whom Peggy had never seen before. She was more puzzled still when Sister and her party made their way to the serving table. The other Sisters also put on big white aprons and began to follow the head nun around the room, handing out plates of Christmas dinner to the girls. Peggy had to admit it was the best meal that she had tasted since their arrival six months ago. The dinner was followed by fruit pudding and custard. When all was eaten, plates were passed to the end of the table where again to Peggy's astonishment senior girls collected them to be placed in the hoist and returned to the kitchen.

It was all over so quickly. Peggy was on refectory orders, so she had to stay behind after grace had been said. Sister Superior clapped for silence. She named and thanked the other nuns for helping to make this such a lovely day, then departed taking the other nuns with her. Once they had gone, everyone who wasn't on refectory or kitchen duty went back to the playroom. The next few hours were spent making their own enjoyment.

In the refectory Peggy was amazed to notice hardly any of the paper on the tables was marked. The food had been too precious to drop any. She helped Josie to fold the paper, and collect and fold all the fancy hats, placing them in a large wooden box. They even had to be counted to make sure that no one had taken one. Josie informed her they would be put away until next year. Thank goodness she wouldn't be here then, thought Peggy. The rest of the orders were finished as quickly as possible; the floor still had to be swept and mopped even though it was Christmas Day; then they went to join the others in the playroom.

That was the end of the Christmas activities. Some songs were sung that afternoon but it was work as usual for the rest of the day. "Thank goodness," Peggy said under her breath. "Irene and Marie have not realized what day it is." They went to bed as usual and Peggy cried herself to sleep.

Chapter Nineteen

For the next few days, rehearsals went ahead for the big concert. A group of girls including Peggy were told to go to the church that night to collect candle wax.

"What do we want that for?" she asked her friends once they had gathered near the Wicked Door.

"We collect the wax that has collected at the bottom of the candle holders and put it in a tin bucket, then take it to the kitchen where it will be melted, and any paper concert dresses or headbands are dipped in the softened wax the night before the concert to make them stand up stiffly." Peggy could not believe what she was hearing. Yuk! Some of the girls were even chewing it like bubble gum. It was dark and cold in the church and she was glad when they had finished collecting the wax. They all trouped back through the door with their precious bucket of wax, stumbling in the dark.

The day of the big concert had arrived. There had been lots of activities over the past few days; everyone had been busy practising their dances and other acts. The previous evening Peggy and a few other girls had gone to the kitchen where she had dipped her dress and headdress in the melted wax and had left them there to dry. An hour before the concert started she was to go and collect her things and be ready in time to do her turn. She stood looking at the tattered old dress; she couldn't see what difference the candle wax had made to it except to make it feel slippery and when she arrived back in the refectory to put it on she soon was in trouble with Sister Brown. "Hurry up, forty two, there are other girls waiting to get dressed." The nun threw the cotton chemise at her. Peggy still had trouble trying to put her clothes on and off under the tent-like garment especially with the waxed material poking out all over. She managed somehow after a few slaps and pushes from Sister Brown and then went to stand with the other three girls who were, like her, to dance the four seasons ballet.

The concert was in full swing. Peggy had caught sight of her two younger sisters as they went in to do their dances but she was not allowed to speak to them. Then it was her turn, and arms above her head she danced through the door. "I am autumn, the time for fallen leaves." As she tried to do her steps in the old ballet shoes the heat in the room from all the people gathered there caused the wax to melt; down came the withering leaves and stuck to her face. She panicked, unable to see a thing; round and round she danced and to her horror she felt herself falling off the end of the stage and landing into someone's well-robed lap. Later she was to learn it was the person who was the honoured guest. Quickly hands came and pulled her away back to the refectory, still suffering from shock. Sister Brown pushed her to the back of the room. "Number forty two, you are an absolute disgrace – how dare you spoil the evening? Go and clean yourself up and be ready for the finale." Peggy was crying as she wiped the wax from her face as best she could and went to join the other juniors waiting in line for the final song. She knew that she would be in a lot of trouble and would suffer the following day.

The final song was sung by all the girls and the guests clapped their hands and cheered them all. Peggy was dreading the next part of the evening. Each girl's name, starting with the youngest, was called out by Sister Superior to come and stand in front of the Bishop, the main guest. The junior and senior girls had been taught how to bow their heads and kiss the Bishop's ring before being presented with their gifts. Peggy had been so looking forward to receiving the lovely present her father had bought her only a few weeks ago but as she glanced at the tree her hopes were dashed; her presents were still hanging on the tree. Somehow she found herself standing in front of the Bishop. He smiled and handed her the gifts from the benefactors which included a pinny, school jumper and a cloth rabbit. A used Christmas card with her name written across the top was all she received. Sadly she returned to the refectory and placed her gifts on the table with everyone else. What would her father say when she told him? He would be so angry and demand that his daughters receive their own presents. Peggy looked around the room: no Irene or Marie – they had already been taken off to bed and whatever presents they had received had already been boxed away until next year.

Sister Brown was still very angry with Peggy. "Forty two, find your and your sisters' jumpers and pinnies, take them up to the sewing room and stitch your numbers on them all, and don't speak to anyone or all your recreation will be stopped for a week."

"What recreation?" thought Peggy, but she would miss talking to her friends very much. She slowly gathered up the garments and made her way up the dark stairs to the workroom, vowing to herself that for the relatives' and friends' concert when her father would be there she would not put any candle wax on her headdress no matter how much trouble she would be in afterwards.

The big day came at last, and thankfully for Peggy everything went like clockwork. "Will I be able to see my Dad after the concert?" she asked Sheila. "I don't know, I have never had anyone to meet me." Poor Sheila, not having any relatives; she would tell her that she could share their father next visiting day.

When the last song was sung she peered over the heads of the rows of girls and then she saw him, sitting in the middle of the third row. Oh, how she wanted to run over to him and tell him how unhappy she was, but they had all been told earlier in the day they could see their relatives for a quarter of an hour after the concert. Irene and Marie would be in bed; no sense in upsetting them with an evening visit.

Peggy changed her concert clothes as quickly as she could (Sheila had offered to put them away for her) and was first in the queue to see her father. Sister Brown was once again in charge. "Now remember, girls, when the bell rings you all return to this room at once." At last the door opened and she was through, nearly tripping over herself in her hurry. Her father was sitting in the same place she had seen him in earlier. He reached out and placed his arm around her and smiled down on her. "That was a wonderful concert, you were all very good."

"Irene and Marie can't come to see you, Dad; they had to go to bed because it was so late."

"I know, love, but I saw them singing and dancing. Your Mum will be so proud of you all when I tell her."

Peggy was quiet for a minute. "How is our Mum, is she nearly better? I do so want to come home. We didn't receive our Christmas presents that you bought us – they are all still hanging on the tree." Peggy turned her head towards the tree but nearly everything had been stripped from it and placed in large wooden boxes so she knew that they wouldn't see their presents any more.

"Never mind," her father was saying. "We will buy some bigger and better things when you all come home; just try and be good for your Mum and me and I am sure she will get better sooner." The bell was ringing.

"Oh no," Peggy cried, "I haven't told you half the things I want you to know: when will you be coming again?"

"As soon as I can," he said, hugging her to him. Sister Grey and

Sister Brown were moving around the chairs. "Say goodnight to your father now, and away up to bed with you." Peggy was choking with tears: all she wanted to do was go home with her father, but it wasn't to be.

Turning away from him she stumbled her way back into the refectory, tears flowing down her face she lined up with the other girls and marched off to bed.

Mr Cairnes was hanging back. He had been shocked at the lack of presents and at the way Peggy had looked. This was not what he had wanted for his children. He wouldn't dare tell his wife about the state they were in, the way their hair had been cut and the old clothes that they had to wear. He would have a word with Sister Superior to see if anything could be done, but he knew the situation was bad. His wife's illness was getting worse; the doctors didn't hold out much hope of her ever getting better and were in the process of moving her to another hospital where she would be able to lie in peace and comfort.

Sister Superior was walking towards him, "Ah, Mr Cairnes, how lovely to see you. I hope you enjoyed your children's performance. They are all very well, so you have no need to worry about them. How is Mrs Cairnes? Is there any improvement in her condition?"

He told her the situation and asked her not to tell the children as it would upset them too much and he thought Peggy had enough to worry about. "Oh, we will look after them for you, don't you worry; are you paying for their keep tonight? It will save you calling again next week."

"I will be coming to see them next visiting day; tell Peggy for me," he said, handing over the money he had brought with him just in case.

"Goodbye Mr Cairnes, see you next time," she said, hurrying away from him. He picked up his coat and sadly walked through the door. Peggy lay awake wondering if her father had gone home yet and if she dare sneak downstairs and ask him to take her home with him. Then she thought of Irene and Marie. Her mother was depending on her to look after them for her. Maybe they wouldn't be here long now; her mother was sure to be better soon, then everything would be back to normal. Perhaps she would be able to go to the grammar school she had worked so hard for.

Chapter Twenty

Peggy must have fallen asleep because the next thing she heard was the ringing of the morning bell. She shrugged her shoulders and decided to get on with things. It was almost three months since Peggy's father had told her how ill her mother was. She had tried so hard to be good both at the orphanage and at school. There had been two more visits from him and although he never said that their mother was getting any better, she always hoped for some good news.

One night, after prayers had been said and all the lights had been turned out, "Fatso" appeared at the side of Peggy's bed. "Get up, forty two, Sister Superior wants to see you. You are to go down to the sweet cupboard door." (This was where all the jars of lovely sweets were kept locked up until every second Saturday afternoon, when Sister Superior would bring them down to the playroom with the big black book in which she kept the records of any money the girls had been given by relatives or friends.) To the girls lucky enough to have any money, she would sell five boiled sweets for a penny. But the girls who didn't have any money got none. This made Peggy very sad so she shared her sweets with her three friends and saved one for Irene who never seemed to be in the playroom when the sweets were being sold.

Now in the dark Peggy ran nervously down the dark cold steps, wearing only her thin nightgown. What on earth had she done now, she wondered. There was a light shining from above the nun's head casting dark shadows all around her. "Yes, Sister?" She hesitated, wondering what was coming next.

"Oh, forty two, your father called this evening."

Peggy felt a moment of nervous excitement.

"Yes, he called to say that your mother died last night and she has gone to heaven. You can tell your sisters in the morning, now off to bed with you."

Peggy stood rooted to the spot. Dead, her mother, gone to heaven? No, it couldn't be true! She was getting better and would be home soon. Sister Superior had got it all wrong.

She felt a sharp push on her shoulder. "Go on girl, back to your bed and pray for your mother's soul." The light went out and she found herself alone on the dark cold staircase. Somehow she managed to find her way back to her bed without bumping into any of the senior girls. There she lay all night, crying silently. She decided not to say anything to Irene, she wouldn't understand and of course Marie was back in the infants' home so there was no point in saying anything to her.

Peggy woke with a jump. The point of the window pole was jamming into her back. "Get out of that bed at once, you bone idle girl." It was the mean face of Sister Brown glaring at her. "How dare you disobey orders?" She fell out of the bed. At first she could not think why she felt so upset. Then she remembered last night and the shock returned to her.

Her mother was dead, gone to heaven. Sister Brown was still glaring at her. Peggy dressed quickly, fighting with the chemise which seemed to be heavier than usual. She was finished just in time to fall on her knees in prayer.

The rest of the day passed in a haze for Peggy. She waited in vain for someone to say that they were sorry to hear that her mother had gone to heaven but not a word was spoken of the event. She had decided not to say anything to Irene, and Marie had already gone back to the babies' home so she wouldn't see her anyway.

When she got the chance, she told her friend Sheila and asked, "What happens next?"

"Oh, nothing," replied Sheila, placing her arm around Peggy's shoulder. "You will just have to pray for her and I will too." Two days later she was once again summoned to see Sister Superior. The nun was sitting in her usual place. "Come here, forty two, I have something to tell you. Your father has requested that you and your sister Irene attend your mother's funeral tomorrow. Sister Grey will go with you, so go and see her now so she can fit you both out with clothes for the occasion. Off you go and remember you must be on your best behaviour."

Peggy's head was in a whirl, She had never been to a funeral before and she felt very frightened. Who would be there? Would she see her father? Sister Grey was waiting for her on the corridor. She liked Sister Grey as she was kinder than some of the other nuns; she was so pleased that it was her going with them and not the horrible Sister Brown.

The nun soon had them fitted out with the same kind of clothes that she had worn on her shopping trip with her father. The senior girl who had brought Irene to Sister Grey was waiting at the end of the corridor. Sister Grey nodded to her and she came and took her back to the playroom. Irene was so used to the senior girls telling her what to do that she didn't even protest anymore.

Carrying the bundle of clothes Peggy followed Sister Grey up the stairs. They stopped two flights up, and the nun took some keys from her pocket and opened a door that seemed to be part of the wall. Inside were three beds and lockers, all painted white. The room had its own wash basin and a lavvy. It looked very cosy. "Put your clothes on that bed and the shoes underneath. In the morning directly after breakfast bring yourself and Irene to the door outside. I will be waiting for you both."

Peggy was looking around her. "What is this room used for Sister?" She knew that she wouldn't be in trouble for asking Sister Grey. "This is the sick room Peggy. Sometimes girls are taken ill and they need to see a doctor." The nun smiled at her. "You can go now. I will see you later." Peggy smiled back then made her way back to her orders. There was no excuse for not doing your work, not even the death of a mother. Irene thought it was all very exciting, she had no idea what all the fuss was about. Peggy was worried, she hadn't told her about their mother and didn't know what to say to her. She will find out tomorrow, thought Peggy, although she had no idea herself what to expect. Maybe Sister Grey would tell them tomorrow.

The following morning she took Irene up to the sick room door. Sister Grey had told her the previous evening that she didn't need to do her morning orders or go to school. She hoped that it wouldn't cause any trouble with her teacher Mrs Ryan.

Once inside the sick room they were quickly dressed in their fancy clothes. Warm brown coats and hats with a brim. Wrapped around the brim was a yellow and purple ribbon. Holding them both by the hands, the nun led them down to the nuns' home. They went through to the big bolted door. This was opened for them by another nun who just smiled at them.

Down the road they went to the tramcar stop. Irene loved it; she was bouncing up and down on the tramcar seat, and Sister Grey just let her do as she wanted. After a long ride Peggy realised that they were near her own home. She could see the spire of the church and her old school building. At last they arrived at the church door. "Now girls, stay by me no matter what happens," whispered Sister Grey. "What will happen?" Peggy whispered back as they entered the church. The sound of the organ playing a familiar hymn reached Peggy's ears as the nun led them into a bench halfway down the aisle. Then she saw it, the big long shiny box. It was standing on two wooden trestles in front of the altar with candles burning at each end.

Just then there was a sound of people coming into the church being led by a priest. Her father was walking towards them between the benches. He had a quick word with Sister Grey who shook her head and said no. But their father took no notice and propelled them both into the aisle and down to the front near the altar where they stayed for the rest of the service. Peggy didn't understand what happened during the service, but she found herself outside the church afterwards with all the other people, some of whom she knew to be aunties and uncles. There was a lot of crying. Father was holding them both by the hands. Sister Grey tried to pull them away but a few words from her father and she soon left them alone.

Then Peggy saw them, Mr and Mrs Oates, their friendly neighbours who had been so kind to them when their mother had become ill. Peggy let go of her father's hand and walked slowly over to them. They too had been crying. Mrs Oates placed her arm around the little girl's shoulder and gave her a big hug. Then Peggy cried; it was the first loving gesture that she had received for a very long time, except from her father. Wiping her eyes she gazed up into the friendly face. "Do you still live in our street and do you see any of my friends?" Mrs Oates gave her another hug. "Yes dear we do, and we will still be here for you when you all come home again and I am sure that your friends will be too." Her father tugged at her arm and led them to a very big black car. Irene was laughing and chattering away as her father lifted her inside. Peggy was frightened, she didn't know why. She gazed around at all the people, then she saw it again, the big long shiny box. It was in another big car just in front of them all on its own. Two of her aunties and a grown-up cousin called Katie entered the car. Soon they were driving slowly up the road.

Suddenly the cars stopped outside their own house. Peggy's spirits rose. "Are we going inside, Dad?" She gazed expectantly at her father's face. "No love, but we will come back later." She wondered what he meant by later, later than what? she thought. Then the cars set off again, driving slowly. Peggy saw many of their other neighbours standing near their gates, heads bowed.

After what seemed a very long time they arrived at the cemetery gates. She had never been in a cemetery before and was unprepared for the sight that met her eyes. Row upon row of headstones, of all shapes and sizes, with names engraved on them. Oh, she thought, if all these people are in heaven, there can't be much room left. I hope our mother has got there all right.

When the cars came to a halt her father turned to her. "I want you and Irene to stay in the car. We won't be long. Katie says that she will stay with you." Peggy watched what happened next. The big box in the front car was lifted out by four men, then her father and all the other people followed behind. They went round a corner and out of sight.

Katie looked at her young cousin's face. "Don't worry, they will soon be back". She was much older than Peggy. "We live in Ireland and it has taken us such a long time to get to Lingford, but I am glad that we came." Irene started crying. "Oh Peggy, I want to go to the lavvy." She was jumping up and down. Peggy looked out of the car window but could not see anything that looked like a lavvy. "Oh quick, come here." Katie took her by the hand. "I'll take you." Irene was so frightened of wetting her pants. Infants usually were smacked very hard if they did. Katie lifted her out of the car and to Peggy's horror she took her quickly behind one of the large upright stones. They were just back in time before her father and all the people returned to the cars.

Everyone was in a more talkative mood as they drove away. Irene was busy telling everyone how she nearly wet her knickers.

The cars once again stopped outside their home. Peggy was excited. Maybe they would be staying at home, their father could always go back later to the orphanage and bring Marie home. He helped her down from the big car, and she ran into the house, so happy. Mrs Oates and another neighbour Mrs Stevens were pouring out tea and handing round food but, although she was very hungry, all she wanted to see was her own bedroom.

Irene was being spoilt by everyone and was loving every minute of it. "Do have one of my special buns, I baked them for you." Mrs Oates was smiling at her. She was so sad to see the state that the girls were in; they looked so thin and what on earth had happened to their lovely hair? "Thank you, Mrs Oates, but I don't really feel like eating."

"Oh go on, love, take two, you must be very hungry and thirsty. I have made some of your favourite lemonade. Have these and I am sure that you will feel better." Peggy took the cup and plate from the kindly woman; she was very hungry and it seemed such a long time since she had tasted a cream bun. Sitting down on one of the wooden chairs, she looked around the room. Nothing had changed except that the door of her mother's room was now open. People were sitting inside eating and drinking tea. Her father was busy talking to people. Irene was running in and out of the door, up and down the garden path with a bun in each hand, being looked after by Katie. When she had finished eating, Peggy ran up the stairs and into her own lovely bedroom. Everything was just as she had left it. All her books and games were neatly stacked on the shelves and in the little bookcase that her father had made for her. She looked in the drawers, the clothes that she hadn't taken to the orphanage were neatly folded and her winter coat was hanging behind the door.

Peggy didn't know how long she had been sitting on her bed when the door opened and her father came in. "I thought I would find you here. People are asking to see you to say goodbye." She smiled at him. "I'm home now Dad, they can see me anytime." Her father looked at her happy smiling face. How was he to tell her that this wasn't how things were going to be? Sister Superior had told him that the girls could go to the church but they must return after the service with Sister Grey. He had got her on his side outside the church, but had promised they would be back in time for tea. He was due back at work in a day or two and had a lot of sorting out to do before then. There was no way he could let them stay at home.

He took a deep breath and sat down on her bed.

"I am really sorry, Peggy, but I have to take you both back this afternoon. I will be in enough trouble with your Sister Superior for bringing you to the house. She had told me that you were only to go to the church but I wanted to spend some time with you both. My hands are tied because of the education inspectors."

Peggy dropped her head onto her arms. "I can't go back Dad, it is so awful there, and we don't get enough to eat."

"I know love, but I promise that I will do my best somehow to arrange everything to get you all home again.

She sat up and gazed around the cosy little bedroom, so different from the crowded dormitory with little beds that she had become accustomed to. He pulled her to her feet. "We had better find Irene before she wears your cousin out." She followed her father downstairs, but she was so upset she hardly remembered saying goodbye to people. Soon everyone except Mr and Mrs Oates had gone home. "Come here, love, and have some more tea before you go back. I know that you don't want to go but it will help your father if you could be good girls." Peggy felt nothing like being good. She wanted to shout, "No no, I am not going, I will only run away if I have to go back." Her father was worried, he had never seen his Peggy act like this before. What was he to do with her?

Irene was still happily eating buns and drinking lemonade. Peggy looked at her then turned to Mrs Oates. "She will be sick, she is not used to eating very much."

"It's all right, dear, don't you worry about her, I will look after her until you are ready to leave."

Soon it was time to put on their hats and coats for the journey back. Father was trying to make her laugh but not very hard. "Are we to have a ride in the big black car again Dad?" Irene was jumping up and down. "I want to go back to my friends, I will miss my turn in the games." Their father glanced at his daughters, standing there in their unfamiliar clothes. "Come on Peggy, Irene is getting restless and we all know what that entails." Taking hold of Irene's hand he steered the two girls to say their goodbyes to Mr and Mrs Oates and their other neighbours. He then led them through the door and out into the street. "We will be going on the tramcar again, won't that be nice?" Peggy was silent all the way back. Nothing her father could say to her would change her feelings; she had once again been taken from the home she loved. They arrived outside the big black door of the orphanage. Father pulled the bell chain and the panel in the top of the door opened. The face of Sister Superior appeared, and quickly the big door swung open and she led them into the visiting room. "Hurry up girls, Sister Brown is waiting for you to change your clothes and be ready for tea." She pushed the two girls towards the shiny staircase. Irene ran on ahead because she wanted to be back with her friends, but for Peggy it was a disaster.

She tried to turn back to her father. He was still standing near the door; he smiled at her and nodded his head. But she saw the look on the nun's face and knew it meant trouble.

She slowly made her way up the stairs. Her chance had gone: maybe they would never go home again now that they had no mother, and their father was to busy with the war work to keep them at home while he was helping to make tanks.

Chapter Twenty-one

That evening, Peggy went about her orders automatically. She had even given her precious bread away to her friends at teatime. She didn't think it was worth saving for later by hiding it inside the front of her dress. Perhaps she wouldn't ever eat again. "Peggy," Josie whispered. They were both on kitchen orders and her friend had not spoken a word since arriving back from her mother's funeral. "Did you have a nice time, was your father there?" She knew that Sister Grey had arrived back without the two girls. Josie didn't know what happened at a funeral, and felt something awful must have happened to her friend. Peggy looked at her worried face. "Oh, I am all right," she whispered back. "I will tell you all about it tomorrow when we are in the playground."

Peggy was still waiting for one of the nuns to speak to her about her mother, but nothing was said. There was such a lot she wanted to find out. It was orders time again. This time she was to help the senior girls to undress some of the infants and to get them ready for bed. But she was not allowed to have Irene in her group.

As Peggy was leaving the infants' dormitory, Sister Superior was waiting for her. "Ah, forty two, I want a word with you, I gave orders that you and your sister were to come straight back here after your mother's church mass. Why was I not obeyed?" Peggy stood her ground: she thought that if she said nothing then she wouldn't get into trouble. "I am waiting for an answer," said the nun, glaring at her. Peggy didn't know what she wanted an answer to as she had not spoken to her about her mother except on the night when she had told her that her mother had gone to heaven. "I'm sorry Sister, I don't know what to say, I only did what my Dad told me to do."

She was rewarded with a flick of the cane around the back of her legs. "Go and kneel on the middle corridor floor and pray for your sins and don't bother to come down to supper." With this she pushed her hand hard into the girl's back, almost toppling her over.

"That is it!" thought Peggy desperately. "I have had enough of this place, somehow I have to run away and get as far away from this place as possible." Kneeling on the hard wooden floor, she dropped her face into her hands and cried for all the things that she had lost. Her mother, her home and her freedom. Thoughts were racing around in her head. She would plan her escape, but it had to be soon, maybe tonight! But how would she manage to steal through the Wicked Door? She would ask her friends – maybe they would know a way out.

Her knees were hurting, she had been on them a long time and it was becoming very dark, but she dared not move.

Just then the senior girl doing the night rounds came from the sewing room and saw her. "What do you think you are doing forty two, trying to sneak off orders? You should be in bed, get up before I report you." The following day, Peggy and her friends were in the school playground. She went to lean against the railing to think. After a few minutes one of the 'other girls', Maureen, came and stood by her side. "Hello Peggy, Mrs Ryan told all the class yesterday that your Mum had died and has gone to heaven. I'm so sorry. If there is anything that we can do to help you please let us know." Maureen was one of the new friends that she had made at the school Christmas party and they had remained friends ever since. Peggy hesitated. Should she tell her of her plans to run away? Maybe she would help her. She took a deep breath. "I need to run away from the orphanage. I must see my Dad again as soon as possible." Maureen didn't know what to say; she had never known anyone who had run away before. Also she knew that the girls from the 'home' didn't have homes of their own to go to like her and her friends, the 'other' girls. She put her hand in her pocket and brought out a penny coin and handed it to Peggy. "Here take this, a penny ticket on a tramcar will take you well away from the orphanage, but how will you manage it?" The same thoughts had been on Peggy's mind since the events of yesterday. "Oh, thank you so much. I have still to find a way but don't worry, I will." She kept the penny tight in her hand and went to join her friends who were playing their game of stones.

That day after school she changed out of her school dress and wrapped it round the penny so that no one could see it. She pushed it as far back in the corner of the drawer as she could. Then she went about her orders with a spring in her step.

That night she lay in her bed plotting in her mind ways of running away and reaching her home, but it would be quite a while before she could put any of her ideas into practice.

The following days passed by quickly. Peggy was determined not to get into any trouble or to bring notice to herself.

Chapter Twenty-two

Senior girls and some juniors, those who didn't get into any trouble, were allowed to spend their Sunday recreation time in the top playground. This privilege was very rare for juniors and Peggy was one of those never to have been there. But maybe if she could there might be a way of escape over the rooftops. Anything was worth looking at. So the next few weeks she did all her orders on time and made sure she wasn't caught talking anywhere she shouldn't be. Her good resolutions paid off. One Sunday after dinner when they were in the playroom, she heard her number being called out. It was one of the senior girls called Molly. She had done a few favours for her in the past week or so. "Now, forty two, I have chosen you to visit the top playground with me." Peggy held her breath hoping she wouldn't change her mind. The precious penny was secreted in the sole of her shoe making walking very uncomfortable. She crossed to where the senior girl was standing. This was to be her big adventure. She was to find out later that one of her best friends, Josie, had also been invited by another senior girl.

She followed Molly upstairs until they came to the senior dormitory door. Leading up from there was another flight of stairs. These were strictly out of bounds to anyone who wasn't invited. Peggy had often wondered where they led. Up and up they went, three more flights of steps until they came to a small wooden door. Molly opened it and they both went through.

Peggy gasped; they seem to be up in the air. The playground was small and round with high railings fitted all around it with nearby roofs pointing up to the sky. The nearest one to the rails was part of the roof of the orphanage.

"Go over there, forty two, and play with your friend. I don't want any trouble from you, do you understand me?" Peggy nodded her head and quickly limped over to Josie who was standing with her back to the railings. The penny was making walking difficult. The two friends sat down in the playground.

"Have you got something wrong with your foot, Peggy?" Josie was looking concerned for her friend.

"Oh no, I am going to tell you my secret." She then took off her shoe and showed Josie the penny. "I am going to run away and you can help me."

"Me, how?" "I am going to climb up on the rooftop and then slide down to the street below." Putting on her shoe she let her gaze roam around the playground. All the senior girls were huddled together talking in whispers and taking no notice of the junior girls. "Come on, Josie, this is my chance, there is a small gap in that railing over there and I am sure that I can squeeze through it."

"You will never do it Peggy, the seniors will see you."

"Not if you stand in front of me, they won't. Come on, we are wasting time."

Josie reluctantly followed her friend. They moved a few inches at a time so as not to draw attention to themselves, and stood for a while near the gap.

"Now," said Peggy. "This is my big chance, keep a lookout for me and if I do get away and I have been home for a while, I will come and visit you all." She then squeezed herself through the small gap and found herself standing on a piece of coping stone. In front of her was a sloping roof leading to the very top of the home. Peggy thought that if she could get to the top, she would only have to slide down the other side to reach the street and would be on her way home.

She climbed to the very top and straddled the ridge tiles. She looked down the other side of the roof. Peggy was shocked, she froze with fright; it was a sheer drop, she could only see the yard where the kitchen and laundry were, there was no sign of the street that she was hoping to see. By this time she was petrified and found that she couldn't move a muscle.

"Help!" she shouted to Josie who was looking at her through the railings with a frightened look on her face. "Go and get some help, I can feel the slates slipping from underneath me and I dare not move." Josie ran as fast as her shaking legs would carry her to where the senior girls were still sitting talking with their backs to what had happened.

"Please get some help, Peggy Cairnes is stuck on the roof," she whimpered. Molly followed Josie to the railings. "Get down from there at once, forty two," she shouted. "Is this all the thanks that I get for inviting you up here as a treat?"

"I can't move, I've lost my nerve," Peggy shouted back.

Molly turned to Josie. "How the heck did she get up there?"

Josie pointed to the small gap in the railings. Molly looked at it and realised that no one bigger than Peggy would be able to go through it. By this time all Molly's friends had gathered around to see what the commotion was. Pushing one of them in the shoulder she yelled, "Go and bring one of the Sisters, she will know what to do." Shortly afterwards, an out-of-breath 'mean' Sister Grey came rushing through the door. She too realised that no one could reach Peggy who by now was very cold and frightened.

The sound of fire engine bells was soon ringing in their ears. More of the nuns had arrived, the girls were panicking and Josie was crying. What would happen to her best friend now?

A large fireman came running across the playground followed by Sister Superior, she was wringing her hands as she explained to the other nuns. "We must get her down safely and quickly. Holy Mother, what can be done? The fireman has told me that they will bring a ladder up the stairs and try to reach her from here." She turned to the fireman. "Great care is taken to see that the children come to no harm in this home, but no one expects a child to get up on the top of the roof."

"Don't worry, Sister, we will soon have her down safely," he answered her.

Three more firemen came dashing through the door carrying a ladder; they all had various tools hanging from their belts. The damaged railing was quickly removed and one of the firemen stepped over to the coping stone. The ladder was passed across to him, and carefully they placed it near the sloping roof. It reached up to the ridge tiles where Peggy was hanging on for dear life. He climbed up towards her while another one stood at the bottom to make sure that the ladder didn't slip.

"Hello Peggy, your Sister Superior has told me all about you. My name is Dave and I think that you have been very brave holding on for such a long time. Now when I place my arm around you just let go, don't be frightened, we will soon have you down from here."

Peggy turned to look at the huge-looking man and her confidence came flowing back. With his strong arm around her she let go.

Arms aching and legs trembling she was quickly lowered to the playground. The rest of the girls gathered around her. Sister Superior's face was red with anger. Dave turned to the nun. "She must see a doctor as soon as possible, she is suffering from shock and she also has cuts and grazes to her hands and legs."

Sister Superior turned to Sister Grey. "Take her to the sick room at once. I will be with you as soon as I can." She grabbed Molly by the arm. "Go quickly to the convent and ask them to send for Dr Quinn." While all this was taking place the fireman turned to the nun, "No one is to be allowed up here again until the roof is repaired and the damaged railings replaced."

Down in the sick room Sister Grey soon had the shivering girl undressed and put onto one of the beds. Peggy felt very sickly and was trembling from head to foot, more with fright at what was going to happen to her. The door opened, and in strode Sister Superior followed by Dr Quinn. He gave her an overall examination and declared that she was to stay where she was for the next two days. After giving instructions for her hands and knees to be bathed he said she was to be kept warm and quiet and to be allowed to get over the shock. He smiled at Peggy and left the room.

Sister Superior glared at her. "I will be back to see you in a few minutes." Saying that she stormed out of the room and followed the doctor. "Oh, what is going to happen to me now?" Peggy was more frightened than anything else of the fact that Sister Grey had found the penny in her shoe and had demanded to know where she had got it from. Peggy had pretended not to hear her and had kept quiet. The door opened once more. Sister Superior came striding in followed by a reluctant Molly who had been given the job of looking after Peggy while she was in the sick room. "Now, forty two, what on earth did you think you were doing?" shouted the enraged nun. "You have caused a great deal of damage and trouble for us all. I will have to ask your father to pay for the repairs to the roof and railings." Peggy slid further down the bed, her hands and knees hurting as they rubbed against the sheets. She was feeling happier now: her father was to be told, he would pay for all the repairs and would know how hard she had been trying to reach him. Being so young, she didn't realize that her father would not have that kind of money.

She was now alone in the little room, and started to feel hungry. She had no idea of the time and wondered if she would be brought anything to eat. The doctor had said that she was to remain in bed for two days. Molly came into the room with a scowl on her face, carrying a cup and plate. "Here you are Cairnes, You have made a lot of work for me and I don't like it. Don't think for a minute that you will get away with it." She banged the cup and plate onto the little locker at the side of the bed and flounced out, slamming the door behind her.

It was just the same food, watered-down tea and a slice of bread without the Sunday jam. Peggy ate the bread and gazed around her. There were no windows in the room, only ventilation gaps high up on the walls. The light had to stay on all the time.

Across the room was the lavvy: dare she get up and go before anyone else came in? She just managed to get back into her bed when Molly reappeared to collect her pots. Staring into Peggy's face she hissed, "I have to turn off the light when I go, and you, Cairnes, have to go to sleep. There will be no supper for you tonight." Peggy wasn't bothered, she was used to being hungry and she was very tired. It had been a long tiring day. Time passed slowly. Even if there had been any light there were no books to read so she spent her time dreaming of how it would have been had she been confined to her bed at home.

She lay on her side thinking pleasant thoughts of home.

She didn't remember anything else until the light was switched on by Molly. It was Monday morning and she wouldn't be going to school. Who would be doing her orders, she wondered? Molly had become more and more angry each time she had to come and minister to Peggy, who knew that there was trouble ahead, but she would deal with that when the time came. Just now she was enjoying doing nothing.

Her rest was soon over, however. Sister Whitey, the 'sick' nurse passed her fit to resume normal activities.

So here she was on Wednesday morning doing her orders in the refectory. She knew that she had to see Sister Superior after breakfast. Sister Brown had already told her that one of her punishments was that she had to stand while eating all her meals and she was wondering what her other punishments would be. Peggy knocked nervously on the sewing room door. "Come in, forty two, I have been waiting for you. How could you have caused so much trouble when you had been given such a treat? You have spoilt it for everyone else. It will be the last time that you will ever go up there. As one of your punishments you will not be allowed to speak to anyone for the next two weeks. You will also do double orders and have no recreation whatsoever. After school you will go to the kitchens and do any orders that Sister Purple gives you. All the other Sisters know that you are to have no free time. Now get out of my sight and back to work."

Arriving at school Peggy found that she was the talk of the playground. Everyone had heard of her escapade on the roof and her rescue by the firemen. She was soon surrounded by a crowd of girls all wanting to hear her story.

Mrs Ryan came striding across the playground ringing the school bell and everyone quietly fell into line. Peggy hoped that Mrs Ryan would not mention her ordeal and that she would be allowed to speak to her friends while she was at school.

Sheila, Josie, Peggy and some of their 'other' friends were sitting in a circle on the playground floor. "I'm so sorry, Maureen, that I lost the penny. I didn't think that I would be able to speak to you about it but Mrs Ryan hasn't said so."

"No," piped in Josie, "she is not allowed to speak to any of us for two weeks at the home but we are going to try and tear a page out of one of our writing books and then we can write messages to one another, it will be our secret."

"I will do it for you," said Maureen. "I will try and find you a small piece of pencil. You can hide them up your knicker leg and don't worry, I will soon find you another penny." Peggy went on to recount the events of the past three days. Her friends were very impressed, each one of them wishing that they had been the cause of all the excitement. "Are you still going to run away?" whispered Maureen. Peggy smiled at her. "As soon as I can. When you don't see me here at school you will know I have done it."

That evening, her friends spent a happy time tearing the sheet of paper into small squares and with the stub of pencil, along with the paper that Maureen had found for them, they happily wrote little notes and secretly passed them between Peggy and themselves.

Chapter Twenty-three

It was the week before Easter. Her father had been to visit them the Sunday before. Irene had played up, being a little bit naughty as usual. Her father soon calmed her down with a sweet, then he told Peggy that the problems with the roof and railings had been sorted out, she was not to worry any more about it. He had been informed that the church authority would pay for all the repairs. It was soon to be Peggy's eleventh birthday, so he would ask Sister Superior if he could take her out for the day but they would have to wait and see.

That week was also the time of year that some of the juniors looked foward to. All the nuns from the orphanage, except the ones who worked in the kitchens, went on a week's "retreat". They kept a vow of silence and prayer and had nothing to do with the children for a whole week. In their places came another group of nuns. They wore the same coloured aprons as the regular nuns but were completely different in their ways of looking after the girls. Peggy was delighted with them; they were very kind and no one was ever in trouble for talking or anything else. The senior girls hated it, because anyone taken to the Sisters for running or talking or any other offence, was simply greeted with a gentle word and a smile. One of the nuns had a very good singing voice and led the girls into impromptu concerts most evenings, and she wouldn't stand for any bulling from the senior girls

The mean Sister Grey and the nasty Sister Brown still slept in their 'cells' at each end of the dormitory. One night when all was quiet, a folded piece of paper was thrown over the top of Sister Grey's cell and it landed on Peggy's bed. She opened it up. The message said. "Forty two, close the window." Peggy glanced up at the high window above her bed. How was she to reach it without the window pole? No one was ever allowed to touch that without receiving punishment. A smile came to her face. This was a way to get her own back on the mean nun, knowing that she wouldn't be able to speak or shout at her. Peggy found the small stub of pencil her friend Maureen had given them. She kept it hidden in one of her socks. She wrote on the back of the note, 'Meany Grey, close it yourself.' Then threw it back over the top of the cell. She knew that she would be in trouble but she didn't care at all. She was soon to find out later that if there had been an emergency in the dormitory, the nuns would be able to break their silence.

She went to sleep happy.

She laughed with her friends the following day at what she had done and wondered what her punishment would be.

It was twelve o'clock on Saturday, the angelus bell was tolling, and everyone in the playground stood still. "What happens next?" Peggy whispered to her friends. "What do we do now?"

The kind nuns had said their goodbyes, and were awaiting the return of the regular nuns.

Five minutes later, they came striding across the playground led by Sister Superior. As they passed the girls, 'mean' Sister Grey shot out her arm, grabbed Peggy by the shoulder and marched her into the building. "So, forty two, you thought that I had forgotten about the window, did you?" She was shaking the frightened girl backwards and forwards. "I had to suffer the rest of the week with a painful stiff neck. Now go and bring me your hard hair brush and I will deal with you."

Peggy could hardly sit down for the next few days but she was pleased to have annoyed the mean Sister Grey.

Lots of the junior girls were in trouble including Sheila and Josie for the things that they had done whilst the nuns were on retreat. The senior girls had put them all in the report book.

Chapter Twenty-four

It was the Easter holidays and one of the benefactors was to provide a treat by paying for some of the junior girls from the orphanage to go to see the pantomime Mother Goose. Peggy, Sheila and Josie were lucky, their names had been pulled out of the box. After all the trouble that Peggy had been in she was surprised to find her name had been entered. But she was learning by experience that once you had done your punishment all was forgiven until the next offence. All the lucky ones chosen for the treat made sure that they stayed out of trouble before the big day.

Although Peggy had received many lovely treats at home she had never been to a pantomime and was really looking forward to the occasion.

The day dawned bright and sunny. Those going on the treat were dressed in their best going-out clothes. Two coaches had been booked to transport them to the theatre and back. It was two hours of pure magic. The highlight for them was when the big white goose waddled into the centre of the stage, sat down, then rose up to reveal a beautiful 'golden egg' on the floor. Everyone gasped in delight. They all had a wonderful time and the happy thoughts were to stay with them for a very long time. Peggy could hardy wait to tell her father all about it when he came to visit them the following Sunday.

Once they were back at school Peggy turned her thoughts to how she could run away. She was quite used to the rules of the home and had done her best as her father had requested of her to settle down and be good, but she missed her home life and longed to be back there again. Her mother would not be there having gone to Heaven, but she was sure that now she was nearly eleven, that they would all manage somehow.

Little Marie along with the other babies had been brought back to the big home for the Easter holidays. Peggy had tried to see her as often as she could but she clung to the senior girls and didn't seem to know Peggy any more. This made her very sad and more determined to make sure that they all returned to their own home as soon as possible. It had been her mother's wish that they all stay together Peggy had made her mind up, This was going to be the day. She had decided not to tell any of her friends her plans. Then they would not get into any trouble. Maureen had not managed to find her an other penny so she would walk home. Once she had found her way to the tramlines she was sure it wouldn't take her long to find the way.

Chapter Twenty-five

After dinner they lined up to return to school. Somehow Peggy managed to find herself at the end of the line. She followed the others, led by a senior girl as usual through "The Wicked Door" and round the corner. In the past few days, she had taken notice of a small gap between the school and an outbuilding. That afternoon, she squeezed herself into it. No one took any notice of her absence. She held her breath as the senior girl came slowly walking back. As soon as she had passed out of sight Peggy made her move.

She quickly walked down the street keeping to the side of the wall with no idea where she was going and hoping no one would see her or notice the blue spotted dress of the orphanage.

She hurried on her way, and luckily she soon sighted the top of a tramcar in the distance. She carried on walking until she came to a busy road, where she saw the tram-lines. Her instinct was to follow the lines going slightly uphill. How long she had been walking Peggy had no idea, but now that she had set off there was no turning back. She slipped in and out of shop doorways. It was Friday afternoon and the shops were full of people doing their weekend shopping. No one took the least bit of notice of the young girl in their midst.

She became very tired as she had been on the go for such a long time. Her feet in the worn-out pumps were beginning to falter. But she dared not stop, or someone might notice her. Her head was drooping, when suddenly she saw a halfpenny lying at the side of the road. Peggy picked it up, glancing around her to see if anyone had seen her. Holding it tight in her hand she made her way to the next tram stop.

A few minutes later a tram with '– MEADOWFIELDS' displayed across its front window came into view and rattled to a stop.

The lady behind her who had quite a few shopping bags gave her a push. "Come on love, we are in a hurry to get home even if you are not." Peggy shrugged and gave her a scornful look.

Peggy climbed up the tram steps and found herself an empty seat. Just then the conductor made his way up the tram with his ticket machine hanging by his side. She took a deep breath; she hadn't been on a tram before on her own and didn't know what to do.

"Fares please," he called out, looking at Peggy. "I only have a halfpenny, how far can I go for that?"

"Oh, for half fare you can go to the terminus, but if you want to be off sooner just tell me and I will let you off."

She gazed out of the window, hoping to see a familiar sight. After a while she recognized one of the shops where she and her father sometimes used to do their shopping. If she got off at the next stop she was sure that it would be easy to find her way home. Peggy soon found herself in her own neighbourhood, and quickly found her way home.

On arriving at the house she found that the front and back doors were locked, and peeping through the window she realized there was no one inside. Her father would still be at work so she would just have to wait for his return.

Swinging backwards and forwards on the garden gate, she looked up the street and saw Mrs Murray, another of their neighbours walking towards her. She was coming back from the shops after doing her weekly shopping. "Hello Peggy, what are you doing here? I didn't know that your Dad had brought you home."

"No, Mrs Murray, I've run away, but I am sure that my Dad will let me stay when he sees me." The kindly woman looked down at the bedraggled young girl in front of her. "Come on love, I will take you to Mrs Oates, she will know what to do." Taking hold of Peggy's hand she walked her up the street and knocked on Mrs Oates' door. "My goodness, how on earth did you get here?" she exclaimed, opening the door. "Do the Sisters from the home know that you are here? Your father will be surprised, he didn't know you were coming, I will have to let him know at once." She thanked Mrs Murray and took Peggy inside. Taking a piece of paper from the sideboard she turned to Mr Oates who was sitting in his chair by the fire. "You look after Peggy while I contact her Dad. I am going to the phone box near the shops." Putting on her coat she dashed out of the house.

Half and hour later there was an urgent knock, the door was flung open, and her father dashed in. "What has happened, how did you get here? Did you come on your own?" He gazed in bewilderment at the sight of his daughter, her ragged dress, worn-out pumps and socks with holes in them. "Oh Peggy, what am I to do? I will have to take you back, the nuns will have the police looking for you."

Peggy didn't care. "I am not going back there, I will be in so much trouble." Then she started to cry. Her father knelt by her side and placed his arms around her. "Don't worry, we will sort something out. Now eat the lovely food that Mrs Oates has prepared for you, then we will go home."

He turned to the worried couple. "I won't be long. I must let them know she is safe." Then he rushed from the house. Little did he know that the nuns didn't inform the police when a girl ran away until seven p.m. They were usually picked up quickly because most of them had nowhere to run to. Peggy had been lucky; Friday was a busy day and no one had noticed her.

Father and daughter walked down the street hand in hand. How was he to tell her that two nuns would be coming to collect her at six-thirty that evening, and she would have to return to the home with them? He would go with her and explain to Sister Superior how unhappy she was. But in his present circumstances there was no way that he could keep his children at their own home.

Peggy spent the next hour happily roaming round her home. Most of her time was spent in her bedroom but it soon became cold, so she returned to the front room and sat next to her father on the settee. He had lit the fire and she was soon feeling warmer.

He gently explained to her why she had to go back, because of his work and the fact she was too young to stay in the house on her own especially when he had to work the night shift. Peggy was the first to hear the knock on the door and she jumped to her feet.

"It's all right, I'll answer it," her father said, pushing her gently back onto the settee. He moved quickly to open the door. There in the dusk, dressed in their black habits, stood Sister Brown and the 'mean' Sister Grey. He ushered them into the room where Peggy sat trembling.

"It's all right, dear child, we have just come to take care of you." Sister Brown was smiling, but Peggy knew that it wouldn't last. "Did you bring a coat with you, child?" The mean Sister Grey was staring at her. She knew that coats were only worn on special occasions and this was not one of them.

Her father looked at her. "Why don't you go upstairs and bring down your winter coat? I think it will still fit you." He was trying to sound cheerful but he was annoyed that the nuns hadn't even thought to bring a coat with them. It was still cold in the evenings.

Peggy sadly looked around the room, wondering if she would ever see her home again. All the things that her father had told her weighed heavily on her mind. Her father fastened her coat buttons and took her by the hand as they all left the house.

On the way back, the nuns sat side by side on the tram, arms folded, staring straight ahead. Her father did his best to engage Peggy in some conversation but she sat silent, head bowed, not wanting to talk to anyone. She was very scared, even with her father there. She dreaded the return to the orphanage and all that it would entail.

On their arrival, Sister Brown pulled the bell chain. The small grille opened, sounds of the bolts been drawn, the key turning in the lock. The door was opened by a young nun who ushered them all inside. The door was closed, locked and bolted, even though her father was still inside. Peggy moved closer to him. She noticed Sister Superior standing very still at the foot of the stairway. What now, wondered Peggy. Would her father be able to speak to the Sisters on her behalf? Sister Brown moved quickly before anyone knew what was happening. She pulled Peggy by the arm and was marching her towards the stairs when her father spoke up. "Just one minute Sister, I would like to say my goodbyes to my daughter."

Sister Superior quickly stepped forward. "One moment Sister. Let the girl come back for a minute." Sister Brown was angry, she had spent enough time that evening chasing after Peggy and had already missed her evening meal.

Peggy stood by her father's side once more. He was angry. "I am not going home until I know why my daughter is so unhappy, enough to make her want to run away." Peggy had never seen him so annoyed before. Sister Superior turned to face him. "Perhaps we could discuss this later, when the child has gone to bed, she must be very tired after her long walk. Say goodnight to your father now and off to bed with you." She didn't know what to do but the look on the nun's face soon made her mind up for her. She hugged her father, and turned to walk away leaving him, she hoped, to deal with Sister Superior.

Sister Brown was pushing her all the way up the stairs, and arriving at the top she turned to see her father and the Sister disappearing into the visitors' room. She was soon back in the orphanage and upstairs in the junior dormitory. Kneeling by her bed she dropped her face into her hands, and cried and cried, thinking that her world had shattered.

The rest of the junior girls began arriving. It was bath night and she had missed hers so there was no clean nightdress or underwear. The dirty nightdress had been collected by "Fatso" earlier that evening. Peeping through her fingers she saw the kind Sister Grey walking up and down in front of the beds. Peggy stood up and walked towards her. "Forty two, what have you been up to this time, missing your tea and the bath?" She placed her arm around her. "Go to the bathroom and ask Sister White to give you your clean clothes, you can take your dirty ones down to the laundry in the morning. Come back here and wash your face and clean your teeth. Sister Superior will deal with you in the morning."

Peggy had hardly any sleep that night. She wasn't allowed to toss and turn, so she lay on her side, visualising the trouble ahead of her the following morning.

A summons to visit Sister Superior loomed once again. With shaking legs she went to stand outside the sewing room door and knocked quietly, hoping that no-one would hear her.

"Well, forty two. Why did you dare to run away from the loving home we provide for you here? You ungrateful girl, I can't understand you." Peggy didn't answer her; she knew very well why she had done it. "Your punishment will be very severe this time. I will not stand for your disobedience any longer." She took down the large punishment book from the shelf above her head. "No recreation for three weeks, no sweets, and as many extra orders that the other Sisters can find for you. Also there will be no visitors for two months. Now go back to your orders and I don't want to see you here in front of me again, do you understand me girl?" Peggy hung her head. She didn't mind the extra work but not to see her father for such a long time hurt her very much. Why had he not sorted things out with Sister Superior when they were in the visitors' room? She had not been aware that they had discussed the situation and he had been told in no uncertain terms that if Peggy was to remain at the home with her two younger sisters, this was her last chance. Mr Cairnes had no option but to agree. There was no way he could bring his girls home and he wanted them to stay together until the time came when he would be in a position to do so.

Chapter Twenty-six

May dawned bright and sunny. There was great excitement in the home and school. This was the month of the May Procession. One girl from Mrs Ryan's or Miss Banners' class would be chosen to be the 'May Queen' with twelve girls to be maids of honour, six from each class. There was always friendly banter among the girls as to who would wear the nicest dress. The group of friends in the school playground chattered away. "I brought a beautiful dress from home, my Mum made it for me," Peggy said excitedly. "I brought it with me when I first came from home, but I haven't seen it since. Will our names be in the box to be picked as the May Queen? That was how it was done at my old school during assembly."

"Don't be daft, girls from the orphanage are never picked." Josie was laughing at her. "We just walk at the back of the procession wearing the dresses chosen for us by the Sisters. You will be lucky to see your own dress."

Back in the classroom all sat in silence, waiting for Mrs Ryan to speak.

"Molly Burns has been chosen to be our May Queen this year." Molly was in Miss Banners' class. "And here are the six girls chosen from my class who will be maids of honour." She read out their names, two of Peggy's friends from the 'other girls', Maureen and Helen, had been chosen. They were delighted and when the next playtime came all the girls gathered around them laughing and talking.

"I wonder which dress I will receive, I expect that my own dress will be to small for me now." Peggy and Sheila were on orders in the kitchen that Sunday morning. "Oh, we just line up in turn and Sister Grey will choose which dress we wear."

After dinner Peggy stood in line with the other juniors. When she arrived at the front of the queue Sister Grey handed her a dress. She looked down at it. It was made of lace and looked almost grey with age. She was so disappointed and was relieved her mother would not be there to see her, but her father would and she wondered what he would think.

All the juniors went up to the top dormitory to put on their dresses.

They struggled with the chemises but were all dressed and ready in time.

At two thirty, all were assembled in the playground. Peggy glanced around her. All the others seemed to be wearing off white dresses too. To her child's mind they seemed to be many, many years old.

"The Wicked Door" was opened. They all passed through and were on their way to the church.

On Peggy's first visit to the church, at early morning mass the first Friday after entering the orphanage, she had thought it a big dark place, but at later visits she had come to see it as the most beautiful place to come and worship and pray.

On this May Day they entered the church and gasped at the glorious sight of the sanctuary which was magnificent and always inspiring to behold. That day it was even more inspiring, decked with flowers all the way down to the front aisle. There was no sign of the 'other girls' from the infants and junior schools.

Peggy wondered where they were. She was walking beside Sheila. "Where is the May Queen?" she whispered. "They all dress in the school classrooms, and will come on later, you will see," Sheila whispered back.

Once again she was disappointed. They were led to the far aisle of the church. From there it would be impossible to see the altar and the crowning of the statue of Our Lady. They were behind a column of stone pillars that graced both sides of the centre aisle. The organ was playing and the congregation was singing the hymn, "I'll sing a hymn to Mary", as girls from the school came processing down the centre aisle. The girls from the orphanage joined on at the end followed by the May Queen and her attendants. The altar boys, dressed in red and white vestments, carrying candles, led the way out to the church grounds. That was when Peggy saw her father, standing amongst the crowds of people. He had not arrived in time to find himself a place inside the packed church. She was hoping to be able to meet him later but was to be disappointed, as it was not a visiting day.

As they were walking around the grounds, Peggy heard a voice in the crowd and saw that it was a ginger-haired lady who spoke. "Ah, here come the poor little orphans; you would think that better dresses could have been found for them." Peggy stepped out of line and pushed the woman to one side. "I am not an orphan, my Dad is standing over there. Orphans don't have Dads and we are not poor either."

Sheila reached out quickly to pull her back to her place. It all happened in a flash, but not before Sister Brown had seen what had taken place. She glided up to Peggy's side, stamped on her toes and hissed in her ear, "Wait till I get you back to the home, forty two. Once again you have misbehaved and let us all down on a great occasion." Sister Brown stayed close to Peggy's side during the rest of the walk until they were re-entering the church after processing around the streets, where the pavements were crowded with people who had come to watch the children celebrate the month of Mary.

Sister Grey was walking with the infants from the orphanage. Then Peggy heard her. It was Irene, she had seen her father and ran across to where he was standing. "Dad!" She was jumping up and down excitedly. "Dad, have you brought me any sweets?" Sister Grey was doing her best to make Irene go back into line but she didn't want to. "I want some sweets, our father always brings some for us." Sister Grey wrapped an arm around the struggling child, and lifting her up she carried her into the church. Once inside she sat her down on a bench. "Now sit still and behave yourself, I want no more nonsense from you." Irene soon realised that she would be in trouble if she didn't do as she was told.

After the crowning of Our Lady and the singing of the final hymn, the girls from the orphanage were the first to leave the church. They filed through "The Wicked Door", crossed the playground and went up the stairs to the dormitory to change their dresses. Each dress had to be brought down on its hanger and handed to Sister Grey who replaced them in the cupboard. There they would stay until the next procession. "Forty two, stand near the wall." Sister Brown had appeared from nowhere. Her hand was holding the top of the cane she kept hidden underneath her apron. Peggy stood with her face to the wall; she knew what was coming next. She clenched her teeth and closed her eyes tight. 'Swish-whack', six times went the cane across the back of her legs. "Take that for now, forty two. I hope the lady that you pushed will complain about your actions to Sister Superior and that you receive further punishment, you wicked girl."

Peggy hoped not, she had been in enough trouble that year. Sister Superior had spoken to her father and had also warned her. If there was any more trouble from her she would be sent away from here to live in a home for "bad girls".

The threat of being in serious trouble weighed heavy on Peggy's mind. She couldn't concentrate on what she was doing for the next few days. As the week wore on her mind eased. Perhaps nothing would come of the pushing incident. Then came the dreaded summons. On returning from school on Thursday she saw the 'kind' Sister Grey standing at the foot of the staircase.

"Ah, there you are forty two, you have to come with me immediately. Sister Superior wants to see you at once in the visitors' room." Peggy's mind was in a whirl. The visitors' room, that was where you were received on your first arrival at the orphanage. It was also the room where you left for good or on an outing. She feared the worst and expected to be confronted by two policemen, come to take her away to the "bad girls' home".

Sister Grey knocked on the door. "Come in." It was Sister Superior's voice. Peggy was all of a tremble as she entered the room. But it wasn't what she had been expecting. She was greeted by the smiling face of Sister Superior and a woman with reddish hair whom she seemed to have seen before.

"Ah, this is the child." The nun reached out to draw Peggy towards her. "This lady has something to to say to you."

The lady was smiling at her. "Hello Peggy, Sister has been telling me all about you and your sisters and I have come especially to say that it was wrong of me to make those awful remarks. I hope that I can be forgiven and I will be more careful what I say in the future. Am I forgiven?"

"Er, yes, miss," stammered Peggy, who was completely taken by surprise. "And I am sorry for pushing you."

"Well then, that is the end of the matter," said the lady. "My name is Mrs O'Brien. Sister and I have been making plans for the school holidays and some evenings in the future. I am to come here and teach you girls dancing in your recreation time. I have two friends who would also like to come to play the piano and help with the making of clothes for dancing and the concerts. So we will be seeing more of each other. My friends and I are looking forward to starting as soon as possible."

"Yes," said Sister Superior. "Mrs O'Brien and her husband run a public house in Lingford, and they now have a collecting box on display for donations to support our home. Every so often one of the sisters in company of one of our girls goes around to collect the offerings by friends of our home." She paused to catch her breath. "You, Peggy, are now getting older so you may be chosen to go with a sister on one of these outings."

Peggy was very impressed. "It's nearly your teatime, so say goodbye to Mrs O'Brien."

"Bye, Mrs O'Brien, and thank you for coming to see me." Peggy smiled at her and left the room. It was the greatest feeling she had experienced for a long time as she seemed to float back up the staircase alongside Sister Grey. A great weight had been lifted from her mind, it was such a relief.

"Wasn't she a lovely woman?" said Sister Grey. "I think we will all have some good times during her dancing lessons."

"Yes," said Peggy, smiling happily.

Chapter Twenty-seven

It was the week before the start of the long school holidays. It was also visiting Sunday. Peggy was excited. "I am looking forward to telling our Dad how much I have enjoyed the dancing lessons and the sing-a-longs with Mrs O'Brien and her two friends." More happy times were to follow. One day in July, at the start of the long summer holidays, Peggy entered the playroom and was astonished to see a group of excited junior girls looking at a list of names that had been pinned to the inside of the door; some were jumping for joy. "What's all this about?" she asked her friend Josie, who was one of those jumping about.

"My name is on the list," said Josie. "I will be going on holiday to the home in the countryside, we all go, thirty at a time for two weeks during July and August; I am to go with the first group. Have a look, Peggy, your name might also be there."

Peggy looked, and to her delight she saw her name printed near the bottom of the list.

When the happy day arrived, they travelled by coach. Peggy gazed out of the window, transfixed by the beauty of the changing scenery. Hedgerows separated the fields, some of which had cows and sheep dotted around grazing. The trees were so green, overhanging the lanes that they were travelling along. The sun was bursting through where there were gaps in the foliage.

The coach started slowing down as they approached their destination. They had arrived at the village called River Vale, and the home was situated just on its outskirts.

St Saviour's was run by two nuns of the same order as the ones at the orphanage. Their names were Sister Martha and Sister Carmel and they were helped by some senior girls who had left the orphanage as they were past school leaving age.

The home was completely different to what the girls had become accustomed to. Once inside they were shown to their bedrooms, each one having six beds and six small lockers. The rooms were bright and airy, and brightly patterned covers lay on the beds. Downstairs was the dining room; Peggy liked the idea that it wasn't called the refectory, it made it feel more homely. Meals were served in sittings and the nuns were very nice to them all and even helped serve the meals. They had lots of fun and games in which the nuns took part. There was a large field where they could play games. Rounders was a great favourite. Special treats were visits to the nearby riverbank which had a waterfall. Peggy loved the sound of the falling water. They enjoyed pleasant walks down country lanes. It was a blissful time. All too soon it was time to say goodbye to the two nuns and to thank them for such an enjoyable holiday.

It was the end of the long school holiday. It was also visiting Sunday. Peggy was excited, I am looking forward to telling our Dad how much I have enjoyed the dancing lessons and the sing-a-longs with Mrs O'Brien and her two friends. Peggy looked down at Irene who was standing by her side waiting to see their father.

"I am very fond of the ballet music that they danced to and Peggy was very good at the Irish dancing, as were some of the nuns who joined in the sessions. Sister Purple was an expert dancer and the ladies who came to help made beautiful dresses in lovely patterns.

They all had a great 'Hooley' as Sister Purple called the Irish nights. It was good fun for all.

When they next saw their father he looked tired and run down. "Are you not feeling very well, Dad?" asked Peggy.

"Oh, I am not too bad, don't worry about me, it's just tiredness. I have been working long hours, plus I am a bit stiff from all the digging."

"What do you mean, all the digging?" asked Peggy, becoming worried.

"I have been making an air-raid shelter in the back garden. I have dug a big hole, and we are to receive an Anderson shelter in case of air raids when the war starts."

"Will we be home by then to go into this shelter?" asked Peggy excitedly. "It sounds like good fun."

"Me too," piped up Irene, not wanting to be left out of anything.

"No love, you see Germany has invaded most of Europe, and Britain has made a pact with France and Poland. If Germany invades either of them we will declare war on them."

"But I don't understand, Dad, why are we fighting? We say our prayers every day and there might not be a war. I don't know what war means. Will you be all right, Dad?"

Irene thought it was time she had a say. "Dad, have you brought us any sweets or anything nice?"

"Oh Irene, you would cheer anyone up! Yes, here are some sweets, and save some for Peggy." Her father laughed at her eager face and placed his arms around them both.

"So, girls, we will all have to say our prayers for Uncle Charlie who is on standby ready to go to France any day now."

"I will pray for him and make a petition before the altar of Our Lady of Lourdes when we go to church, It's my favourite part of the church. It is where I always remember our Mum in my prayers and leave petitions asking for us to come back home again soon."

Chapter Twenty-eight

During school assembly at the beginning of September, Mrs Ryan stood up to speak. "I have something to tell you that is very important. Mr Chamberlain, the Prime Minister, had broadcast to the nation on the wireless that we are now at war with Germany." Prayers were said for the soldiers, sailors and airmen who would be fighting for their freedom. Some of the 'other girls' were near to tears and worried because their fathers and older brothers would have to go away from home to fight in the war and would be in great danger. Peggy told her friends about her petitions and prayers for her Uncle Charlie and said she would include all her friends and their families in her thoughts and prayers.

Peggy and Maureen were leaning near the lavvy wall. "My Dad may not have to go away to fight in the war because he is needed to work in the production of tanks. He works at a big factory in Lingford where tanks are to be made." "I'm so pleased for you Peggy, maybe my Dad will do war work too," said Maureen.

On the next visiting day, her father reassured her that he would not be called up mto the army as he was doing essential war work but some of the men who worked on the lines had been drafted into the armed forces and that they were to be replaced by women. He also told them that in his last letter Uncle Charlie had written that he would be leaving England but he was not allowed to reveal his destination so more prayers were needed. Peggy had kept to the promise that she had made to the 'other girls' at school by helping them with their school-work. Her friend Maureen had re-sat the scholarship exam but unfortunately she had failed again. "It must be exam nerves," Peggy had told her, "because you are a bright girl."

Peggy was doing well at school and was very popular and well thought of by her classmates as well as her teacher. In the home she made sure that she kept out of trouble, because if you were in disgrace, you were not allowed to attend the dancing or sing-a-longs with Mrs O'Brien and friends. She enjoyed the music and dance and didn't want to miss out on any of it.

Because of her good behaviour, she was given less demanding orders.

On one occasion she was working in the convent, the nuns' home. She was in a small room that was used as an office. It was very quiet and peaceful, just the pleasant ticking of the pendulum clock hanging on the wall facing the highly polished table. Peggy was humming contently to herself as she bent down to polish the curved legs of the table with a soft yellow duster.

All of a sudden, there was a loud startling 'brr, brr.' The shrill ringing of a telephone, very near to her head as she bent close to her work. Peggy nearly jumped out of her skin. Straightening up quickly she banged her head on the side of the table, staggered into the wall just below the shelf, on which was perched a statue, just missing knocking it to the ground. Her heart was thumping, then she realized that it was the first time she had been in a room with a telephone. That was why she had been so startled. The door opened, Sister Superior came dashing in and went to the table to answer the telephone.

After the conversation the nun asked, "Are you all right, forty two? You look pale, and why are you rubbing your head?"

"It's the first time I have been close to a telephone, Sister. It made me jump and I banged my head on the edge of the table."

The nun came to take a closer look at her head. Placing her hand on Peggy's head, she declared, "Well, there is no blood."

She then looked into her eyes, and raising a hand she asked, "How many fingers am I showing?"

"Three," said Peggy. "That's all right then, you don't appear to have concussion, so carry on with your orders. We have the telephone loud so that we can hear it in the sitting room down the corridor. It was a friend of our home ringing to inform me that the collecting box in their public house is full. I will be sending a Sister and one child to visit a few places to bring back the money collected for our home. You are doing good work in here and have not been in trouble lately, so as a reward I will be sending you on the outing. Come to the visitors' room on Saturday morning after breakfast. Oh, and you will be excused the Saturday senna."

"Will I have to go to the big cupboard to get some going-out clothes?" asked Peggy, hardly daring to breathe. "No, not at all, you will go as you are dressed now; we don't want you to look too well turned-out, otherwise people may not want to give; we need all the money we can get."

Peggy was so excited, she could hardly wait to tell her friends the good news. She was to go on an outing with Sister Brown who was the sister who always visited the public houses to empty the collecting boxes.

After breakfast on Saturday morning Peggy presented herself at the visitors' room door. She was dressed as usual, spotted dress and pumps on her feet. She knocked on the door. Sister Superior opened it, and inside was Sister Brown waiting for her. She had a thin well-worn cardigan over her arm. Approaching Peggy she held it out to her. "Put this on, forty two, it can be quite chilly outside at this time of year." While Peggy was putting on the cardigan Sister Brown was adjusting something a leather satchel round her waist under her apron. The cardigan was rather big for Peggy's small frame. It had three buttons at the front and two large hip pockets.

As Sister Superior was opening the big door to let them out she said to Peggy, "Some people might give you money, but remember it is all for the home and not for you, so put it in the pockets of the cardigan and leave it there until you return, and then hand it back to Sister Brown. Do you understand me, girl?" Peggy nodded her head; she just wanted to get through the door.

"Oh, and remember to walk just behind Sister Brown."

As she walked down the street, Peggy recognised it as the route she had taken on the day she had run away. But its appearance had changed. Some of the houses and shops had brown sandy-coloured sacks stacked around the doorways that she was told later were sandbags. Also the lamp posts had white bands painted around them so that they could be seen at night as the street lighting was not allowed during the "blackout".

Walking slightly behind Sister Brown, Peggy realised that they were approaching the main road, where the tramlines were. At the junction to the main road they came to the first public house on Sister Brown's list. "Now stand there in the doorway, forty two, and don't dare move until I return." Peggy stood to attention as Sister Brown swished in through the doors. Not knowing what to do she fixed her eyes on a large poster stuck on a nearby wall which read "Dig for Victory". She wondered what it meant. Girls in the orphanage had not been given any information regarding the war except for saying prayers for those in conflict. While she was standing there two ladies who lived nearby approached her. "Hello dear, are you waiting for the sister who does the collections?" Peggy nodded her head. "Here is a sweet for you," and she handed her a pear drop, "it will help you pass the time." Peggy looked longingly at the sweet but knew that she could not eat it, so she placed it in the cardigan pocket. A few minutes later Sister Brown reappeared. "Has anybody given you anything while I have been inside?" Peggy nodded her head and produced the sweet It had bits of fluff from the cardigan pocket sticking to it. Sister Brown took the sweet and placed it in her own large pocket. "Come on then, let's get moving, we have lots more places to visit. Try to look more woeful, that is what you are here for, if they think that you are a sorry sight people will be more generous." They crossed the road and started walking up the hill, but far from feeling sorry Peggy was elated; they were heading in the direction of Meadowfields, which was where her home lay.

They were to visit a few more pubs in the busy area. People passing by seeing Peggy waiting in the pub doorways handed her pennies and halfpennies and on one occasion gave her a threepenny piece. Eventually, they arrived at a public house that she recognized as the place where they used to alight from the tramcar on their way home from shopping in Lingford city centre.

The cardigan pockets were heavy with loose change. Peggy felt happy looking across the road; she could see the field with a footpath worn along the route they always walked along, leading to the street where she lived. While Sister Brown was inside the pub, Peggy was fondly remembering the times that she had walked across that field. She was deep in thought when she heard a tram approaching, coming from the direction of the city. She immediately turned her back as the tram stopped hoping none of the alighting passengers would recognize her. She didn't want any of her friends to see her – she was beginning to feel like a street beggar. Sister Brown came striding through the door and glared at Peggy. "Are you looking for trouble, forty two, why are you crouching down with your back to the people? Are you hiding something that you have been given?"

"No, Sister, but I live just across the fields and I didn't want anybody who knows me to see me and tell my Dad, he might think that I have run away again."

"Time to start making our way back to the home, otherwise we will be late for dinner," the nun growled at her as she adjusted the bag underneath her apron. It looked very full, making her look rather plump.

"It is a good job it's downhill going back, I am weighed down with all this loose money. Your cardigan pockets are also full so make sure that you do not lose any coins on the walk back."

As they crossed to the other side of the road, Peggy took a long last look at the footpath across the fields. There were two figures a long way off, walking down in the direction of the main road. It was a man and a woman holding hands; she thought the man looked like her father. She was still looking over her shoulder to see if it really was him when Sister said, "Come on forty two, look where you are going." Peggy walked just behind the nun still wondering if it was her father that she had seen coming down the footpath with a woman. Now she would have to wait until the next visiting day to ask him.

On the way back Peggy saw something that she had not noticed on the outward journey. Up in the sky were large silver whale-shaped balloons. I wonder what they are for, she thought.

They left the main road and tram tracks. "We will go by the park, it is a quicker way back," the nun said. Just after they had passed the park, coming in the opposite direction towards them was a column of marching soldiers three abreast, rifles over one shoulder, the other arm swinging in perfect unison. As they marched they were singing:

"There'll always be an England, and England shall be free."

They both stopped to watch the soldiers marching by, along with other people. Peggy felt very proud and wanted to clap and cheer them but Sister Brown said, "Come on, we are going to be late for dinner." She pulled on the chain of the door bell when they arrived back at the orphanage. The big door opened, and as soon as they entered the nun said, "The cardigan, forty two, take it off and hand it to me carefully. The pockets seem to be well filled, we have had a good day. Off you go now, it is your dinner time."

Peggy hurried up the stairs to meet her friends, eager to tell them of her morning out with Sister Brown. But she was still wondering about her father.

Was it him she had seen and if so who was the lady walking by his side?

Chapter Twenty-nine

She would say nothing to her friends until she had asked her father herself on his next visit. Days turned to weeks and it was coming up to Christmas. Peggy's father had told her on his last visit, "I am going to take you out shopping in Lingford for your Christmas presents. But this year, I am not telling the nuns that I am going to take you and any presents that we buy will go back to our own home: it will be something for you all to look forward to when eventually you do come home for good."

Peggy was very excited. "Oh yes, it will be our little secret. Sister Superior will be very annoyed."

"Well, don't you say anything to anybody or else they won't let me take you out at all."

"I won't," giggled Peggy, keeping a close eye on Irene who was once again busy sucking on a large sweet that her father had brought her, she was oblivious to anything else being said or done around her. Peggy hugged her secret to herself. The only other event that she had to look forward to was the singing and dancing, organized by Mrs O'Brien and her friends for the Christmas concert. This year she was to dance in an Irish reel and sing in the final song along with the rest of the girls. But the mainstay of her days was work, prayers, and more work. Peggy was now thirteen, and had learnt not to get herself into as much trouble as she had in the past, so her orders were not quite as hard. She had already been allowed to work in the convent and to go out collecting with Sister Brown.

Then she remembered, she had not asked her father who the lady was walking by his side that she thought she had seen on her day out with Sister Brown.

On the following Saturday he was to take her out Christmas shopping so she would ask him then. She was looking forward to their outing and was so pleased that they would be taking the presents to her own home. The last two Christmases she had also gone shopping with her father, and he had bought them lots of lovely presents, but they had never received them. He had bought Irene and Marie lovely dolls, books, pencil cases, coloured crayons and lots of little presents to put in their stockings but at the orphanage they didn't hang up their stockings; in fact, as usual they would receive a gift on 6 January, after the big concert. A gift that Peggy didn't want. It would be a new pinny and a new toy which was removed from her soon afterwards and put away until next year. She didn't care, because this year her best presents would be safe at her own home. Her father was to come for her at one o'clock. She was ready and waiting dressed in her going-out clothes when the senior girl came to collect her and take her to Sister Grey, who took her to the visitors' room. "Now don't forget forty two, you must be back here by five o'clock and bring all your shopping with you." Peggy just nodded her head, she did not tell the mean Sister Grey that she would be taking all the presents to her home. She would just have to deal with that problem when she arrived back. In the meantime, she just wanted to enjoy her time out with her father. Sister Grey opened the door and her father came striding towards her. He placed his arm around Peggy's shoulder and gave her a big hug. Sister Grey was giving them orders, how she was to behave and what time that they had to be back but neither of them was listening to her. Peggy tried to look interested, but all she wanted was to step out of that big black door with her father.

Once outside they quickly made their way down the street. Peggy gazed up at her father's face and noticed how much better he looked since she had last seen him. "Dad, can I ask you something?" she asked tentatively. He looked down at her earnest little face.

"Of course you can, ask me anything you like, I will answer you if I can," he said smiling at her. She took a deep breath. "Well, when I went out with Sister Brown collecting money, I thought I saw you walking towards the tram stop, but there was a lady with you. Was it you, Dad, and who was the lady?"

Her question came as a shock to Mr Cairnes; he had wanted to tell her all about his new friendship with a lady who was a fellow worker at the big engineering factory where they both worked. But he had been too afraid to approach her with the news. Peggy needed careful handling; she wouldn't want another person taking her mother's place.

"Let's do the shopping first, and when we get home I will explain it all to you." He took hold of her hand, swinging her arm back and forth; he needed time to collect his thoughts. "Tell me all about your morning out with Sister Brown, had I known that you were so near home I would have come to meet you." Peggy, in all innocence, told him all about how she had to stand outside the public house doors and how people filled her cardigan pockets with money while Sister Brown was inside emptying the collection boxes. As she chattered on her father became more and more annoyed. How dare the nuns use his daughter as a begging bowl? He paid good money every week for their upkeep. He would have something to say to that Sister Superior when they arrived back at the orphanage.

By this time the tram going to Lingford city centre had arrived and they were soon on their way. The shopping was done much more quickly that year, as there was not a lot to buy in the shops because of the war. They bought what they could and were soon on a tram heading for Meadowfields.

Peggy was so glad to be in her own home again and was soon busy helping her father to put away the presents that they had managed to buy. "I am going to make some tea now. Mrs Oates knew that you were coming and she wanted to make you some of the cream buns you like so much but with the rationing and the shortages she could only manage some oat biscuits, though I'm sure that you will enjoy them just the same. She hopes to see you if there is time before we return to the home," he said, glancing at the clock.

When they had finished the tea and biscuits, Peggy's father led her into the sitting room and sat down next to her on the settee. Looking her straight in the eye and smiling he said, "Well Peggy, you know the question that you asked me regarding the lady you thought that you saw me with? It is true, her name is Betty and she works at the same factory as me." There was silence for a moment. "But why were you with her during the day?" This is going to be difficult, thought her father, playing for time. He was also keeping his eye on the clock. He wasn't in a hurry to take Peggy back but didn't want to cause her to be in any trouble with Sister Superior or any of the other nuns. Sister Grey had told them to be back by five o'clock so it had to be. He had about an hour and a half left to get things sorted out.

Peggy sat with her hands folded in her lap and was thinking to herself, "Why does my Dad need to go out with another lady?" She was puzzled because when she came home for good he wouldn't need anyone but her to look after them. He had an idea what she was thinking, and was a very troubled man. He sighed, then continued. "Betty is a very nice lady, I have told her all about the three of you and she would love to meet you all; wouldn't that be nice?"

"Meet us where, Dad? We only see you on visiting days and anyway we don't know anything about her."

"Well, I do," he answered, feeling as though he was losing the battle. "As I said she is a very nice lady who has been very helpful to me, doing my washing and cleaning the house, you can see how everything is clean and tidy; she wanted everything to be all right for today when you arrived home."

Peggy was silent. "So," she thought, "his friend Betty has been in our house doing things for him." She looked at him. "Where does she live? Has she no children of her own to look after?"

"Betty lives here in Meadowfields with her elderly mother and father and no, she has no children of her own or any other relatives, and she is sometimes lonely." He was quiet for a moment. "When this war started, lots of ladies had to go and work in the factories, to take the place of all the men called to active service." He glanced at her face wondering if she knew what he was talking about. "I met her when we were all walking home from the tram stop. You don't know this, Peggy, but it is very dark on the streets at night owing to there being no street lighting, and lots of ladies are frightened to walk home in the dark. So I see Betty to her home and make sure that she is safe, that's when I told her all about you three."

He looked at the clock once more; it was nearly time for them to go. "But you won't need her to look after you when I come home, Dad, will you?" He nodded his head. Peggy felt better, Betty was only looking after her father for her so she must be all right. She wondered what she looked like. "Are you going to bring her to see us next visiting day, will you have to ask Sister Superior if she can come?"

Her father gave a big sigh of relief. "Yes, I will bring her, Peggy and no I don't have to have permission." He pulled her to her feet. "Come on, we had better get a move on; we don't want any trouble now, do we?" Peggy laughed and ran to get her coat; wait until she told Sheila and Josie that her father was bringing a lady to visit them. Her father smiled. "We have been talking for so long there is no time to visit Mrs Oates, but I will tell her how much you enjoyed her biscuits."

They arrived back at the orphanage just in time to meet the five o'clock deadline. This was when Peggy began to feel nervous. Sister Superior would be waiting for them to hand over their gifts as was the normal procedure. They stepped inside the big door to be greeted by by the look of anger on the nun's face.

"Where are your Christmas presents, forty two? You were told to bring them back with you." Peggy partly hid herself behind her father's back.

"Well," Mr Cairnes was looking straight into the nun's face, "my children have never received any of the previous presents that I have bought them, so I decided this year to take them to our own home and there they will stay until the children return home. I think that it will be for the best, don't you?"

Sister Superior had a face like thunder. "How are we to present them with gifts when the Bishop comes?" Mr Cairnes stood his ground. "The same as you do every year, give them some old toys and remove them after the concert." Peggy was getting worried; she had never seen her father look so angry, and she wondered what would happen to her once he had gone home. Her father took something from his coat pocket and handed it to the still-angry nun. "Here is the money for my children's upkeep, and don't you dare send my Peggy out begging for money ever again."

"Mr Cairnes!" Sister raised her voice. "We will not discuss such matters in front of the child, and you," she pointed her finger at Peggy, "upstairs at once; I will deal with you later." Taking no notice of the nun's angry gestures, Mr Cairnes bent down, drawing the frightened child towards him. "Don't worry Peggy, you run along now, I will sort things out with Sister."

She gave him a hug and a kiss and quickly scampered away wondering what the outcome of today's events would be.

Chapter Thirty

As Peggy was slowly walking along the corridor, the mean Sister Grey was standing near to the refectory door. "You are too late, forty two, tea is already finished; I told you to be back in good time. Now go and change your clothes then carry on with your orders, there will be no tea for you today."

Peggy didn't care, she was still full from eating Mrs Oates' biscuits and was more concerned with what her father had said to Sister Superior after she had left them. He had looked really upset and angry.

Later carrying her going-out clothes over her arm on her way to return them to the cupboard she saw Sister Superior waiting for her near the sewing room door. "In here, forty two. You have really done it this time. Was it your idea to take your Christmas presents home?" she growled at poor Peggy. "I never gave your Dad permission to go anywhere but shopping and you have come back with nothing."

"No Sister, my Dad just thought that it was a good idea, as we never seem to receive any of the presents that he buys for us and I am sure that our Mum would have wanted us to have them." Sister Superior stamped her foot in rage and gave Peggy a push. "You are the most ungrateful girl I have ever come across, and your father is not much better." She took a deep breath. "Now listen to what I have to say to you. This home is run by Sisters who have left their good homes in a lovely country. They dedicate their lives to care for children who have nothing and nobody. We feed and clothe them in a safe environment with the help of the public and our benefactors and we teach them love and sharing. Your presents in the past were displayed on the Christmas tree so that all could enjoy them. Do you understand me forty two?"

Peggy nodded. "I do share my things whenever I can, but I would like to share them out myself, and I would like Irene and Marie to have their own toys to play with and not just to look at."

"You have decided to be selfish, which is sinful. Go and kneel at the end of the corridor and pray for forgiveness of your sins. You will be on double orders from tomorrow, and no recreation until I say so." The following morning Sister Brown was on duty. She sneered at Peggy, grabbed hold of her hair and started pulling her backwards and forwards. "Sister Superior told all of us about your conduct yesterday, and your disobedience after being given the treat of an afternoon's shopping. You are a bad girl and will receive lots of punishments. It will serve you right if you are sent to the home for bad girls. After you have washed yourself, go down to the kitchens and receive the first of your punishments." Peggy didn't care; she knew that she would be in trouble. But seeing how angry her father had been yesterday when they had returned, she had the feeling that he would soon have them all out of here and back home for good.

As far as Peggy was concerned, Christmas as usual was a non-event. The tree was once again erected in the playroom and she could see their presents from the past two years displayed among its branches. Irene and Marie's dolls, her sewing box and all the other little presents that her father had bought them. She knew that they would never receive them. They still went to church, and sang the Christmas hymns. The church looked beautiful, lots of lovely flowers decorating all of the altars. But the spirit of Christmas didn't penetrate Peggy's thoughts. She was still thinking about her father and wondered if he was spending his Christmas with his new friend Betty.

One thing brightened her days; Marie and all the other infants had been brought back to the orphanage for the holidays and the Christmas concert, rehearsals for which had been going full swing for the past four weeks. Marie and all the other infants had learned their songs and dances in the infants' home, and Peggy couldn't wait to see what she would be doing. Irene, along with seven other eight-year-olds were to do a song and dance act dressed as little wooden dolls. Peggy and her friends had had many a good laugh watching them rehearse. She herself had learned all the steps to the Irish reel they would be dancing as well as the words to the final song. She would be glad when the whole night was over. But the following week would be parents' and friends' night, and she was hoping to see her father. She was still doing double orders and was worried in case Sister Superior decided that not seeing her father would be a punishment.

The two concerts went without a hitch, but as they all filed in for the final song for the parents, Peggy was disappointed when she saw her father. He appeared to be on his own, sitting between two elderly ladies, neither of whom looked like a Betty.

It was very busy in the refectory as the concert finished, girls pushing and shoving trying to change their clothes. Peggy swiftly slipped through the door, back into the playroom where her father was sitting waiting for her. He hugged her to him. "I really enjoyed tonight Peggy, you all did so well."

"I'm so glad that you had a good time Dad, wasn't Irene and her group funny? We could hear you all laughing behind the scenes."

"Yes," replied her father. "It really cheered me up."

"Why didn't you bring Betty with you? When are we going to meet her?"

There was a small pause. "It will be visiting Sunday in three weeks' time, I hope to be able to bring her then. I am sure that you will like her and she is so looking forward to meeting you all."

At that moment the bell rang, announcing the end of her brief time spent with her father.

Peggy was one of the last girls to leave the room after bidding her father goodnight, with the pleasant thought in her mind that on his next visit he would bring his friend Betty with him and they would all meet at last.

She had lots of questions to ask of her. One was, how often did she visit their house? And also to thank her for doing her father's washing and cleaning the house for him. She would also tell her that she wouldn't be needed once they were all home again as she herself would look after everything and everybody. In that frame of mind, she made her way up to the dormitory and bed.

Chapter Thirty-one

Visiting day came at last. All the children were out in the playground. Peggy and Irene's numbers were called out by a senior girl. Marie had already returned to the infants' home. She had danced beautifully as a fairy at the concert. She was almost five and would be ready to start school after the Easter holidays, but Peggy hoped that they would be home before then. Peggy went to the far side of the playground to collect Irene who was playing a game with her friends. "Come on, you, our Dad has come to visit us and I want you to behave yourself. He may have brought a lady with him and we want her to like us, don't we?" Irene nodded her head. "What lady, do I know her?" she asked, jumping up and down as usual. Peggy turned to her. "No, we don't know her yet, and if she comes, don't you dare ask her for any sweets." Saying that she took her by the hand and hurried her across the playground.

They made their way towards the refectory where their father would be waiting. "Ah, forty two and forty three, your visitors are here," said the senior girl who was on duty. She quickly opened the door and they stepped inside.

Peggy looked across to where her father was sitting. Next to him was a lady, looking as nervous as Peggy herself was feeling. She had fair wavy hair and was wearing a red coat and holding a black handbag.

Peggy and Irene made their way across to where they were sitting. Their father stood up and placed his arms around both their shoulders. He turned them both towards the now-smiling lady. "Betty, these are two of my girls. Peggy and Irene. You will meet Marie later." They all looked at each other in silence for a few moments. Betty was the first to speak. "I am very pleased to meet you both at last, your Dad has told me so much about you that I feel I know you already. I hope we will soon become friends." Opening her handbag she produced two cone-shaped paper bags twisted closed at the top containing small sweets. They didn't know she must have used her sweet coupons to purchase them.

Irene sat facing her father happily eating the sweets, but Peggy had other things on her mind. She wanted to ask Betty so many questions but didn't know how to start. She took a deep breath. "Has our Dad told you what happened to our lovely Mum? I promised her that I would look after all of us and that is what I will do when I come home."

"I'm sure you will," replied Betty. "I know all about your Mum, and don't worry, I promise to look after your Dad for you."

She looked across at Irene, who was still tucking into her sweets. "I can see that you like sweets! Had you better save some for later?"

"No," replied Irene quickly. "Someone will take them off me when we go back into the playground, you gave them to me and they are mine."

"Don't be so naughty, Irene, the lady has been very kind to us and we haven't even said thank you to her yet," said Peggy.

Betty smiled at her. "Oh that's all right, I hope that I have helped to make you both happy."

"Well," said their father, "I am so pleased to see that we are all getting along so well. Would you like Betty to come and see you again?"

Irene was still busy eating. Peggy just nodded her head. There was still a lot more that she wanted to know about her father and Betty but it would have to wait until the next visit.

She turned towards her father. "Have you heard anything from Uncle Charlie, is he still away fighting in the war? I remember him every night in my prayers and hope he returns home safe."

Her father looked at her worried face and tried to sound cheerful. "No I'm sorry love, I don't get any letters now, but no news is good news so they say. We just have to hope and pray."

He carried on making conversation, including Betty as often as he could. He knew Peggy wasn't quite sure about her feelings towards her yet. Irene was different, she would take to anyone who brought her sweets. Just then the bell rang, bringing visiting time to a close.

After goodbyes and promises to come on the next visiting day Peggy hurried Irene back to the playground and handed her over to the senior girl in charge of her group. She wanted to get back to her own friends; she knew that they would be eager to hear all about the visit. "What was she like then?" Sheila asked her. "Did she look rich, does she live in a big house? It must be lovely to have a nice lady to come visit you as well as your Dad." Then Josie joined in. "Is she going to live at your house, so that you can all go home?"

Peggy was shocked. "She was very nice and even brought us these," taking the sweets from her knicker pocket. "I hid these from Irene otherwise she would have eaten the lot."

Opening the packet she shared them with her friends. It was a treat for them, as they had no family or friends to give them money to be entered into the ledger book. "I like Betty," said Peggy. "She is looking after our father doing the washing and housework; she is a big help to him because he works such long hours. But there will be no need for her stay when we return home, I will do everything for all of us."

Sheila sighed. "I wish that I had a home to go to and someone to visit me." Peggy looked at her friend. "I can imagine how you feel, but some day you will have a home of your own."

They all went about their orders before supper. Peggy was still doing double orders, and she hurried about her tasks not wanting to miss her supper, meagre though it was.

That night lying in her bed, she went over in her thoughts the events of the afternoon. She liked Betty but she was still worried that she didn't know enough about her or her family. She also realized that Betty was younger than her father. She also wondered how they would all get along together once they were all back home. Would she still want to come to a house with three children messing it all up? Irene and Marie would need looking after but she was quite capable of looking after herself. With these thoughts on her mind she fell asleep.

The following day they were all back at school after the holidays. Peggy decided to tell her friend Maureen all about Betty. At playtime they were leaning near the lavvy wall. "My Dad brought a lady friend to visit us yesterday; her name is Betty." She paused, then went on to tell her all that had happened on the visiting day.

"Ooh," said Maureen. "Do you think your Dad will marry her? That will make her your new Mum. There is a girl in our street called Lily, who has just got a new Mum and she likes having her at their home. Lily has a brother and sister who are younger than her. Their grand-mother used to look after them all when their father was at work, but she was very strict with them. Their new Mum is very nice and they are all much happier now. If that happens to you and your sisters I will be very happy for you all."

"Oh, I don't know," Peggy sighed. "My Dad never said anything to me about getting married or having a new Mum." To her way of thinking she didn't think that there was such a thing as a new mother. If there was, why hadn't Sheila, Josie and all the girls who were in the orphanage received one? She would speak to her father about it. Not knowing anything about the facts of life, she often wondered what the nuns meant when they told them to sleep with their legs closed "to keep the devil out". She still believed that babies came from heaven and were placed under a gooseberry bush by the angels. That was what she had been told as a little girl and she still believed in such things.

The bell rang for the end of playtime. "Come on," said Maureen. "What is going through your mind, didn't you hear the bell?" She pulled her friend back into line, she didn't want her to be in trouble with Mrs Ryan. She was still in Mrs Ryan's class because of a shortage of teachers during the war.

Chapter Thirty-two

The days seemed to drag by very slowly, and it seemed to be ages before the next visiting day arrived. Peggy had been turning things over in her mind. She had a few sleepless nights, wondering what she would say to her father. Would he be getting married to Betty, and would she be their new mother? It was the same routine, their numbers were called and they were ushered as usual into the refectory.

Once again their father was sitting with Betty by his side. Today she was wearing a blue coat and on the table in front of her was a brown paper bag. Peggy made sure that she sat next to her father, and Irene sat next to Betty who was opening the brown bag. Irene was very excited; she wondered what Betty had brought her this time. They were busy emptying the bag, and while they were occupied sorting the treats out Peggy took her chance to speak to her father.

"Dad," she whispered into his ear. "Are you and Betty going to get married, will she be coming to live with you at our house? My friend Maureen said she would be, she also said that Betty would be our new Mum, is it true, Dad?" Her father quickly glanced to where Betty and Irene were still busy. "No love, nothing has been said or settled yet, we are just good friends, but would you like it if we did get married? It would make things different at home. But Betty still lives with her mother and father so there would have to be changes there. It is all pie in the sky at the moment, we will just have to wait and see what happens. Hey, look, Irene has nearly emptied the bag, there will be nothing left for you if we don't stop her."

Betty looked up. "Come on Peggy, change places with Irene and see what I have brought for you. I do hope you like comics and girls' journals, and I have managed to save your sweets from Irene's grasp." "Thank you, it is very kind of you to bring us such nice sweets. I hope you are not working too hard at our house, you must have a lot of things to do in your own home." Betty just smiled at her; she knew it was going to be difficult. Peggy had had her father all to herself for such a long time. The two younger children had been very young when they had lost their mother. It was easier for them to accept other women into their lives. But with Peggy it would be different. She would take some careful handling. When they left after visiting, she would discuss with their father whether it was a good idea for her to continue visiting with him.

Marie had now returned to the orphanage to stay and was ready to start school with the rest of the infants.

Peggy had quite a few problems with Marie since her return to the home. She was used to the senior girls looking after her and at first she didn't want anything to do with Peggy who even now was not allowed to look after her youngest sister. One day Peggy saw her sitting on the bench in the playroom. "Hello Marie, I am your big sister Peggy. Our father is coming to visit us next Sunday, won't that be nice? You, Irene and me all together, won't he be surprised?" Marie looked at her. "I can't come with you, I don't know you." Peggy felt like crying. Her little sister, who she had promised her mother and father she would look after, didn't know her. She composed herself, and decided they would get to know one another again before they went to see their father. She would try and see Sister Superior and ask her if she could spend more time with her younger sisters.

A senior girl came striding across the playroom floor. "What do you think you are doing, forty two, you know you are not allowed to speak to your younger sisters."

"Yes, that's right," confirmed Peggy. "But she is my sister and it should be me looking after her."

"Well, you can't," said the angry senior girl. "Go and do your orders before I report you." She took Marie by the hand and hurried her out of the room. Peggy followed slowly behind. On the following morning, just after breakfast, Peggy made her way upstairs to the sewing room to try and find Sister Superior. She was usually sitting at her big desk writing out reports. Peggy gave a light knock on the door, didn't wait for an answer and crept slowly into the room. "What do you want, forty two, you can see that I am busy, and why didn't you knock?" "I did knock, Sister, but you didn't hear me. I would like to speak to you about my sisters, I need to know them better; they are not babies any more and I want them to know who I am."

"Well, forty two, it does not work like that, rules are rules and they can't be broken just for your family. You can mix with them on visiting days, now go about your orders and let me do my work," said the impatient nun, dismissing her with a sweep of her arm.

Visiting day came round again. Peggy collected Marie along with Irene. She had been getting along much better with Marie due to the fact she had managed to spend time getting to know her unseen by the nuns. The senior girls hadn't bothered her, it was one infant less for them to care for. She hurried her two little sisters along to the refectory. Inside their father was sitting on his own. His face lit up with pleasure when he saw Marie was with them. He took her on to his knee. Irene didn't like it – she was used to being the centre of attention. "Where's my sweets?" she demanded. "Have you brought me some, Dad?" He looked down at her expectant face. "You are becoming very cheeky, you will have to learn you don't always get what you want. Now, sit there with Marie," he said, lifting his youngest daughter from his knee and placing her on a chair. He then produced little bags of sweets and handed them to the waiting girls. They both sat contentedly swinging their legs and eating their sweets.

Now it was Peggy's turn, and she moved up close to him. "Dad, why hasn't Betty come with you? Does she not like us any more, is it because you have asked her to be our new Mum? Perhaps it would be too hard for her to look after these two. I can look after myself."

"Oh no," he replied, wondering what was going on in her mind. "Betty likes you all very much and would love to look after you all, but if it does happen it won't be for quite a while. There is a lot of sorting out to do, it can't happen overnight. I will tell you everything as we go along. Don't worry I will only do what is best for all of us. Now come on, eat your sweets before these two get their hands on them."

By this time, Marie and Irene were back on his knees, trying to find out if he had brought them anything else. Peggy sat with thoughts running through her mind of what her father had just said. Turning back to her father she said, "It's all right Dad, we all like Betty and would love her to visit us again." He smiled down at her, nodding his head in agreement. The rest of the visit was spent trying to keep the two younger ones quiet but entertained. She didn't want Sister Brown, whose eyes were everywhere, coming to put a stop to the visit.

Every visit after that, Betty accompanied their father whenever she could. She brought them treats and seemed to enjoy entertaining the two younger children. Peggy was pleased for her father was looking much happier.

Chapter Thrity-three

One morning as they all filed into the washroom, Peggy was standing in line waiting her turn for the lavvy. As she turned her head she saw a younger girl of about nine standing near to the big sink holding her bed sheet rolled up into a bundle; she was crying and looked very upset. Peggy forgot about the lavvy and went over to where she was standing. She placed her arm around the crying girl's shoulders and said, "Don't cry, you're not the only one to have wet the bed. What is your name? You have only been here a few days so I haven't had a chance to speak to you." The young girl wiped her eyes on the corner of the wet sheet and looked at Peggy in fear.

"Please don't shout at me, I didn't do it on purpose," she sniffed, still looking terrified. "My name is Joyce, me and my little sister Alice had to come to this place because our Dad, who is in the air force, is away flying aeroplanes. and a bomb blew up most of our street, we were in an air raid shelter, our mother had gone back to the house for something, she was in the house when the bomb landed, her legs were hurt and she was taken away in an ambulance. There was no one to look after us so here we are." She started to cry again. Peggy smiled at her. "How old is your sister?" The younger girl looked up at her. "She is only just three and I haven't seen her since we arrived here. Oh, can you tell me where she is? We both used to sleep together in the same bed at home, and I used to sing songs to her until she went to sleep, and I never wet the bed before."

"I know just how you feel, the same things happened to me when we first came here. Don't worry about Alice, she will have gone to the babies' and infants' home and will be well looked after. My youngest sister Marie lived there but now she is five and old enough for school so she is now back here with us."

"Will I be able to she her again?" Joyce asked. "Yes, when the infants are brought back here again for the next holiday. Don't upset yourself, she will be all right and I will look after you."

Peggy hoped that she could keep her promise to the younger girl who had stopped crying and was looking at her hopefully. "Give me your sheet, I will wash it for you," whispered Peggy. The mean Sister

Grey was watching them. Taking the wet sheet from her arms she pushed her way to the front of the queue. One of the senior girls saw her. "What do you think you are doing, forty two, started wetting the bed, have you?" Peggy took no notice of her and plunged the wet sheet into the big sink. The sheet was made of calico, a very heavy cotton material. Squeezing as much water as she could from it and grabbing the bewildered Joyce by the arm she took her down to the kitchen area where there was a yard with clothes lines strung across it. She flung the dripping sheet over the nearest one. "You will have to come and collect it after tea and just hope that it dries," she said to Joyce who was nodding her head. "Now come on or we will be late for breakfast and school."

One of Peggy's orders was to clean the sinks and lavvies, and wash the floor of the washroom before going down for breakfast. She knew she wouldn't finish that order but would try and do as much as she could, and managed all but the floor and would try and finish it after school. She was also on kitchen orders after breakfast which didn't leave much time before school.

"Come on, Peggy." It was the voice of her friend Sheila. "We don't want to be in trouble and miss breakfast." Peggy dried her hands on her dress and followed her friend. No one would notice that the floor had not been washed, she hoped, as they hurried down the stairs as fast as they dared and into the playroom just in time to hear the bell rung for breakfast. Peggy had a lovely day at school, especially in the afternoon. It had been her favourite subject, art, and she and her friend Maureen had painted part of a mural that was to be placed around the wall of the classroom. She had really enjoyed herself and hadn't given a thought to the fact that she hadn't washed the floor of the washroom that morning. That was until she stepped through the Wicked Door on her way back from school. Sister Brown was waiting for her just inside the door. She grabbed Peggy by the collar of her dress dragging her all the way across the playground, at the same time slapping her across the back of her legs with a bamboo cane.

"Forty two, I have been waiting for you, you deserted your orders this morning."

Peggy tried to get a word in. "Please Sister, I was only trying to help a new girl to wash her sheet."

"Don't try to make excuses, I don't believe you." She carried on hitting Peggy with the cane. "You can now resume your normal orders, and complete the washroom order during teatime therefore missing your meal as an extra punishment." By this time Peggy couldn't care less, the weals on the back of her legs were beginning to stand out and she ached all over from the pushing and shoving she had received from the angry nun.

"This is it," thought Peggy, "I am going to run away for good this time and if I can't live at home I will find somewhere else to stay."

With these thoughts in her mind she painfully went about her orders. She couldn't wait for the following day, and vowed to herself that she would be away from this place. She spent a very uncomfortable night, unable to sleep because her legs hurt so much.

In the morning, she rose painfully. Would the pain in her legs prevent her making the long walk home? She hoped not. Later that morning, during playtime she told her friends what had happened to her and showed them her legs.

Maureen gasped at the sight. "Oh, I wish I could help you to run away, but I haven't got any money."

"Don't worry about me," replied Peggy, "I will manage somehow, just don't tell anyone that I am going. I'm sure I can make it to my home."

On their way back to school after dinner Peggy hung back and managed to hide herself in the same gap that she had used the last time she had run away, and waited until the senior girl had passed on her way back to the home.

This time she knew the way and hurried down the street until she came to the main road and the tramlines. Crossing the road she started her steady walk uphill in the direction of Meadowfields and home. It took her much longer this time, her legs hurt and she had no money to take a tramcar ride. It took two hours before she arrived at the familiar sights of her home.

Passing through the front gate and round to the back garden, a surprise awaited her. There was Betty, hanging out her father's washing on the clothes line.

"Good grief, what are you doing here?" said Betty in a shocked voice. Then Peggy started to cry; she had been through so much in the past two days that the events had become overwhelming and she couldn't take any more, and she sat down on the back doorstep hiding her face in her hands. Betty dropped the washing on the ground and came rushing towards her. "Oh Peggy, what have they done to you? Look at your legs! Come on, I will take you indoors and sort you out."

Seating her on the settee, she made her a warm drink. All Peggy could say was, "I'm not going back, I'm not going back."

Betty didn't know what to do; she wasn't used to dealing with children. "Would you like a nice hot bath? It will help to ease your aches and pains," was all she could think of saying.

Peggy was wondering what would her father say this time. Surely he wouldn't send her back once he had seen the state she was in. Later Betty helped her out of the bath and placed a nice warm towel around her. Sitting her back on to the settee, she said, "You sit there while I go to the telephone box to let your Dad know that you are at home."

Half an hour later her father came dashing through into the room where Peggy was waiting for him, still wrapped in the towel. As he looked at her a look of horror came over his face. "What on earth have they done to you, was it Sister Brown?"

Peggy nodded her head. "I thought so, this time they won't get away with it."

"But I am not going back, Dad, so it does not matter, if you say anything to them it will only make it hard for Irene and Marie until we can get them home too."

He had to calm her down. She would have to go back for at least a short while to give him time to acquire some new bedclothes for their beds as the children's bedding had been used to stock the air-raid shelter; also she had no decent clothes with her.

The main thing he would have to tell her was that he and Betty were to be married next Saturday. He had wanted to allow Betty to become used to living at their home if just for a short time. Then the two of them were to visit the three girls in two weeks' time to tell them they were married and all about their plans for the future. He and Betty had discussed bringing the girls home once everything was arranged for them.

Betty brought in some tea and biscuits and sat herself down next to Peggy. Her father cleared his throat. "Er... Peggy, Betty and I are going to be married next Saturday. We wanted it to be a nice surprise for you all."

"Married?" cried the astonished Peggy. "Where, when?"

Her father did his best to calm her down and explain.

Betty spoke up as much as she could. "It will all work out, love, we think that we could all live together and be very happy."

Peggy was ecstatic. "Are we all coming home, Irene and Marie as well?"

Her father tried again to calm her down. "Now Peggy, the first thing I have to do is to let the nuns know you are here. As we have tried to explain, you have no clothes or decent shoes, not even a coat, so you will have to return and I will ask the nuns for some new clothes for you all. Betty and I would like to buy them for you but we can't buy anything without clothing coupons. The nuns have yours, though by the look of you they haven't spent many on you."

Peggy became excited: they were all coming home, her father and Betty were to be married. She forgot all about the thoughts she'd had of looking after them all herself, it would be lovely to live as a family again. She really liked Betty and knew that they would be happy.

Her father broke into her thoughts. "Now, Peggy, I am going to telephone the orphanage and I will tell the nuns not to come for you, I will take you back myself, and I will have something to say about how you have been treated by Sister Brown. She won't hit you like that again in a hurry."

Betty brought a big wool cardigan from the kitchen that she had knitted for herself and placed it around Peggy's shoulders. "This will help keep you warm until you arrive back at the home; your Dad can bring it back for me." She gave Peggy a hug. It was the first time that they had been close and Peggy liked the warm cosy feeling that it gave her. "Thank you so much Betty. I am so glad that you and our Dad are getting married. When we come home I will make sure that Irene and Marie don't make any trouble for you." Betty gave her another hug. "Don't you worry about anything, Peggy, I will manage, they are lovely children and only need love and a bit of a fuss making over them." Peggy sighed; at last it seemed that everything was going to be all right.

"Let's go, Peggy," said her father, pulling her to her feet, "and sort those nuns out. I don't want you to do any worrying. I will do all the talking." Betty came and stood next to them. "Goodbye for now Peggy, we are sorry that you have to go back but we will do everything we can to bring you home for good as soon as possible."

Peggy looked at her and noticed how kind and concerned she looked. "Thank you Betty, I am really looking forward to our new life together. I don't mind going back if it's only for a few weeks. I don't care what they do to me from now on as long as I know my time in that home is coming to an end. I wish it could be the same for my friends."

"Come on you two, there will be plenty of time for talking later. We don't want to be too late. I have a lot to say to Sister Superior. Betty and I will be commg to visit you all in two weeks' time and we hope to have everything sorted out by then and maybe a date for your return home."

They both left the house and turned to wave to Betty who had come to the door to wave them off. They walked side by side down the street, across the fields, on their way to the tram stop.

"Dad, did you know that I will be leaving school in July? Some orphanage girls, when they leave school, are sent out to work in posh people's houses as maids to do domestic work. Others stay in the home and become seniors. They help to look after the infants and juniors, but some of them can be very mean and are always putting us on report. It's sad really, because they have no homes to go to, so they don't know what it is like to live at home with a family of their own."

She linked her arm through her father's. He was smiling. "Oh, we have got plans for you. You passed your scholarship so we know that you can use your brains. How would you like to go to a commercial college and train to be a secretary?"

Peggy stood still and gazed up into her father's face. "A secretary, how will I do that? I won't have to go away from home again will I?" she said with a tremble in her voice.

"Oh no Peggy, you will live at home. This college is in Lingford and you will travel there and back by tramcar. I have found out that two of your old school friends from the estate will be starting there in September. I have had a word with them and they said that it would be great if you could join them. They are looking forward to seeing you again after all this time. I have worked it all out; you will sit an entrance exam in July which I am sure you will pass."

Peggy grabbed his arm. "But who will take Irene and Marie to school if I am not there?" Her father laughed. "You are still the little mother, aren't you? Don't worry, Betty will take them until they become used to the new routine. After a while they can take themselves, now they are older. There is just one more thing; Betty would like you all to meet and get to know her mother and father. Like her they are kind and gentle and would very much like to help us all. They live on our estate, not very far from us, but all these things will have to be sorted out before you can come back home."

As her father pulled on the chain that rang the bell on the big black door, he bent down and with a smile whispered, "This will be the last time we will be doing this together. Hopefully the next time you come out through this door will be for good and we will be on our way home to start a new life."

The door was opened by the kind Sister Grey. "Do come inside, both of you, and I will let Sister Superior know you have arrived." The big black door was closed with a bang. The sound of the bolts sliding shut and the key turning always made Peggy shudder.

Sister Grey was leading the way to the visiting room when Mr Cairnes spoke. "I would like Peggy to return to her friends as I want to speak to Sister Superior alone."

Sister Grey smiled at them. "Of course, I will take her there myself. Say goodnight to your father, Peggy and then come with me."

Peggy turned to her father and they hugged one another. "I will see you all soon, just do as you are told and everything will be all right."

Saying this he let her go, turned and walked into the visitors' room to await his meeting with Sister Superior. Peggy walked in a carefree manner with Sister Grey, hoping this would be the last time she had to return to the orphanage. Soon she was back among her friends and was eager to tell them her good news.

In the meantime Sister Superior was confronting her father in the visitors' room. They glared at each other. Mr Cairnes was the first to speak. "How dare you allow one of your nuns to treat my child with such cruelty?"

The nun replied, "We have over a hundred children in our care in this home, and we have to teach them discipline, or they would soon be out of control."

Mr Cairnes was still glaring at her. "Well, it won't happen to my children again because soon I hope to bring them all home." He went on to tell her about Betty and their plans to be married.

She looked surprised and a little taken back. "Well, well," she said. "I can only hope that you will all be very happy. Peggy has sometimes been a trouble to us, she is very strong-willed."

"I know," replied Mr Cairnes, "but she was never in any trouble when she was at home."

The conversation carried on for a few more minutes. Then Mr Cairnes wished her goodnight and turned to leave, saying he would visit his children on the next visiting day and pay her the money for their keep. Just as he reached the big door he turned. "When my children do come home I hope they receive adequate clothing, including coats, night-clothes and shoes."

The nun nodded curtly, turned her back on him and walked away. As he walked through the door, opened for him by Sister Grey, he was left with the thought that the way forward was not going to be easy for any of them.

Chapter Thirty-four

The following morning Peggy woke with a jump. Sister Brown was on duty again. She walked menacingly towards Peggy's bed. "So, forty two, you decided to come back I see." She prodded the bed with the window pole she was carrying. "Sister Superior has given instructions you will not be allowed to speak to anyone." Peggy looked at her. "I don't care, I will be going home soon and I will be able to speak to anyone that I like, at any time."

"Get down on your knees, you wicked girl, you will be severely dealt with later." Peggy did as she was told and knelt, but not caring. Soon all this would be behind her and she would be able to live her life again.

That same morning, in the school playground, all her friends gathered around her asking questions. Maureen was the first to speak. "Did you really make your way home, and did you see your Dad?" Sheila chimed in. "We want to know as well. Peggy is not allowed to speak to any of us in the home but after today we will use a trick that most of us have learned."

"What trick?" asked Maureen. "Speaking without moving our lips," replied Sheila, demonstrating. "That was amazing," said Maureen. "Can you do it, Peggy?"

"Yes I can," said Peggy, also not moving her mouth. Josie did it too. The 'other' girls all laughed, it was so funny, their voices sounded strange coming from the back of their mouths with no movement of their lips.

"Well," said Peggy, speaking in a normal voice, "here goes." She went on to tell them all that had happened from the time she left the home to when she was brought back by her father. She then went on to tell them the best news, that she and her sisters would be going home in a few weeks' time.

Sheila was the first to react to her news. "Oh Peggy, we will all miss you so much, we have had some good laughs together" – she gazed around at the 'other girls' – "won't we?" There was a chorus of, "Oh yes, we will all miss you."

Life became very hard for Peggy for the next two weeks. Sister

Superior had made it clear that she had plenty of extra orders to do. There would be no recreation and she would not be allowed to speak to her friends.

Peggy was careful not to involve any of her friends in any trouble by speaking to them when there was a nun or senior girl watching them, but they still had their secret way of speaking to each other.

Visiting day came around. Peggy hoped she would not be banned from seeing her father as an extra punishment. When visiting time arrived, she had just finished one of her extra orders, and went down to the playground just in time to hear her, Irene's and Marie's names being called by a senior. Quickly she collected her two sisters and hurried them as fast as she dared to the refectory where all the visitors were waiting. Peggy's heart sank when she saw who was on duty outside the door. It was "Fatso" and she was always putting Peggy on report. "I don't think I should let you in, forty two. You are on punishment. But as Sister Superior has not said anything to me I suppose I will have to let you pass." Saying this she opened the door. Peggy moved fast, pulling Irene and Marie in behind her. Her father and Betty were sitting together. Betty raised her arm and waved to them. They hurried across the room and were soon together in a little group. Irene and Marie were soon rummaging in the brown paper bag that Betty held out to them, eager to see what was inside.

But Peggy was more interested in what her father had to say to her. She sat gazing at him in anticipation. "Well Peggy, Betty and I have been to see Sister Superior and told her that we intend bringing you all home a week on Saturday. We have sorted everything out at home and all will be ready on that day. We will come and collect you all at one o'clock and Sister Superior has agreed to all our arrangements."

Peggy couldn't speak, she was so excited, and grabbing hold of her father's hands she cried, "Are we really, really coming home, Dad? I can't believe it after all this time."

"Yes Peggy, Betty and I are now married and we are really looking forward to having you all home." Peggy turned to Betty. "I am so pleased we are going to live as a family again! I will help you to look after these two." Betty laughed. "As I have told you before, I will be so happy to look after you all. You will be too busy with your college work and enjoying yourself once more with your old friends."

The rest of the visit passed very quickly, and then the bell rang to signal that it was time for the children to leave. There were hugs and kisses all round. "Thankfully, this will be the last time we meet in this room. The next time I come it will be to bring you all home. In the meantime be good," he said with a wink and a smile.

Holding her small packet of sweets tightly, Peggy took the other two by the hands and almost danced across the room. Reaching the door she turned and waved, she was so happy and didn't care what happened to her from then on. No one would be able to stop her going home this time. In the corridor, she was once again stopped by "Fatso's" big hand pushing her in the chest. "What are you smiling at, forty two? Give me whatever you have in your hand." Her fat face lit up when she saw what Peggy was holding. "Here, you can have them," said Peggy, throwing the packet at her. "I am going home soon and will have as many sweets as I like." She didn't realise that people had to have sweet-coupons to buy them from the shops as it was war-time.

She pushed past "Fatso" who was still busy looking inside the sweet bag and took Irene and Marie out to the playground.

On Monday morning, during morning playtime, Peggy gathered her friends around her in the school playground and told them all that her father and Betty had said. Her friends were both happy and sad at the same time. Happy for her that she was going home, but sad to be losing a good friend.

Although Sister Superior and the other nuns knew of her imminent departure, she was still to be given double orders, no free time and no conversation with any of her friends.

One day, just before teatime, Peggy saw Irene standing in the corridor. Looking around quickly to make sure no one was watching, she went up to her. "Irene, you know we are going home next weekend, don't you?"

"Oh yes," replied Irene excitedly. "I'm so happy, I can't wait. Will we be going back to our old school?"

"Yes," said Peggy. "You and Marie will but I'll be going to a different school; but don't worry, Betty will look after you both. I have to go now and fmish my orders before someone sees me talking to you."

With that she quickly left to continue with her work.

Two days later Sister Superior sent a senior girl to bring Peggy up to the sewing room. As she entered she noticed three separate piles of clothing stacked on the big table. Peggy stood still, not daring to move in case she did something wrong. "Well forty two, your father has requested adequate clothing for you all to take home." Saying that Sister Superior started lifting the garments up one by one. Peggy was horrified, she had never seen such old-fashioned clothes in her life.

They were dark dingy clothes ones her mother would have given to the rag-and-bone man years ago. Then the nun produced the shoes from behind some boxes. She gave Peggy a pair to try on; they were even older that the ones she was wearing and only just fitted her feet. There was a strap that fitted around her ankle and she had to stretch it to make it reach the side of the shoe. The next thing she had to try on was a coat, made of a dark green woollen material which seemed to have been washed a few times. Peggy was thin, but she found it very hard to fasten the big buttons at the front, the sleeves had shrunk, and only reached halfway down her arms. She was worried about what the people living on their estate or her friends would think of her in these clothes. When living at home, the girls had always been nicely dressed. Sister Superior broke into her thoughts. "Now forty two, here are three carrier bags, I will leave you to sort out the clothes that you and your sisters will need to wear when you go home. The rest of the clothes I want you to pack into these bags." Saying this she swept out of the room, leaving Peggy alone feeling bewildered, staring down at the carrier bags and the piles of clothing.

She had wanted to ask Sister if any of the clothes would fit Irene and Marie. As she looked closer, she became aware that they had only been given one set of everything and she wondered what would they do when they needed a clean change of clothes. They were lucky it was the summer because the dresses and underwear were very thin. The only garments that were thick were the knickers. Dark blue flannel, with a pocket at the side of one leg.

Peggy sorted out the garments, placed them in the carrier bags and left them on the table. She turned and left the room and went about her duties. In one way she would be sad to leave. She had grown quite close to Josie, Sheila and the twins and hoped that some day she would be able to help them.

The following week passed in a whirl for Peggy. She had been sent for by Sister Superior on various occasions, who gave her instructions on what had to be done on their day of departure. The three of them were to go to the sick room where their going-home clothes would be laid out on the bed, with three chemises for them to use for dressing.

On the morning itself, they were to dress, put on their coats, and wait until one of the nuns came for them to take them to the visitors' room. This was to be done while all the other children were occupied elsewhere. She didn't want any of the other children to see them leaving. Later in bed that night, Peggy let her thoughts run wild. She was

171

excited at leaving, but even more excited that she may be going to a college. Did they wear uniforms, and where would she acquire all the books that she would need, and would her father be able to pay for everything?

But one thing she didn't know was that Betty, just like their mother, was great at sewing and making clothes, and mother's sewing machine was still in their front room, so she had no need to worry. Thoughts were going round and round in her mind but at last she fell asleep.

Chapter Thirty-five

In the days leading up to the Saturday, Peggy became concerned. Every time she met with Sheila, Josie or the twins they became weepy at the thought of losing their friend. She would have liked to promise them that she would visit one Sunday. But the thought of coming back into the orphanage filled her with dread. It was sad, but she knew that she wouldn't be able to do it.

Saturday arrived at last. Peggy had hardly slept; she was worried in case something went wrong at the last minute. She jumped out of bed and knelt to say her prayers, saying an extra prayer, asking God's help on this day of days.

Although she was going home she still had her orders to do before breakfast. She did them cheerfully with a smile on her face. Peggy managed to say her goodbyes to her friends before collecting the excited Irene and Marie and taking them up to the sick room. Once inside and because no one was watching, she quickly helped them get changed without using the hated chemises. Taking her own clothes she went into the lavvy and dressed herself. As the three of them stood together they looked more like orphans than they had ever done.

The mean Sister Grey came into the room and stood them in a line to examine them. Peggy felt brave; she was not afraid of the nun any more, and decided to speak. "Sister, where are our own clothes and suitcases that we brought with us to this home? I know that my clothes won't fit me any more, but I am sure some of them will fit Irene or Marie." Sister Grey was livid. "You ungrateful girl, we have clothed and fed you for years. Your clothes were given to other children who were in need."

"Who were they?" Peggy asked. "I have never seen anyone wearing them."

Sister Grey was becoming very angry. "Forty two, give your sisters their bags and all go and sit on the bed until someone comes to collect you." She turned and left the room.

There would be no dinner for them. They were to stay in the sick-room when the dinner bell was rung, which was at eleven forty-five on a Saturday. Irene and Marie were becoming hungry, and wanted to go downstairs to the refectory. "You can't," cried Peggy, "we have to sit still and wait. Our Dad will be coming soon, we will have our dinner at home today." At long last the door opened, and Sister Superior swept into the room, holding a large brown envelope in her hands. "Are you ready, forty two?" Peggy nodded her head. "Then bring your sisters and follow me." Peggy pushed her two sisters in front of her. She was still struggling with her own and Marie's bags; Irene carried her own. They followed the nun down the stairs and along the corridor. The only person they saw was "Fatso". She was standing at the entrance near the lavvies, not allowing anyone access to them. She looked at Peggy. "Good riddance forty two, I will be glad to see the back of you."

"Ugh, and I will miss you too," laughed Peggy, knocking into her legs with one of the bags as they hurried past. Sister Superior turned round. "Stop messing about forty two, we don't want to keep your father waiting, do we?" she said with a sneer. They passed through the door, down the convent steps and arrived at the visitors' room door.

Opening the door, the nun pushed the three girls inside the room. Standing in the middle of the room was their father, a broad smile on his face. They rushed towards him, Irene dropping her bag on the floor. "When you take us home, Dad, will we be able to have some sweets?" Her father laughed. "You will just have to wait and see." Marie stood looking up at him. "Me too, Dad?" she asked. "Yes, you too, now be good while I arrange everything with Sister Superior." The nun walked towards him. "Mr Cairnes, I have some forms for you to fill in and some documents to be signed for before you leave." Saying this she walked towards the small table which stood in the centre of the room. Opening the brown envelope she had been carrying in her hand, she spread the contents on the table, counting them into three separate piles. She turned to Mr Cairnes. "You must sign for the release of these important papers. Included are birth and baptism certificates, also each of the children's ration books, which we have kept up to date." Mr Cairnes quickly leaned over the table and took the outstretched pen from the nun's hand. "Thank you Sister," he replied, placing all the papers back into the envelope after he had finished signing them.

He turned towards his daughters, picked up their bags and ushered the girls towards the big black outer door. "I have ordered a taxicab to pick us up at quarter past one, so it should be here any moment now."

Sister Superior pulled back the big bolt. Peggy held her breath; the door was about to be opened.

They all stepped outside, and Peggy gave a big sigh of relief. The nun spoke first. "Now girls, be obedient to your father. Remember that you have had a good upbringing at this home and always remember to say your prayers for those less fortunate than yourselves." She then closed the door on them with a bang. They all stood there in stunned silence not knowing what to do next. The taxi had not yet arrived. "Is this really it, Dad, have we passed through that door for the very last time?" asked Peggy. "Yes, you have, we are all going home together; Betty will be waiting for us. Look, here comes the taxi," he said as the big black car glided towards them. They all piled inside while their father and the taxi man stored their bags in the boot. Peggy turned her head, looked at the big black door and shuddered. 'I hope I never have to see you again in my life,' she whispered to herself. Their father climbed into the car and sat next to the driver. He closed the door and they were off to begin a new chapter in their lives.

It was a happy journey. Their father kept turning round with a smile and giving them the thumbs-up sign, meaning everything was OK.

The car came to a stop outside their home. Betty was standing at the gate waiting for them. She opened the car door and they all stepped out. "Welcome home, I hope you are all hungry," said Betty. Father paid the taxi driver and they all made their way excitedly up the garden path and round to the back door.

On entering the house they were met with an aroma of fish and chips. "What is that lovely smell?" cried Irene. "I am hungry." "Me too," said Marie. "It's making my mouth water," Peggy said. Betty smiled at the sight of their faces when they saw the table. It was covered with a fancy tablecloth. Plates, knives and forks were all set out neatly. Betty sat everybody down and served out the fish and chips: what a feast it was. Halfway through the meal Peggy became uncomfortable and stopped eating. Irene and Marie were also struggling with their food.

"What's the matter?" asked Betty. "Don't you like fish and chips?" She had tried so hard to make everything go well for their homecoming.

"They have not been used to eating so much food, but I am sure they have enjoyed the little that they have eaten, haven't you girls?" said their father.

"Oh yes," replied Peggy, "but we are just so full up."

"We will have to do things gradually, and remember that they have been away from home for a long time. It was a very different way of life for them and they are still very excited, but this is a very happy day for us all."

A short time later, when their dinners had settled down, their father suggested they go and look at their bedrooms and sort out their clothes. Betty went upstairs with them to help.

Peggy was to have her own room again and Irene and Marie were to share one. The first bag to be opened was Marie's. Irene tipped hers onto the bed. Their father was shocked at the sight of the contents. They were old and worn. His first instinct was to gather them all up and put them in the dustbin. He turned to Betty. "What can we make of these, I can't let them wear these clothes. Their mother would have been very upset, they were always dressed so well."

"Leave it to me," said Betty. "I will try and make some alterations, just leave the clothes on the bed and I will sort them out later. Now take the girls downstairs and I will go and see how Peggy is coping."

She tapped on Peggy's door. "Can I come in?" She opened the door. Peggy was sitting on her bed crying. "Oh Betty, I can't wear these clothes."

Betty sat beside her. "Don't you worry, Peggy, I will alter them for you. I know that you can sew, so you can help me; we will make a start on them tomorrow."

Chapter Thirty-six

Once they were all back downstairs again Irene and Marie wanted to go and explore the back garden. They also wanted to see inside the air- raid shelter that had been erected during their absence from home. Peggy needed some time to herself to ponder on the day's happenings. She went to the front garden and stood near the garden gate. A few minutes later a boy, about her own age, came walking down the street. He looked very smart and well dressed, his hair parted down the side and a little quiff at the front. He was carrying some rolled up comics under his arm. As he drew level with Peggy he stopped, turned to face her and burst into song. "Eye-tiddly-eye tye-pom-pom" he sang, tapping her gently on the forehead to accompany the words, "pom-pom". "Have you got any comics to swap?" he asked.

Peggy blushed. "Er, I don't think so, I have been away and have just arrived home today."

"I think I know you," said the boy, "you used to go to our school. I haven't seen you for a long time. Have you been evacuated?"

"No," replied Peggy, "we have been living in a home in another part of Lingford, but I think I remember you. You and your brothers used to sing funny songs in the school playground."

"We still do, always singing for a laugh. Do you remember us when we had no socks to wear and had holes in our jumpers, that was before the war. We are much better off now; Dad, Mum, our Fred and Uncle Harry are all working down the pits or in the factories, working all the hours that God sends."

"Do you still play games in the fields after school?" she asked him. "Sometimes," he replied. "But now we have spending money, we go to the pictures quite a lot, and sometimes we go down the back road at the far end of the estate to watch the soldiers drilling in the army camps."

"I saw some soldiers once," said Peggy. "They were marching and singing."

"Was it near the park?"

"Yes," said Peggy.

"Oh," said the boy. "They march from the railway station on their way to the camp. I will have to go now and see if I can swap some comics. See you later." Then he sang out. "TTFN!" and was gone.

When Peggy returned to the house she asked her father, "What does TTFN mean?"

Her father and Betty smiled. "You have been cut off from the world in that home," laughed her father. "Didn't you have a wireless to listen to?"

"No, we only had a gramophone, which we listened to on Thursday evenings. We listened to ballet music and Irish songs which we danced the Irish reels to. I am very good at Irish dancing, Sister Bluey and one of the ladies who came to teach us dancing taught me. You saw me at the concerts, doing Irish dancing and ballet, I am very fond of ballet music, do they play it on your wireless?"

"You all did very well in the concerts, I enjoyed them very much. We have everything on the wireless, Peggy. News, music, plays and lots of comedy shows. One of the most popular is called 'It's that man again' with Tommy Handley. It is also known as ITMA, and at the end of each show he says 'TTFN' which means ta-ta-for-now."

"I have just been speaking to a boy who goes to our old school. He seemes to be much better dressed these days."

"Yes Peggy, everyone is working very hard, helping the war effort, the home front it is called; it is very important to support our fighting forces who are facing the enemy."

"Where is Uncle Charlie now?" asked Peggy.

"We will have a talk about that later," said her father. "Irene and Marie are enjoying themselves outside, Let's join them."

Betty took a ball out of the cupboard, and they all joined in playing a game of donkey. There was much laughter every time their father or Betty dropped the ball. Six drops and you were the donkey. Father made sure that he was the first to drop out.

Peggy was starting to unwind. She realised that the orphanage days were behind them. It was a long time since they had laughed and played together.

"I will have to go inside and stoke up the fire, you will all need a bath before going to bed," said her father. "We will have a light tea, a glass of milk and a biscuit for supper," Betty told them as they all went back indoors.

After their bath and supper, Irene and Marie went up to bed; they were very tired and were soon asleep. Peggy had a lovely bath and came down to supper and a talk with her father. It was then he told her.

"When you were in the orphanage, you always asked about Uncle Charlie. I told you a little white lie, because I didn't want to upset you. I had received a telegram from the war office informing me that my brother was missing in action. I feared the worst so I asked you to pray for him. Some time later I received another telegram, saying that Uncle Charlie had been taken prisoner. It seems that their unit had been cut off trying to make their way to Dunkirk. They had been helped by some nuns who had sheltered them in their convent. But when France surrendered, they were handed over to the Germans who were winning all the battles then, but we have won a major battle at a place called El-Alamein, and now it looks as though we will win the war. All the prisoners will be freed, and Uncle Charlie will be home soon I hope."

Peggy's head was nodding. "I am very tired Dad, I feel like going up to bed now." She went to say goodnight to Betty who was still busy in the kitchen.

"Oh," said her father, "I have put something on your pillow. See you in the morning."

Peggy went upstairs, and peeped into Irene and Marie's room; they were fast asleep. She entered her own little room and saw it straight away, it was laid on her pillow. Her mother's prayer book, the back and front covered in mother of pearl. She picked it up and read the inscription on the front, scratched into the mother of pearl. "To Kate from Charlie". She turned it over, and there on the back were the words, "From mother to Peggy". She held it close to her as she knelt to say her prayers, then placed it on the bedside table, climbed into bed and lay there thinking: we are home at last, no more orders or rules.

A whole new way of life lay before them.